Stimulosis
Mark Time

STIMVLOSIS

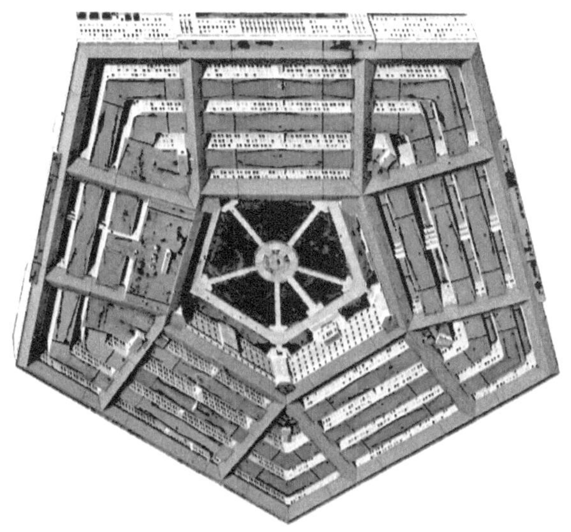

A Novel by
Mark Time

JACKALOPE HILL

An imprint of Antelope Hill Publishing

Mark Time can be contacted via Telegram
(@Mark_Time_Author)
or followed on his channel: t.me/MarkTimeAuthor

Cover art by Swifty
Edited by Lute Currie
Published by Jackalope Hill
The fiction imprint of Antelope Hill Publishing
antelopehillpublishing.com
Paperback ISBN-13: 979-8-89252-051-5
EPUB ISBN-13: 979-8-89252-052-2

AUTHOR'S NOTE

The journey for this book has left an indelible mark on my soul. As bizarre as it may seem, the premise for the novel came from a series of dreams spanning roughly a year. The vision of its central horror continues to haunt me to this day. Perhaps the reader will share in my continued sleepless nights.

I wrote the book in a white heat of inspiration in two phases. I averaged two thousand words per day early in 2024 until I had to stop at around thirty thousand. The subject matter was too heavy, and it was taking a toll.

However, I had almost weekly nightmares until I finally took up the book again. Over the course of three weeks in October of that year, I wrote more than sixty thousand words to finish the novel, averaging four thousand per day.

The stock one puts into or withholds from dreams will translate to the reader's approach to the novel. Regardless, one must concede the parallels of the scenarios revealed in my fevered visions and the nightmarish, demonic system we find ourselves under today.

They say truth is stranger than fiction. Well, *Stimulosis* is certainly some strange fiction.

May God bless you and our people.

Mark Time

CONTENTS

QUID EST VERITAS?

"Wake up," a voice said. "The time is very short."

Richard Malden awoke in a cold metal folding chair. A single glowing lightbulb swayed imperceptibly above him. The plastic folding table before him was blotched with unidentifiable stains. He could not tell the exact size and shape of the room. Shadows writhed and gesticulated in otherworldly forms on objects just beyond the reach of his vision.

"Richard!" the voice commanded again. "It's very important that you tell me everything you know."

There was little left of Richard. Malnutrition and constant fear had taken a toll on his body. His auburn hair— once a bronze crown atop a proud man—lay in thinning strips over a starkly creased brow. His pale eyes darted listlessly, staring into the opaque spaces beyond the light. His mind was busy conjuring ghastly visions and possibilities.

"Who are you?" Richard shouted.

He looked up at the lightbulb, stunning his retinae and leaving a blinding afterimage. He heard only silence. Then he detected a shuffle in the darkness as a silhouette appeared by a stack of old boxes.

"I'm the one who got you out of that hell," the man began. "God told me what you saw."

Richard furrowed his brow. "God? I think I've had enough of both the seen and unseen."

He noticed he was bound to his chair. His mind felt dim and hazy, as if coming off a cocktail of strong drugs. A noise pierced the musty, strangling air. The silhouette grabbed a metal chair and dragged it across the cracked concrete floor until it came to rest on the side of the table across from Richard.

The air shifted. The lightbulb swayed as if caught by an incoming tide. Its rays oscillated across the man's face like a scanning document, each pass revealing greater detail.

"You can call me Edwards," the man said, crossing his arms. "I know I certainly seem like an enemy, but I promise I'm a friend."

He was a towering figure, around six-foot three. His salt-and-pepper hair sat resolutely in as generic a haircut as one can imagine. He wore a simple red-and-grey flannel shirt and faded jeans. Stubble covered his face—stubble that, if left untamed, would have grown into the beard of an Old Testament prophet.

Richard peered deeply into his captor's crystal blue eyes. "That's why I'm bound up, right?" the captive looked up defiantly, concealing a growing sense of fear.

For an instant, the light revealed a grin—quick, sharp, and gone again.

"I needed you to stay put," Edwards replied, taking a deep breath. "Most don't react well to waking up alone in a cold warehouse."

"Why am I here?" Richard shuffled in his chair, acutely aware of the tightness of his bonds.

At last, the man took a seat. The scraping of the metal chair on the floor reverberated through the space until it dissipated into the silence of a tomb.

"Do you remember where you were before I picked you up?" Edwards interrogated.

Richard clenched his teeth. Vague memories of a medical facility sprang to mind. He looked down and saw he was still wearing a hospital gown. "A hospital," he answered.

Edwards let out a slight chuckle at the reply, scratched at his stubble, and leaned forward. "If that was a hospital, this is the Ritz," he gestured to the space around them. "You were in Walter Reed—room 384."

Richard narrowed his eyes.

"Same place, same reason, same room as James Forrestal back in '49," Edwards continued. "If I hadn't yanked you out of there, probably the same fate too."

"He killed himself, didn't he?"

The man pursed his lips and shook his head slowly while maintaining piercing eye contact. "We'll get to that," Edwards began. "What I need from you right now is everything you know about the engine room."

The last two words hung over them like a cloud of exhaled smoke, filling the captive's nostrils and stinging his lungs.

"The engine room . . ." Richard murmured, his gaze lost in the distance.

"The boy?" Edwards clarified.

Richard widened his eyes until he had no lids at all. His heart raced, and his blood ran cold. A deep shiver overtook him as the memories came flooding back. "No!" he cried. "No! It's not real. That never happened!"

Edwards sat back, crossing his arms. "And you are correct. He is . . . or at least was a boy."

"It's not real! I-," said Richard, tilting his head back slightly—a hellish dread consuming him as clarity began wringing out his memory like a wet dish towel. "It was . . . in the basement of the Pentagon."

"Go on," Edwards replied, nodding slowly.

Richard agreed at first, but halted. "How do I know this isn't a trick? How do I know I'm not still in Walter Reed?"

"In the name of God," Edwards clenched his fists. "I'm here to help you. If you ever want to see the horror you witnessed come to an end, you'll do as I say and tell me what you know. What position are you in to bargain?"

Slumping his shoulders, Richard held back tears. He was at the end of a long series of life-altering experiences beyond his control. "What can I even tell you?" he said quietly.

Edwards lowered his tone. "Every last little detail. I don't care how small or insignificant. The color of your socks, the time of day, what you were thinking at every stage, that little itch you had on your arm. I don't care how small the piece of information is. I need *everything*. Time is running out, but we can't afford to skip details."

Richard nearly rolled his eyes. "What's the point?"

"The truth," Edwards said assertively, tapping the table with his finger. "Just start talking."

Richard relented. After all, what he knew was forced upon him without his consent. It gestated and grew in his soul until he could no longer contain it. He felt he might exact some revenge on his tormentors by baring their every design. His mind cleared as he prepared to tell his wretched story from stem to stern.

&

"The truth, Richard," Edwards repeated.

Truth is a funny concept, after all. I used to think truth was something aspirational—a peak, a zenith. I found truth wallowing in the gutter. I could not grasp it unless I tripped over misfortune and landed face first in the muck. The truth is, I hate the truth. It is a wild animal that trespassed in my skull and daily claws to get out. All I want are the warm, summer days of ignorance—when the truth was something tame and distant. When I didn't know it, I could retreat into soft, permeable platitudes about objectivity's shortfalls, just as Pontius Pilate quipped in his moment of decision: *Quid est veritas?*

A fool's errand—I have gone up on Mount Sinai. I have seen what I have seen. I return to the base of the mountain with white hair and all faiths in man shaken.

When I introduce the hard reality to you, I'm sure it will send you spiraling. There's something to be said for the buildup of suspense, though it gives me no more pleasure to tell you this story than to put down an ailing dog. There are things that must be done, regardless of the agony.

To be honest, I don't know where to begin. Childhood? When I joined the Navy? My whole life has occurred only in the past few months. The preceding years are only whispers and clouds of smoke. They have all been overwritten by those inerasable eyes. Those eyes, pleading and pallid, begging me for a release. When I discovered him, I found the truth. Disgusting, regrettable truth. I resisted its implications harder than I have struggled with anything else. I know I've got to do something, but what? I'm not even sure I could find him again, much less do anything to help.

Here I go getting ahead of myself again. I ought to tell you the story, not just vomit my misgivings and trepidations.

ALL FOR A LITTLE BIT OF FUEL

I suppose I'll start with my journey to the Pentagon. I was a lieutenant commander then. I suppose I still am. I had just come off a department head tour on a destroyer out of Mayport, Florida. We gave a good, distant thrashing to some rebel group I've forgotten the name of somewhere, and left. When we pulled into port after the long deployment, I already had orders for my shore tour in DC. Ever the careerist, I understood the need to get face time with the brass during what was supposed to be a restful break in my life between taxing sea tours. I wanted command. I wanted recognition. I wanted me.

I left Mayport on a radiant September day marked by swaying palm trees and the gentle caress of the Florida sun. All of my personal effects had been loaded up and shipped north to await me in a storage unit. I chose to drive to DC in my car a few days earlier than my report date so I could look for an apartment. I got a terribly late start due to a dead battery. With a little help from a jump pack, I was on my way.

As I lumbered up I-95, my front left tire blew out just as I crossed the Georgia state line. Digging through the assorted luggage and uniforms in my trunk, I managed to extricate the full-sized spare. Daylight waned as dark clouds rolled in. The lug nuts had been fused to the studs by the salty Florida air. After considerable sweating and swearing, I broke all five loose. By the time I got the new tire on, it was completely dark. Vehicles passing far too close to the shoulder kicked up rooster tails of spray from the growing rain storm. When I finally slumped into the driver's seat again, I was soaked, exhausted, and beaten.

"What a start," I said, rubbing my face and realizing too late how dirty my hands were.

My hands drifted to the ignition. An aggressive turn was answered by a pathetic click from the engine bay. I sat back in amazement for a moment.

Maybe the hazard lights drained the battery, I mused with doubt.

The car had been sitting for eight months, after all. There were bound to be some issues. Fortunately, the jump pack still had some charge left—just enough to get me going. As I joined the northbound traffic, the raindrops made a gentle patter on the windshield. Checking the GPS, I saw that I still had about ten hours to go on the wet roads.

"No sleep on shore duty either," I joked to myself aloud.

The last of Georgia passed into the rearview mirror without incident. Things going horribly wrong were just part and parcel of my time in the Navy. Looking back now, I can see what all that trouble really was. I don't know if it was heaven or hell trying to stop me that night, but something desperately wanted to keep me out of DC. I so dearly wish I had driven off a bridge or a semi had careened into me as I ignorantly changed my tire. Every obstacle I surmounted was just one more log I heaped onto my funeral pyre.

I decided to call it a night somewhere in South Carolina. The GPS showed a little bed and breakfast just a short distance from the interstate. As I pulled off the exit and away from the main roads, the surface changed from asphalt to compacted sand. Furrowing my brow, I zoomed out to see where I was heading. The blue route line wound its way deeper and deeper into dense live oak growth and draping Spanish moss.

"You have arrived," the tinny GPS voice reported abruptly.

"What?" I shook my head and strained my eyes in the darkness.

I slowed the car and rolled my window down. The rain had stopped, and silver moonlight started to peer through the clouds. The low rumble of the uneven road blended with the unknowable chirps and distant screams of unseen wildlife deep in the swampy mist. Moths and mosquitos swarmed in clouds around my headlights.

Stopping my car completely, I rechecked my bearings, carefully searching "hotel" once more on my phone. To my bewilderment, nothing came up for many miles. The bed and breakfast I previously set as my destination failed to show up at all. Worse still, the road I was on did not even have a name.

The engine hummed in the heavy, humid Carolina night air. I set about turning around. Just as I regained my heading, I noticed my fuel was perilously low.

But I just filled up?

I impotently clenched my hands on a steering wheel which felt increasingly like a prop. In rapid succession, the low fuel warning and check engine lights glared on the dashboard. I would have pushed past the low fuel light, but the second warning caused me to halt. The touch screen displayed a command to restart the engine due to an ECU fault. I anxiously eyed the jump pack in the passenger seat. I shifted the transmission into park and contemplated my options. I was stopped on a small, aging concrete bridge over a stagnant creek.

The onboard computer took this action as consent to shut down and initiated a countdown. I wrestled with the shifter, but the car's benevolent computer had locked it in place. As soon as the thirty second timer expired, the engine shut down while the screen showed the contact information for the dealer for a few fleeting seconds before the car went totally dark. My frustration mounted as my sleep-deprived mind raced.

It just wanted a restart, so I should be good to get going again, I bargained.

Gingerly turning the key, my heart dropped in tandem with the pathetic click I received.

"This piece of…" I kicked the tire on my trip out to the hood.

Attaching the jump pack once more to the battery, my brow began to pour with sweat as the bugs swarmed. The pack's light failed to even turn on. In anger, I slammed the hood as hard as I could as soon as I disconnected the cables. I cursed myself for being too cheap to just get a new battery back in Jacksonville.

By now, my skin was a sopping mess of sweat, mosquito bites, and road grime. Even if I could get the car started, I doubted that I had enough fuel to get back to the interstate. Every movement was punctuated by the incessant needling of my insect tormentors.

My thoughts drifted to my recent deployment. At sea, refueling was a careful dance of coordination as the ship and its oiler sailed in parallel courses, connected by a lattice of delicate cables and cranes. I couldn't stop thinking of the last underway replenishment we completed before returning to port. There were rumors of an extended deployment circulating, and we had just been served steak and lobster the previous night. We had already been at sea for months as whispers of trouble in the Western Pacific beat against the hull of our ship. Many took this rendezvous with the oiler as final confirmation of the extension. Morale was already in the gutter.

The meetup appeared to go off without a hitch. The crew had completed this evolution enough times for it to be second nature. I was standing Officer of the Deck, keeping a careful eye on our course and speed. The captain hovered nervously over my shoulder, micromanaging every minute shift of the rudder. I had little respect for her, and neither did much of the crew. She had been featured in newspapers, magazines, and tabloids for her status as a commanding officer and a single mom. I personally couldn't have cared less about her personal life. I worshiped competence and found her unworthy of veneration.

The cables and hoses were all set to go, and cargo and fuel began to transfer on our port side. I suddenly heard commotion behind me as I stood on the bridgewing. One of the sailors had climbed up on one of the cables and was inching his way to the cavernous, churning space between the two vessels. I recognized him as Machinist's Mate Third Class Sloan.

I had heard his wife was initiating divorce proceedings while he was away. He also was under investigation for the possible accidental killing of a civilian on our last port visit. Wrapped around his shoulder was a length of wire or rope, I couldn't tell. One of the chiefs attempted to grab his ankle, but to no avail. By the time I processed what was happening, Sloan was already well beyond the railing and perilously suspended above the rushing, foaming channel of ocean between the ships.

"Emergency breakaway!" the captain called out.

Nobody moved.

"Ma'am, if we sever that cable, we'll never recover him!" I sputtered rapidly.

All the while, Sloan wormed his way to the middle of the expanse. He began to wrap the cord he brought around the cable and then around his neck. Everyone froze in horror as they realized his intention.

A considerable amount of shouting and chaos erupted in the pilothouses of both ships.

"Emergency breakaway, that is an order!" she repeated "We'll handle it like a man-overboard."

"Ma'am, you have the deck," I relinquished control and refused to carry out the movement.

Panicked, the captain entered the pilothouse and announced her taking of the deck after a series of grave threats to my career. She ordered that communication be passed to the oiler for an emergency breakaway. After some perceived hesitation, the oiler affirmed. The ship's whistle blew five short blasts as its turbines roared. The cables strained and screeched as Sloan jostled considerably, hung by his neck between the ships. When the captain gave the order for a hard right rudder, a horrific crack announced the cable's failure. I couldn't bear to look as the cord swung his body into the side of our ship on its way down.

The metallic thud of Sloan's gruesome death would haunt me to this day if it were not supplanted by worse horrors. As the destroyer made its circling turn, lookouts observed MM3's corpse being dragged along the surface of the water by his neck. The captain ordered a steady course and slowed the ship. The small inflatable boat was deployed to pick his body up. The crew was ultimately unable to untangle Sloan's mangled remains. The captain ordered the first lieutenant to reel in the corpse with the cable to deal with it on ship. Not a soul who witnessed the scene could keep control of their stomachs. The deployment ended up not being extended after all.

"What a way to go," I reflected just before climbing back into my stranded car. "All for a little bit of fuel."

Of course, Sloan's turmoil extended far beyond that shipboard evolution. As I pulled the door handle, the air shifted. A cold air mass rushed over me as the swamp's nocturnal symphony went utterly silent. My sweat, formerly hot and sticky, turned to an icy flow. I felt as though there was something directly behind me. I whipped around only to see the dark outline of a few trees laden with moss.

"Who's there?" I called out.

The sound of my voice seemed to be entirely absorbed by the air only inches from my face. No amount of screaming in the world would help me. All I could do was try to control my mounting confusion and fear.

Why don't you do something? my internal voice pleaded, Move!

I rushed inside the cabin of my car and slammed the door. Fumbling with the lock, I slumped down in the seat. Shivers overtook me. I became acutely aware of the windows' transparency as shadows overtook the night. I closed my eyes as tightly as I could.

THE SHORT CONTRACT

Death must be terribly similar to what I experienced that night: the feelings of powerlessness as all earthly accolades and prestige melt away under the numinous, tectonic movement of the supernatural. Or perhaps death would be more pleasant. When I opened my eyes, I found myself drifting into the rumble strips on I-95. Gripping at the steering wheel, I managed to get back into the outside lane. My breathing was still deep and tortured. The dash showed a full tank of gas and no warning lights. I was cruising at a cool 70 mph. The GPS indicated my position just shy of the North Carolina border.

Just a dream, I reassured myself.

Even then, this explanation succeeded only in worsening my fear. The miles that had passed under my car without my awareness sent my mind spinning. A rest stop appeared a few miles down the road. I pulled off to see if there was any damage to the bodywork from a sleep induced engagement with a guard rail. When I pulled into the parking lot and exited the vehicle, my pulse rose. Caked along the wheel wells was compacted sand.

There's a perfectly good explanation for that. I kneeled to examine the soil. It must be from the beaches around Mayport.

I shook my head and rubbed my face. If I had fallen asleep, it did nothing to alleviate my exhaustion. My multitude of mosquito bites itched terribly as I climbed back into the car. I froze.

Mosquito bites!

I turned on the interior light and examined my arms. They were pockmarked from dozens of red bumps. The heaviness in my chest returned.

Get it together. You're in the South. It happens. I clenched my jaw and left the rest stop parking lot.

The itching became unbearable. Every time I scratched the bites, I was reminded of my apparent experience. The sand and the bites both had very simple, easy explanations, though. I had just left Florida, after all. Sand and mosquitos were never in short supply. I explained away my memory of the car's clean appearance just before I left as faulty recollection. The bites must've occurred while changing the tire. Nodding to myself, I breathed a deep sigh.

"Welcome to North Carolina," the GPS interrupted my contemplation.

I tried to find a hotel. Whether this was my first or second attempt, I preferred not to know. I avoided a rundown motel and stopped at the nearest chain that I recognized. Breathlessly, I trudged to the counter. All I could think about was a hot shower and a clean bed.

"Do you have a reservation?" The dead-eyed woman at the counter lifted her gaze from the computer screen for a second.

Looking through the glass doors at the empty parking lot, I tiredly replied, "No?"

The woman typed away at her computer as I told her my name and how many nights I needed.

"We don't have any rooms available with two beds. Is that fine?" she asked, looking at me with black, sleepless eyes.

"I don't see why it wouldn't be," I shook my head.

Her focus drifted behind me. She raised her eyebrows and sighed. With a few more clicks, my room was ready.

After paying the exorbitant rate, I entered the elevator. On the safety card, a seemingly cultured vandal had scratched a small yet profound message: "The essence of human interaction is the short contract."

I repeated the inscription aloud. I supposed there was some truth to it. After all, mundane phrases like, "see you later," or "have a good day," have an element of mutual agreement. Having signed on for department head, I was in for the "long contract" with the Navy, among other things.

I finally arrived at my room and collapsed into the bed after a quick shower. Ignoring the mosquito bites, I managed to fall asleep. I awoke the next morning with a terrible headache. The weather took a turn for the worse as well. Freezing rain made an early debut and sounded a racket on my room's window. I shuffled over and shut the curtains, considerably darkening the room. Hunger pangs reminded me that I hadn't eaten since my departure yesterday. I got dressed and gathered up my things to head to the lobby. A different, even more sullen face greeted me at the counter.

"Malden, checking out," I looked aimlessly out of the lobby window at the driving rain.

The attendant nodded and typed slowly.

"Everyone has left the room?" he struggled to piece together the sentence.

I rolled my eyes, "You're looking at him."

This reply was met with a scowl and a few more sullen clicks.

"Have a nice day," he repeated apathetically. "We'll check on the room."

Brushing this off, I hurried to the automatic sliding door. Stopping for a brief pause, I took a deep breath before getting soaked with rain. The car managed to start without incident.

After a lackluster breakfast from the nearest drive through, I bought a new battery from the adjacent auto parts store. The rain broke just as I tightened down the last terminal. It was still unseasonably cold, but at least things seemed to be looking up.

I was just five hours from DC when I received a call from my buddy who was stationed in Norfolk.

"Hey, brother!" Ben Conger's cheerful voice grated my headache. "How's DC?"

I put the phone on speaker and set it on the dash. "I will let you know if I ever get there. I've had nothing but trouble."

"You're still on the road? Why don't you swing by Norfolk on your way up? Me and the guys will show you a good time," Ben laughed.

I shook my head. "I still need to get my apartment sorted. I have a few to look at, but I'm already late. I've had a blown-out tire, dead battery, a detour–"

My friend interrupted. "That sucks man. Hey, I heard what happened on your deployment. That sailor? MM3 what's-his-name."

"Sloan," I replied mechanically.

Ben spoke rapidly. "I knew him when he was undesignated on my ship. Weird kid." he continued in a hushed tone. "Are they going to string you up?"

"There's an ongoing investigation," I replied, "but that was my CO's circus. I handed off the deck and washed my hands of it. I told the quartermaster to make a record of my objection in the log. That should do it for me."

"Geez, man. Must've been rough. Anyways, come on down to Norfolk when you're not kissing some admiral's butt, okay?" Ben chuckled, apparently getting pulled away to do something.

"Will do," I replied.

We concluded with a few pleasantries before I hung up. Ben's pushy conversation style wore me thin. I just wasn't in the mood. When I placed the phone back in its holder, a notification caught my eye. My news aggregator spat a headline reading, "Chinese vessels conduct largest ever exercise around the island of . . ."

I slammed my brakes as hard as I could. The anti-lock system struggled to maintain traction on the wet roads. The bright red taillights of the truck in front of me approached at an alarming rate. At the last moment, I swerved onto the shoulder to avoid collision. I came to a stop even with the driver of the truck I would have hit. He was an older man with sunken blue eyes. He gave me the finger and edged forward. After waiting for him to pass, I sheepishly joined traffic. No one was moving more than a few miles per hour. The GPS indicated an accident several miles up the road, further delaying my arrival in DC.

Resting my head on the steering wheel, I moaned, "I'll never get there at this rate."

I still had a few days before I needed to report to the Pentagon, but I was losing valuable time needed to set my affairs in order. I set about glaring at the bumper stickers on the truck I nearly collided with. I ascertained that the driver was an Air Force veteran, avid gun rights advocate, and lifelong Republican. I never thought much of politics then.

I usually made vague homages to "the American way" or "democracy" when asked by family and friends, but my analysis never went any deeper. I felt almost a sense of obligation to give a recruitment-poster answer when asked about political questions. I only wanted more prestige and authority. Whose bidding I did made no more impact on my daily considerations than the color of my shoes. It wouldn't have made a difference if someone told me anyway. I was a cynical careerist through and through.

When I interviewed for my spot at the Naval Academy all those years ago, a retired Marine colonel posed a scenario to me:

"You're leading a convoy of Humvees through a dangerous area. You've been given strict orders not to stop for any reason, and a child runs out in front of you. What do you do?"

His eyes peered at me with unwavering interrogation.

I was just eighteen at the time, but I knew I needed to show my loyalty.

"I would do what was required of me," I replied.

The colonel nodded imperceptibly and continued the interview.

When Sloan's body slammed against the hull, I suppose I had done all that was required of me.

I stated my objection and forfeited the deck, I reassured myself. There's nothing else I could have done. This is on her conscience, not mine.

Traffic continued to move at a snail's pace. Not learning my lesson, I passively scrolled listings for apartments for rent. To my surprise, the housing allowance for the area would barely cover a one room studio near the Pentagon. Zooming out and lowering my standards as I kept a loose eye on traffic, a few results started to crop up in the remote suburbs.

The thumbnail of one listing caught my eye. It showed an ornate mansion with decorated gardens. The complex had an oxidized copper roof and a granite facade in the Beaux-Arts style. I slammed on the brakes again. Chastising myself, I tossed my phone to the passenger seat. The listing remained open on my phone. I stole another glance. The listing indicated the price as being well below my allowance.

No way.

I furrowed my brow and grabbed the phone as the cars started to move a little faster.

My eyes flitted between the road and the beautiful mansion on my screen. Scrolling through the description, I chuckled when I found the true nature of the rental. Only the small loft apartment above the three-car garage was available. I rolled my eyes and once more tossed the clickbait aside. Traffic resumed its regular pace just before I stopped for lunch.

As I ate my indiscernible slop, I found myself looking at the mansion again. The loft was fully furnished and had modern, up-to-date appliances. One picture showed the view out of the expansive window. I checked the location and found it to be near the town of Aldie, Virginia. My app calculated the commute time to be just under an hour.

Unthinkable, I scoffed.

The commute, with gate traffic, would make for an exhausting daily ritual. I was once again able to dismiss the listing and get back on the road. After some uneventful travel I was now just an hour from DC, with very little idea of where my true destination was. I debated sheltering in another civilian hotel or biting the bullet at the base transient lodging at Anacostia-Bolling.

I found myself thinking of the loft once more. Anything else I was likely to get would be terribly small, depressing, and ultimately unsafe. Despite it being the nation's capital, DC and its surrounding area had been racked with instability and crime. The Beltway served as a moving demilitarized zone where commuters could precariously make their way to their insulated office buildings and prestigious appointments without thinking about the violent urchins below too much.

I stopped at a gas station somewhere in Virginia. The listing was still pulled up on my phone. It displayed a number with instructions to ask for the loft.

What have I got to lose?

THE POTTER'S WHEEL

"Hello?" A soft female voice answered my call after just two rings.

I hesitated. I expected to be on hold for hours. I figured the number was for some large property acquisition firm.

"Yes . . . hello?" Her voice seemed to hold back tears.

"Hi, yeah, my name is Richard Malden," I continued with a creeping, inexplicable embarrassment. "I am interested in renting the property on Bowie Avenue."

My inquiry was met with silence. I could just make out the sound of her taking a deep breath.

"Hello?" I repeated.

"Yes, it's available," she resumed, "you will need to fill out an application."

I agreed.

Her voice cracked as if delivering news of a death in the family, "And then there's the interview."

"Interview?" I raised an eyebrow.

She remained quiet, unable or unwilling to reply.

"Okay, I can do that," I assented.

The woman waited a few seconds before replying, "You will be contacted after filling out the application."

She hung up without any further conversation. When the call cleared, my screen reverted to the listing.

What am I thinking? The commute alone would make this hell on earth.

I switched back to the GPS and got back on the road.

I didn't bother filling out the application. The seeping temptation to rent the loft was easily kept at bay by the prospective daily grind to and from the Pentagon. As I approached DC, I ultimately resigned to staying at the Navy Lodge. Passing gate security, I pulled up to the nondescript concrete building. I checked in and arrived at my room. Logging in to the Wi-Fi, I opened up my laptop to look at more apartments. Before I could set any filters or even enter a zip code, the mansion came up as the first result.

Thanks for tracking my data, I thought with disgust.

As I clicked away from the listing, I saw that I wasn't even signed in. My sign in was interrupted by an email notification. It read: "application deadline."

I clicked the notification and opened the email.

"Good afternoon, Mr. Malden," the email began. "Your inquiry has been received."

I looked at the email address and found it to be a generic string of letters and numbers.

The email continued: "Complete this application no later than 9:00 a.m. tomorrow. We await your response."

The message concluded with the logo of a company known as "Green Holdings." At first confused how they got my email address, I remembered how libertine the rental app was with personal data. I opened the document attached to the email. The application was the standard song and dance about proof of income and employment history. I decided to passively fill it out while streaming a show on the hotel TV and eating a paltry ramen dinner. The swift deadline was bizarre. I figured that the place probably had dozens of applications. Why would they reach out to me directly and impose a sense of urgency?

When I got to the end of the document, I observed a disclaimer that stated the property was under legacy covenants that governed the behavior of tenants. This did not strike me as odd. Every lease has provisions about things like dog ownership, appliance usage, or other mundane aspects of residency. I checked the box and saved the application. Feeling nihilistic about the whole affair, I dropped the file into my reply. The apathy lasted right up until my cursor hovered over the "send" icon.

I recalled a memory from when I was young. Laying in the coarse autumn sage grass, I sighted in an antelope. I was eleven or twelve and on a trip with my father to Wyoming. My heart pounded with the anticipation of the kill. I was roughly 200 yards away and the crosshairs rested on the animal's heart. Remembering the basics, I focused on slowing my breathing until I could perform one last exhale before pulling the trigger. In the stillness of that moment, the world went silent as the antelope perked up its head. My finger drifted from its position on the stock to the trigger. I let out the final breath.

Perched atop the mouse was that same finger. I started to increase pressure on the button. The same potential energy of a kinetic blast made the movement weighty and slow. The muscles of my finger fought each other for the dominant direction. At last, impulsivity won out: I pulled the trigger. I watched with bated breath as the button shifted to a loading graphic. The blue "undo" button sounded the alarm of a five second countdown.

As the time expired, my thoughts drifted once more to the antelope. From 200 yards, the size of the animal was difficult to discern. Its coat indicated it was an adult. When I approached, the antelope laid stoically in the dust. By its size, I ascertained it was freshly weaned, having just shed the markers of a fawn. My bullet had torn a path at the very bottom of its stomach. My father handed me a knife. Together, he guided my hand between the antelope's ribs. The animal called out in agony as repeated, slow, and deliberate stabs cut its life short. At last, it turned over on its side. I tested to see if the antelope was still alive by using a piece of grass to gently brush against its eye. The lid twitched slightly, then not at all. Any trepidations I had about the antelope or submitting the application faded away as I set my mind on my upcoming tour at the Pentagon.

I was set to be an executive assistant for the Deputy Chief of Naval Operations for manpower, personnel, and training education. This was an elaborate word salad to describe a secretary's job. The Navy specialized in this type of resume padding. At the time, I believed every last savory word of my title—and relished it. Just as I was nodding off, a phone call jolted me awake. The caller ID read, "private number."

"Your presence is requested at 613 Bowie Avenue at 11 p.m."

I recognized the voice from when I first called the listing.

"Tonight?" I interrogated.

She made no reply and simply hung up. I reckoned that the call got disconnected. I searched for the original number I called in the listing. To my immense confusion, the listing was nowhere to be found. I opened up my email and tried to see if there was a number in the message. With my luck running out, I searched, "Green Holdings" in my browser. No results. Before I could forget, I scrambled to write down the address. I looked back through my phone call history to try and call the first number. No answer. Next, I looked up the place on my phone's GPS. It was roughly an hour drive and the clock showed 9:58 p.m. For no discernible reason, I felt that there would be immense consequences for being late.

I dug through my seabag and found a reasonably nice button up shirt. I did my best to shake out its wrinkled appearance. Jumping into a pair of jeans and leather shoes, I was out the door. The desk attendant gave me a disapproving look as I ran toward the exit. My actions sailed out of control on the icy surface of imposed exigency.

Why is this so important? I directed my question as much at myself as my situation.

My car reluctantly came to life in the darkness. Not wanting to get hemmed up by base police, I reserved my recklessness for when I joined the Beltway. To my chagrin, every other driver on the road had the same strategy. As I rounded the northbound turn toward Merrifield, I attained the requisite escape velocity to leave DC's orbit. Coasting along I-66, I eventually made it to the back roads leading to the mansion. It was already 10:48.

The narrow turnpike road wove along stone fences and what would have been idyllic pastures in the daytime. The full moon poured a silver veneer on the countryside. It surprised me that such an untouched landscape could exist so close to the sprawling metropolis on the Beltway. With only a few minutes to spare, I caught a glimpse of a huge house beyond the trees out of the corner of my eye. The GPS indicated the entrance being just up the road, but the nighttime silhouette of the edifice against the starlit sky was unmistakable. I did not find the mansion. The mansion found me.

I turned into an unlit driveway. A small sign compelled visitors to turn off their headlights. On naval bases, this was common practice when approaching a guardhouse. I thoughtlessly complied, leaving me to creep along the drive in icy moonlight. Curiously small five-petal white flowers lined the drive and relayed the night's illumination to my eyes. All the while, the mansion's silhouette stood backlit beyond the trees like a gaping jaw. I found an intercom at the gate and pressed the button.

"Name and reason for visit," the metallic speakers broke the silence.

The voice seemed to be the same woman on the phone.

"Richard Malden," I started. For my reason, I could only wince as I said, "interview."

The electronic gate slid out of my path with almost no discernible sound. I gathered that the owner of this mansion was quite a particular man. I felt compelled to drive as slowly as I could to avoid making unnecessary noise. My eyes had adjusted to the light and I was able to navigate the driveway to the house. Even my breath reverberated at an uncomfortable volume. I became acutely aware of the sound of my car's engine and tires. I could just make out the outline of the garage to the right. In the loft's window was a solitary lit candle– the only other source of light besides the moon. When I pulled up to the grand staircase leading to the entrance, I shut the vehicle down. Unsure of how to proceed, I exited the cabin with deliberate movements. I grasped the door with both hands and gently guided it to the frame. When the latch clicked, the moon and stars vanished in a torrent of illumination.

At once, every light in the facade erupted. None of the monuments in DC could compare with the sheer spectacle of the luminous procession. I was blinded by the wall of harsh radiance that washed over me like a tidal wave. After adjusting slightly, I observed the outline of a man standing in the doorway. Whether he had just opened the door or watched the entirety of my entrance, I couldn't be sure.

"Mr. Malden," he called out. "The door is open."

His tone indicated that I should have already known this. Regardless, I perceived an invitation to ascend the granite steps to the entrance.

"Good evening, sir," I reverted to formal Navy parlance as I approached the titanic bronze doors.

The man remained silent and stepped back into the dim light of the foyer as I climbed the last steps. He was middle-aged, with hair the same color as the mansion's stone. He wore it slicked back above hawkish, narrow eyes of imperceptible color. His eyebrows hovered like birds of prey while his lips curled in a perverse smile. The closer I drew, the more I felt my heart compress within me like the hull of a submarine in the blackest reaches of the ocean.

"Good evening, Mr. Malden," he straightened his dark jacket over his turtleneck, "I am the owner of this estate. I wanted to interview you personally. Come along."

I had every impulse to about-face and run out as fast as I could. The deeper I walked into the mansion, the more I felt forbidden to leave. In the reflective surfaces of chandeliers and vases, I could sense my guide checking my progress. After an interminable journey through the lengthy galleries and hallways, we ended up in the same foyer where we started. We had made a circle. The man continued on as if nothing had changed. As we passed the bronze doors once more, still open to the cold night air, the urge to escape left my body. This was not out of relief—but despair.

The man cocked his head and observed me following with the corner of his eye. I saw the last vestiges of a grin as he faced forward again. The second lap brought us to a carved wooden door flanked by blue and white striped columns. We entered and found a cavernous dining room. The space was only lit by a crackling fireplace at one end.

The ceilings stretched to unknowable heights above my head. I could just barely see an elaborate fresco surrounding a dormant chandelier. A mahogany table the length of most houses commanded the polished masonry floor. I estimated it could seat more than a hundred people yet only a large, commanding chair sat at the head near the fireplace with a subordinate seat off to the side. In the flickering light, I saw paintings the height of the room on the walls. I could not discern what they were other than their abstract resemblance to children of all ages in various states of emaciation.

"Do you like my paintings?" the man asked as he led me to my seat.

I struggled to think of a good response. "I'm not sure I understand them."

"The irony," he began as he took his place at the head, "of starvation in the presence of plenty. Privation in the face of prosperity. The light of life holding on," he lifted his eyes to the nearest painting, "despite the divine desperately trying to extinguish it."

I could only nod politely. The man rotated his chair to face me directly. Our shadows danced in gesticulating forms on the walls.

"Jacob Green," he introduced himself.

Seeing as he did not extend his hand and already knew my name, I simply stated, "Pleasure to meet you."

Green pursed his lips and continued his analysis. "Man is master of his environment. If we choose to bind, it is bound. If we take, it is taken. If we burn"—he turned to look at the fire—"it is burnt."

Struggling to keep up, I replied, "I suppose that's true."

"You suppose," Green observed with disgust. He drew a pen from his jacket and began rotating it in his fingers as he continued, "What a bore."

"Sir?" I furrowed my brow.

"I gather you want to rent the loft," he rolled his eyes.

I had no idea how to reply. In all honesty, I just wanted to flee. Green's unflinching gaze forced me to speak.

"I filled out the application," I attempted to give a non-answer.

Green stopped twirling the pen and clenched his jaw.

I continued, "Yes, I would."

His demeanor lightened slightly. "You're a lieutenant commander in the Navy, correct? At the Pentagon?"

"Yes, but I don't start at the Pentagon until next week," I relayed.

Green tilted his head back and set the pen down. "I don't like it that you're working there."

"Why is that?" I attempted to project confidence.

He stated matter-of-factly, "You don't deserve it."

I was taken aback, "What?"

Green changed his tack. "It's just that it's a very special place. Hallowed ground so to speak."

"I suppose so."

"There you go supposing again," he snipped. "And you intend to rent my loft while you're there."

I couldn't understand if he was declaring it as fact or mocking the idea.

He continued, "How are you with following rules you don't understand?"

"I suppose—I mean, I generally am pretty good at it. I'm in the Navy, after all," I stumbled.

Green remained silent for a moment, as if to punish me for saying suppose again. With a summary click of his pen, he resumed. "And you won't tell anyone what you see or hear in the Pentagon?"

"Of course not," I stated adamantly. "That's all going to be classified."

My host stood up and walked over to the fireplace. He took a poker and prodded the logs to keep the fire alive. With the flame in his eyes, Green turned to me and said, "See to it that you hold your tongue."

I was utterly bewildered. I at first assumed he was going to try to extract privileged information from me. Now he was imploring me to keep my mouth shut.

"I've decided to let you stay in the loft," Green faced the fire once more, "I hope to see you grow into your role. I am displeased with where you're at."

"Look, if this is about what happened on my recent deployment," I started.

"What?" he interrupted. "Oh, yes, that. That did come up when I checked up on you. That's got nothing to do with it." Green approached me rapidly and loomed over my chair. "I never wanted you here. You were never supposed to make it here. Everyone agreed with me. We did everything we could to keep you from being here," he spit venom with each word, "But here you are like an advanced cancer. I'd rather keep an eye on you if you must be here."

He settled down and sat in his chair.

I remained dumbfounded. The sheer number of questions swirling in my brain kept me from speaking at all.

"It's settled. You'll be staying here, starting tonight. The leftmost spot in the garage will be yours. The stairs on the wall lead up to your quarters. I've seen to it that a key and garage door opener has been placed in your car's sun visor. Lights out at sunset. Rent is due on the first of the month. A security deposit of two months' rent is due tonight. You must provide advanced notice of any late nights or early mornings. No visitors unless they are personally approved by me." Green rattled off his intricate demands.

"Now hold on," I objected. "I don't feel comfortable with this arrangement."

He slapped the table, "Neither do I!"

The impact of his hand echoed throughout the great hall. We sat mute until the sound dissipated in the hall like distant thunder.

"But I don't suppose," he broke the silence with a mocking tone, "that either of us have a choice. Wisdom has revealed that to me already. If you are wise, you'll understand this too."

"Are you threatening me?" I attempted to show resolve.

Green continued to stare into my eyes with an unblinking gaze. He imperceptibly picked up the pen and tightened his grip until his knuckles showed white even in the amber light of the fire. My heart dropped and my blood ran cold. I was not physically intimidated by him at all, yet I knew there was nothing I could do to touch him. My body sat limp in the chair, utterly powerless to affect my situation. The way he held that pen evoked such inexplicable fear in me. At any moment I felt that he would lunge across the table and plunge it into my neck.

"You must be understanding, Mr. Malden," my host returned the pen to his coat pocket. "At the present time, you are an unmolded lump of clay spinning out of control on the potter's wheel. I never would have selected you, but I've already made my preferences clear. I am sure you can empathize with being told to shut up and follow orders."

I nodded carefully, without the slightest idea of what he meant. I was just relieved that he sheathed his weapon and shifted his tone.

Green continued, "I must play Eliyahu Ba'al Shem. Indeed, an Eliyahu to mitigate this disaster."

I attempted to regain my bearings. He spoke as if he had some kind of institutional authority over me.

"Are you an admiral?" I sheepishly inquired. "Or a detailer of some kind?"

The man leaned forward and stroked his chin. He narrowed his eyes and lowered his brow. With a small, contemptuous chuckle Green stated, "If that's what you need to see me as to grasp the gravity of my words, so be it."

I remained silent and suppressed a shiver despite the warmth of the fire.

"Enough talk for now. It's off to bed with you. I've already sent for your things."

At once, I was grasped firmly on the shoulders. I turned my head to see a tall, muscled man. I never heard him approach. He instructed me to stand up. As I turned to walk to the door, the large man stopped me.

"You must ask permission," he menaced.

Reeling from the unpredictability of the night, I elected to submit.

"Requesting permission to go to my quarters," I tried to avoid servile language.

Green silently waved his hand and swiveled his chair to face the fire. The embers started to wane as the room darkened even more. The last thing I saw before exiting the great hall was my host repeatedly thrusting the poker into the fire, creating a horrific percussive tempo that echoed throughout the house and my innermost anxieties.

I WON'T BE BACK

The burly man escorted me as far as my car. He returned up the grand staircase and shut the bronze doors. As soon as the entryway was shut, the blinding light show of the mansion's edifice extinguished. I once again stood alone in the soft, predatory gaze of the full moon. I felt as though I had passed like a carcass through a meat processing plant, only exiting as a stripped husk. My car stood idly by as a mockery of my imprisonment. There was nothing physically deterring me from leaving. With a good head of steam, I was confident I could bash through the gate. Nevertheless, I felt an impassible, velveteen barrier surrounding the estate. My incarceration was spiritual.

I reluctantly entered my car to make the short drive to the garage. Just as Green said, a key and garage door opener were wedged in my sun visor. I pulled up and pressed the button. It was no surprise that the door operated without any discernible sound. When I pulled into my bay, I noticed a temporary wall separating it from the rest of the garage. The garage automatically shut behind me as I stepped out of my car. I ascended the stairs to my room's door and looked closely at the key for the first time.

I could tell it was quite old, much older than the garage itself. The door appeared to be of similar age. The body of the key bore a symbol I did not recognize. The shape looked to be some kind of star but had eleven circles distributed throughout. The lines interconnecting them overlapped and darted every which way. The centermost circle had eight spokes connecting it to the other nodes. Each circle had fine inscriptions which I presumed to have worn away by decades of use.

I inserted it into the lock and opened the door. The room looked much as it was depicted in the listing when the motion detecting lights turned on. It was nicely furnished, clean, and modern. Nearly every surface was white. The floors were polished marble, with the vaulted ceiling hosting brushed aluminum fixtures above a sitting area. The lightbulbs were a harsh, fluorescent tone. In the corner was a kitchenette with slate cabinets and countertops that matched the floor. A stack of papers sat on the small dining table. I assumed this was the lease agreement. In any other circumstance, the loft would have been exquisite lodging. Beyond a small partition, I saw a black steel-framed bed with pinstripe sheets. The walls were decorated with some abstract paintings, all of which unsettled me.

What disturbed me most of all, however, was the large stack of boxes to my right. Upon closer inspection, I recognized them as the same ones I signed off on in Florida. My personal property had already been diverted here without my authorization or request. To my left, I saw the bags I had left in my hotel room. From these facts, I deduced two things: First, Green or his underlings have free access to military bases. Second, he has enough sway to give orders outside the normal operating procedure and have them followed.

Thoroughly fatigued, I collapsed on the bed. I left the lights on. Though a lieutenant commander and veteran of several deployments, I rediscovered my fear of the dark. As I laid there reeling, the lights shut off on their own accord. At this point I noticed the small window above the headboard. The moon intruded into my space through this portal and pointed its silver finger at the painting next to the bed. It was a simple black square. Two red dots, no larger than periods on a page beamed on the canvas. They were eyes.

I couldn't decide whether to sleep facing toward or away from this painting. This consideration was cut short by the understanding that I wouldn't be sleeping at all. Instead, I tried to keep my mind occupied as fear eroded my courage like the rushing of a great river swollen by rain.

Who is this man? I thought to myself.

I had the idea to play some white noise on my phone to ease my nerves. I shuffled through the darkness to find my phone charger. When

I returned, I found that my phone would not charge. Given that the lights did not turn on either, I reckoned that the electrical panel for the loft had been switched off.

That's what he'll be doing every night at sunset, I shook my head.

I left my phone on to play some comforting rain noise. I could charge it in the morning.

He has some kind of power, I mused, hard power.

I turned up my phone's volume to full blast. Any loss of situational awareness this caused was an added benefit in my mind.

He could be some kind of appointed official? Although I don't understand what kind of oversight an appointee would have over the selection of an admiral's executive assistant, I grappled with an unknowable reality.

The immense gravity Green lent to my relatively small position at the Pentagon made very little sense. I combed through my memory to see if there was anything else to indicate some special importance to my tour.

Sure, I had to pester my detailer for the spot. That's just how the system works. I am going to be setting appointments, taking phone calls, and coordinating meetings. I will be in proximity to some privileged information, but really nothing more than what you could guess.

My mind sailed through the possibilities, each one passing by uneventfully like a ship in the night.

Could Green be an intelligence operative?

This last thought seemed to make the most sense. The concealed nature of Green, it that was his real name, offered a fruitful avenue for speculation. Not only was it likely, this worldly possibility offered a backdoor away from my encroaching spiritual duress.

Perhaps CIA or even Mossad, I mused.

The latter prospect was something I would never discuss aloud. I was no stranger to the close interoperability between American and Israeli intelligence services. At the time, I assumed it was just because of the two countries' close regional cooperation. This was technically true. Even then, however, I knew not to speak too loudly about Israeli interests. I formulated a plan to contact a security representative at the Pentagon when I checked in. If this was all above board, I could at least rest easy with cooperating. If this was some kind of espionage, I could leverage some institutional backup to get me out of it. With a small feeling of control returning to my mind, I could at last get some harried sleep.

But he wanted me to conceal information?

My mind sputtered as I drifted away.

Taking the offensive the following morning, I found the original copy of my orders and suited up in my dress uniform. This was customary for one's first day at a new command. It was earlier than my report date, but that wouldn't be a problem. If anything, my command would look on this action favorably.

As I straightened the tie of my dress blues in the bathroom mirror, I contemplated how I would actually leave. I gathered a few things into an overnight bag. The rest I could retrieve when this was all over. Seeking to reclaim some lost masculinity from the fearful previous night, I chose to confidently exit my apartment, climb in my car, and drive to the gate. I would report Green and the whole matter would be resolved. Perhaps I even would get a medal for exposing a foreign intelligence operation.

The metal fence remained closed when I pulled up to the entrance. My adrenaline rose as I questioned my course of action. A red button sat impassively on a brickwork pillar next to the driveway. I rolled down the window and pensively pressed it with my fist. Nothing happened. I pressed it again, this time holding it for a few seconds. The gate remained unmovable. Just as I was about to exit the car and try to pry the gate open, a hidden speaker challenged me.

"Where are you going?"

"I am checking in early to my command," I stated calmly.

I heard some shuffling on the other end.

"You still have not paid your security deposit," she stated tersely.

Any attempt at sarcasm evaporated when I remembered Green aggressively stoking the fire.

"I will make sure you have it by tonight," I replied with no intention of returning.

The speaker remained quiet, and the gate sat immobile. I pressed the button a few more times in frustration.

"Your security deposit, Mr. Malden," she repeated. "The bank wiring address is in your lease agreement."

I clenched my jaw as I weighed my options. I considered my abortive plan from the previous night of ramming the fence. Not wanting to arouse suspicion in my captor, I decided to pay the extortive fee. After a curse-laden phone call with my bank, I wired the money to Green Holdings following my return to the room. I figured it was a small price to pay to leave the compound. Rushing back down the stairs, I again made an assault on the gate. Even though it was roughly 40 degrees, I began to sweat under the many layers of my uniform.

I pressed the button and tried to remain calm. "Okay, I paid the security deposit. I need to get to work."

The voice replied, "You said you were early."

My frustration mounted. "I don't want to show up in the middle of the day."

"Did you provide advance notice of leaving early?"

I closed my eyes and grimaced. The road sat at a tantalizing distance beyond the gate.

"No, I did not," I said in a defeated tone.

The woman did not reply.

"I was never informed how to do that," I pleaded.

"I am going to do you a favor," the sound of the speaker distorted.

I clenched my teeth and braced for what would come next.

The woman continued, "I will fill out the paperwork for you and let you go."

"Great, thanks," I shifted the car into drive and set my eyes forward.

Her tone lowered as if collapsing down a rocky hillside. "But you owe me."

She grasped his microphone like she would wring the neck of a bird.

My gaze returned to the immobile pillar with anxiety. I could not see a camera but was certain I was being watched.

"Swing by the guest house behind the mansion sometime and introduce yourself," the speaker called out.

The gate moved silently along its rails. I gripped the wheel tightly and lifted my foot off the brake. As I breached the plane of the fence, I was hit with a gust of air despite my windows being closed. At last, I was outside the walls. I could almost feel a hand reaching out to yank me back inside as I stepped on the gas.

"I won't be back," I said to myself like an incantation, as the mansion drifted away in my side mirror.

CHAIN OF COMMAND

After the hour-long drive, I pulled up to the gatehouse. The guard scanned my ID and gave me a salute. I returned the gesture and started looking for a parking spot. Seeing as it was well after 10 in the morning, empty spots were at a premium. I ended up needing to exit the gate and park in the overflow lot outside the base. This meant a long, brisk walk across the breezeway over the road to the Pentagon. I began to sweat again.

When I finally entered the enormous building, I set about looking for the Chief of Naval Operations' office. I was quite proud when I was promoted to lieutenant commander. At the Pentagon, though, I might as well have been an ant. I scurried through the flurry of activity and walked in a clockwise fashion around the perimeter of the building. Seeing as I was going to be in one of the deputy chiefs' offices, I figured I should search in E-Ring, the outermost ring of the Pentagon. Only the much higher-ranking officers were permitted to view the outside world from their windows.

When I found the CNO's office, a sailor rudely informed me that the Chief of Naval Personnel was in a temporary office all the way in A-Ring at the very center. His original quarters were being renovated. Frustrated and mentally spent, I got lost several times before making it to the inner ring. Several other corridors and offices were blocked off for renovations. I tried to find a directory of some sort before realizing that a temporary office was unlikely to be listed. I asked several people who looked reasonably competent only to be disappointed. Finally, a young female yeoman informed me that the CNP was located in the basement of all places. I descended to the subterranean level by the nearest ramp.

At long last, I found a cramped office space in corridor three of the A ring's basement level. A wooden sign with decorative fancywork bore golden letters reading: Deputy Chief of Naval Operations for Personnel, Manpower, and Training, Vice Admiral Kevin Simmons.

I entered the corridor and found a dour personnel specialist fiddling with paperwork. His name tape showed the name "Rodriguez."

"Hey PS1," I addressed him by his rank. "I'm LCDR Malden. I'm checking in early."

Rodriguez acknowledged my presence and took my orders. He rotated in his chair to grab a sheet of stickers. Peeling one off, he slapped it haphazardly on the front of my orders and signed it.

"Okay, sir," he recounted in the most disinterested tone he could muster, "I am going to have you fill out some extra paperwork."

This rigmarole was standard operating procedure. I sat down at a small round table to fill it out. I hesitated when I came to the address box on the first sheet.

"What should I put if I haven't found permanent lodging yet?" I asked.

PS1 sighed, "Just leave it blank."

My hand remained pinned in place.

"You can leave it blank," he repeated.

Inexplicably, I wrote down the address of the mansion. I shook my head and moved on. I repeated the same information dozens of times over the course of several forms, each time cementing the permanence of my residence there.

"All done," I handed in my paperwork like a failing student at the end of class.

The sailor took the stack and placed it on his desk.

"Where is the admiral's office?" I asked after a period of silence.

He gestured with an inarticulate grunt to the opposite wall, where two desks sat in front of a door behind a partition. I nodded and passed rows of colorless cubicles on my way to the office. The sailors occupying the desks alternately gave me blank stares or dumbfounded expressions. When I arrived at the partition, the admiral's door was closed. I presumed I would be spending a great deal of time at one of the two empty desks in front of me. I sat down in a row of waiting chairs on the side of the partition and looked around. The distinct lack of windows made the space feel cramped.

When I heard the door open, I shot up and straightened my uniform. A female officer exited first, using her manicured hands to redo her hair. The admiral, close behind, concealed a lascivious grin when he noticed me. He was a short man of unknowable ethnicity with graying brown hair. Coffee colored eyes floated like refuse above pronounced dark circles. The epaulets of his jacket, bearing three stars, bowed considerably from his rotund figure. His khaki pants were wrinkled and his shoes scuffed. If he were a junior officer, I would have sent him home to fix his uniform.

"You must be Malden," he used an authoritative tone.

"Yes sir," I replied eagerly while maintaining a posture of ignorance.

"Miss Katz, check him in," the admiral instructed the woman before returning to his office.

The female officer wore heavy makeup concealing deep acne scars. Foundation sat like a dusting of snow on her black jacket. Her hair skirted the ragged edge of regulations concerning highlights. She looked more at home in a Los Angeles shopping center than the Pentagon. Her uniform bore the insignia of a human resources officer. I mused that she looked quite young to be holding the same rank as myself. She managed an artificial smile to reveal perfectly straight, white teeth.

"Did you already get your orders stamped?" Katz asked with obnoxious vocal fry.

"Yes, all done."

She nodded and inserted her ID card into the computer. Typing in a few credentials, she grabbed a pair of glasses from the desk.

"It looks like Admiral Simmons is busy until 1200," Katz placed the glasses on, emphasizing her protruding nose.

I checked my watch again. It was 1115.

"Okay," I pursed my lips.

She motioned to the other desk to her left. "That'll be your desk. I've been doing his appointments until you could get here. I also handle in-house admin."

Uninterested, I sputtered, "Hey, who's our security manager?"

Katz looked up from her screen. "Oh, that's Commander Brown. He's on the second deck of E-Ring."

I clenched my teeth in frustration. I was just in E-Ring, all the way at the rim of the building.

"I am going to head over there real quick," I informed her and turned to leave.

"Don't be late," she called out in a tone meant to humiliate me.

A yeoman chuckled at me as I walked quickly out of the space into the hallway. I ran my fingers through my hair as I again rushed through the labyrinthine building. Weaving around slow walkers, my resolve wavered the closer I got to the outer ring. It was as if I could sense Green's hungry eyes the more I approached the outside air.

Could he find out about me reporting him? I anxiously wondered as I climbed a set of stairs.

With my quads burning, I found Commander Brown's office. Checking my watch again, I judged I had ample time. His door was open.

"Afternoon, sir," I knocked on his door frame.

"What's up, man?" his casual verbiage surprised me.

I inexplicably peaked over my shoulder. "I need to report something."

Brown lowered his brow and took on a grave look. He instructed me to sit down and close the door. "What's going on?" he asked with concern.

I realized I did not even have words to describe my situation. I did my best to recount the odd circumstances of the listing, the meeting with Green, and the threats I received.

"But he said he wanted you to keep your mouth shut?" Brown brought his hand contemplatively to his chin.

"Well yes, but there's just something off about this," I exclaimed despondently.

The commander began swiveling back and forth in his chair. "I agree. There's something really weird going down here. What was his name again?"

"Green. Jacob Green," I replied.

Brown squinted at his computer screen and searched the name. Unsurprisingly, he found nothing. He proceeded to look the address up on the map.

"Nice place," he muttered.

I glanced out his enviable window at the sun. The celestial ball sat impotently behind a layer of low-lying clouds

"Well," Brown sat back in his chair and put his hands behind his head, "You're not wrong here. Something's very strange."

I nodded with a pleading look.

"I assume you're not going back there tonight, are you?"

I stated emphatically, "No. Absolutely not."

Brown tightened his lips and nodded. "I am going to get this rolling up the chain of command. Just sit tight, we'll get this figured out."

The desire for an immediate resolution clawed at my chest. "Sir, I don't know how much time we have."

"Relax," he assured me. "I am taking this very seriously."

I didn't have any reason to doubt his sincerity. I realized I needed to go if I wanted to make my meeting with Admiral Simmons.

"Well, I need to head back to my work," I stood up, "I'm really not sure how to proceed."

Brown perceived my anxiety. "I am going to type up a report and take this straight up the chain. You'll have some guidance by the end of the day," he affirmed.

I thanked him for his time and began my sprint back to the basement. As I weaved through the swarm of personnel, the idea of a paper trail discoverable by Jacob Green gave me pause.

It was 1201 when I breathlessly arrived back at the admiral's office. Katz scowled at me the whole length of the corridor.

"You're late," she screeched at an uncomfortable volume.

My mind was in too much of a daze to reply.

Her eyes gestured to the office door. "Go on in."

I tried to perform a mental reset before checking in with the admiral.

"Take a seat, Mr. Malden," Simmons sat with his back to the door, typing an email.

I pulled up a chair next to his desk. He continued to clack away for several minutes. My eyes drifted to the various plaques and awards hanging on the walls. A cardboard box next to the desk contained even more. A display case showed dozens of challenge coins. I recognized the crest of my previous ship. A solitary picture and a silicone wedding ring were the only indicators he had a family. When Simmons finished the email, he loudly clicked the send button and sat back. Nodding for a moment, he swiveled to face me.

We drifted through various pleasantries, formalities, and expectations. Simmons, like all admirals, had the opportunity to lend the full institutional weight of the US Navy to his most pernicious idiosyncrasies.

"I hate bright sticky notes," he droned. "The pastels are better. If you put a bright one on my desk, I am going to throw it out without reading it."

I attempted to listen closely, but Green's voice kept haunting my every thought.

"Are you going to write any of this down?" the admiral creaked his chair.

"Yes sir," I fumbled for my notepad and pen.

I realized I left the pad at the mansion. When Simmons perceived that I didn't have it, he frowned and clicked his tongue.

"I expect more from you going forward," he turned to grab his phone. "Miss Katz?" he called her extension despite her being just outside of the door.

"Yes sir," she piped up.

"Reschedule LCDR Malden for another check-in tomorrow."

My disappointment at having made a bad first impression sullied any hopes of this tour being a good networking opportunity with the admiral. Katz agreed and set me up for the same time the following day. Simmons dismissed me, and I drifted to my desk. Katz raised her eyebrow and gave me a disapproving look.

"Get logged in, and I'll show you how to work the calendar," she ordered.

So much of my grand expectations for my time at the Pentagon collapsed in short order. The rest of the day consisted of passive-aggressive badgering from Katz, cold critiques from the admiral, fear of Green, and ultimately silence from the security manager. I didn't take a lunch break because I figured it would expend any goodwill I had left. Simmons left the office around 1700. Katz followed shortly after, but not before reminding me that someone needed to man the phones until 1830.

When I peeked my head above the partition, only one sailor was still in the office. He was gathering his things to leave.

I clicked my pen anxiously. Though I could not see the sun, I felt a sense of foreboding as the terminal traces of daylight sloughed off the Pentagon's limestone facade. Just as a rock left out in the sun runs cold after sunset, the deep bowels of the building took on an icy chill. I was alone now. As the seconds ticked away on my desk clock, I tried to find a phone directory. To my immense relief, I found a cell number for Commander Brown.

"The number you have dialed is no longer in service," the automated message stated.

JUST ONE MORE NIGHT

I swore bitterly as I slammed the phone down. Weighing my options, I decided to risk leaving the phone unattended to try and find him. For the third time, I scurried through the Pentagon though there were few personnel left in the building. When I found Brown's office again, he was nowhere to be found. I peeked my head around the corridor. An Air Force captain was gathering his things to leave.

"Have you seen Commander Brown?" I asked.

The captain shook his head and mentioned something about Brown rushing between several different offices. I sighed and made the exhausting shuffle back to my desk. At least the security manager was doing something. Nevertheless, I had very little idea of what to do if I heard nothing before the end of the day.

A blinking light on my desk phone indicated I had missed a call. I rushed to open the voicemail. To my immense disappointment, the message was not from Commander Brown.

"LCDR Malden, this is the admiral"—I rolled my eyes at this self-aggrandizing moniker—"I am calling to see if you're at your desk. We will discuss this tomorrow."

I stood dumbfounded for several seconds before slumping into my chair. "What a start," I exclaimed.

The mounting anxiety of what to do after 1830 caused my hands to shake. I could at least pretend nothing was amiss for the short remainder of my workday. I decided it was best to find a hotel and try to contact Brown again in the morning. Just before calling the Navy Lodge, I stopped myself.

Green had free access to my room there, I thought as I furrowed my brow and tapped my finger on the desk anxiously. He probably has access to the guest list too.

I would try to find a motel sleazy enough to not check my ID. At last, quitting time arrived like a judge exiting his chambers to deliver a sentence. I stood up to exit the vacant office space after taking a few breaths to calm my nerves.

As I went out to the corridor hallway, I shut off the buzzing fluorescent lights for the office. Deep in the belly of the Pentagon, silence mastered the hallways much in the same way it lorded over Green's estate. Only a few overhead lights in the corridor were left on to conserve overnight electricity. The gaps between the lit areas yawned with unconquerable darkness.

I started walking toward the stairs, my shoes making sharp clicks on the polished tile floor. As I passed a supply closet on my right, I felt the oddest sensation—one that I recognized. The same heaviness I felt when stranded in the swamps of South Carolina stopped me dead in my tracks. The last echoes of my footsteps dissipated into the opaque blackness.

That didn't happen, I clenched my fists and closed my eyes. I fell asleep at the wheel. Weird things happen on little sleep.

When I opened my eyes, I discovered that the remaining lights had been extinguished. There was no light at all except the sickly glow of the exit signs. The closet, just over my shoulder, radiated dread. I could have found it with my eyes closed using only that peculiar sensation to navigate.

Do something, my internal voice repeated. Do something!

I broke into a run. The clacking of my shoes sounded a terrifying drumbeat. A dim light hovered like a lighthouse at the entrance of the stairs. I focused my gaze on it as the night pursued me. As the sound of my footsteps reverberated on the hard surface of the floor, it sounded as if I was being closely hunted.

When I at last made it to the light at the foot of the stairs, I briefly turned my head to check the hallway. This succeeded only in causing me to trip on the first step and fall. The echoing steps crescendoed to an agonizing volume as I turned on my back as fast as I could. Only those who have experienced the raw, animalistic terror of an inexorable pursuer can understand how my voice pleaded without my conscious consent.

I put up my hands and yelled. "Get away! Get away!"

I squeezed my eyes shut, bracing for an unknowable danger. For an interminable moment, I floated adrift at the mercy of the darkness. The tightness in my chest subsided, and I noticed a glimmer of light through my eyelids. I also perceived a calm silence once more in the corridor. When I opened my eyes, the hallway was again lit intermittently along its stretch. I could just faintly make out the door of the closet.

I sat up, my limbs trembling with fear. "I'm losing it," I whispered, rubbing my face. "Scared of my own shadow. Just the sound of my footsteps."

I consoled myself in fragmentary shudders.

Once I was calm enough to stand, I looked down at my uniform. I found that my ribbon rack had torn off, taking a substantial patch of my jacket with it. This new disappointment, at least, gave me something else to stress about. Trembling legs bore me up the stairs to the ground floor. I took one last glance into the darkness of the basement before setting about finding my way to my car.

The pale, cloudy sunlight I saw in Brown's office was long gone by the time I made it outside. The temperature hovered just above freezing as I struggled over the breezeway to the overflow lot. My car sat under a solitary lamp post at the far end of the space.

The night appeared darker than it had ever been in my life. A few other vehicles sat across the quiet parking lot like a scattering of seeds. When I passed a nondescript late model SUV, I heard its door open.

"Mr. Malden," a voice startled me.

I turned to see the same large man who escorted me out of Green's dining room.

"Where are you going?" his face was shaded in the peculiar shadows of the lamp post.

I stood without saying a word for a moment.

"You're late," he informed me.

"I don't get off work until 6:30," I protested.

The man stepped forward and crossed his arms. At last, I could study his appearance. His sable hair stretched over a dark-complexioned skull in a tightly bound ponytail. His black eyes were punctuated by a small teardrop tattoo. The man's tawny arms bore an unknowable mess of ink, mostly of calavera motifs. The hilt of a large combat knife protruded just above the inside of his waistband.

"You're late," he repeated obtusely.

I shrugged slightly. "I don't have control over that. What time was I supposed to be back?"

The man rested a hand on the knife. After a brief stare-down, he turned to enter the SUV after muttering something in Spanish. The man started his car and turned on the headlights. He motioned for me to get into my car. My plan of avoiding the mansion fell apart before my eyes as I resignedly trudged to my vehicle.

The man honked impatiently. I gripped the steering wheel tightly and unwillingly pulled away from my spot. The SUV pulled in close behind, its bright LED headlights glaring in my rearview mirror. He remained only a few feet behind my bumper the entire anxiety filled drive back to the mansion.

When we were only a quarter mile from the gate, he inexplicably passed me and made preparations to dart into the driveway. The SUV turned off its lights and passed through the entrance unhindered. I followed shortly behind and begrudgingly shut off my headlights just as I noticed the gate closing behind him. It was theoretically possible to slam the car into reverse and dart off into the night. The realm of the theoretical seldom intersects with the practical. I was caught in the magnetic field of the mansion and was drawn to the gate like a hooked fish.

"An early start and a late night," the woman greeted me once more.

I rested my head on the steering wheel. "I work until 6:30 and have to make an hour drive to get here."

"That's going to be more paperwork," she sighed. "You're going to have to stop by tomorrow morning before work."

I clenched my teeth and muttered, "Fine."

The gate retracted swiftly as the enclosure swallowed me whole once again. When I arrived back in my room, I took off my torn jacket and sat dejectedly at the dining table. I was desperately hungry. I got up to examine the fridge. To my surprise, it was well stocked with provisions. Reaching for a microwavable lasagna, I stopped. Anything I took I was likely liable to pay for. Given what I could perceive about Green's nature, payment could take many forms. Hunger ultimately got the best of me.

How much could a premade lasagna cost anyway?

The plastic tray rotated as the microwave hummed right up until the moment the power shut off. I slammed my fist on the countertop and fumbled around in the darkness.

"Lights out after sunset," I sighed.

I figured the motion activated light must start a timer to cut power to the loft if I arrive after sunset. The light switches all toggled uselessly. The fridge was still working, but its internal light refused to turn on. Too hungry to care, I removed the lukewarm pasta from the microwave and consumed it like a savage in a cave. Under any other circumstance, I would have been revolted by the taste. Upon finishing my meal, I reassessed my situation. I needed to visit the guest house before I left to be allowed out in the morning.

Probably more money I have to cough up, I thought in disgust.

I intended to head back to the Pentagon in the morning and start my workday like nothing was amiss. Commander Brown would surely have an answer for me by then and this nightmare would soon be over. I held on to hope once again as I braved another night in the loft. While waning from its fullness, the moon peaked from the clouds and once more illuminated the red eyes of the painting adjacent to the bed. I clenched my fists under the covers

"Just one more night," I tried to remain brave.

LITTLE TOY SOLDIER

I awoke early in my room to birds chirping in the crisp morning air. After putting on my khaki uniform, I ventured outside to find the guest house. It was considerably warmer than the previous day, but the grounds remained cloaked in a damp fog. I could see a branch of the driveway sprouting around the far edge of the mansion. As I passed the grand staircase, I looked up at the imposing doors. Every window had curtains drawn. I made my way around the main building to the back lot. The decorative garden at the rear dwarfed the front in scale and grandeur with trimmed hedges and exquisite sculpture. Set beside the garden was a modest cottage with gray wooden siding to match the color of the mansion's imposing masonry.

I approached the door and mentally prepared to do battle with whatever waited inside. A burnished brass knocker sat on the burgundy door below an engraved sign. The letters spelled out "admin office."

I rapped the knocker three times. An electronic buzz signaled that I was permitted to enter. I discovered a sterile atrium about the size of a storage shed artificially dividing the hallway from the rest of the house. At the end stood a counter with an opaque one-way partition.

"Richard Malden," the voice I recognized from the gate chirped through the speakers in atone I distrusted.

"Good morning," I replied, stepping away from the counter.

"Come closer, I don't bite," the woman coaxed.

Her tone was vastly different from the first mournful phone call.

Reluctantly, I inched to the counter. I noticed a small slot where the counter met the partition, presumably where paperwork could be transferred. Above me sat the unblinking eye of a security camera. I didn't know whether it was appropriate to address the voice facing the camera or the partition.

"I'm here to do my paperwork," I stated meekly.

The slot opened suddenly, making me startle. A wooden ruler slid a piece of paper through. A pen sat neatly on the top page as the slot closed without any further explanation. Unfazed, I set about filling the sheet out. The Navy conditioned me to be unperturbed by banal paperwork and byzantine administrative processes. The sheet asked me to list my regular work schedule and a work phone number. Hesitating for a moment, I put down the number for the Pentagon quarterdeck. This at least would provide a few layers of call transfers before they ever got to me, if permitted at all. The backside of the page was a simple form to request a late night. It was retroactively dated for the previous night. I mindlessly filled it out and placed it in front of the slot.

"Done," I tersely stated.

The same ruler protruded from the slot and slithered the page behind the partition. I waited for several minutes and checked my watch.

"You still owe me," she reminded as the volume of the partition's speaker snapped.

"What do I need to do?" I shuffled my feet and put my hands in my pockets.

I could almost sense a smile on the other side of the plastic. I heard the door buzz and unlock behind me. I realized I had been previously locked in. I turned to look cautiously at the door then back at the camera. I waited for a few seconds.

"You're quite pliable, aren't you?" the woman prodded. "Little toy soldier waits patiently for orders."

I shook my head and stormed out. I caught the last ripples of laughter as the door closed behind me. When I arrived at the gate, I angrily pressed the button.

"Mr. Malden," the woman piped up again, "I will be seeing you again."

Her tone made the statement sound imperative. Before I could manufacture a reply, the gate opened. I drove through and made my way back to the Pentagon. I was still quite early as I wanted to get a proper parking space inside the gates. I secured a good spot and headed inside.

Before I went down to the basement, I navigated to Commander Brown's office. When I got there, I found that his nameplate had been removed from his door. Moreover, his office was completely cleaned out. Confused, I went next door.

"Hey, good morning, sorry to bother you," I addressed the Army major in the next office. "Where did Commander Brown go?"

The major cocked his head to the side in confusion. "Commander Brown?"

"He was right next door," I gestured toward the office.

"Honestly I don't even know what my job here is," he joked. "There might've been a Commander Brown there, but I just moved into this office today. The whole Pentagon is getting reshuffled from these renovations."

Disheartened, I let out a frustrated sigh. I turned to fight the swells of slow walking traffic in the labyrinthine corridors once more. I averted my gaze from the supply closet I fled from the previous night. I arrived at my desk fifteen minutes early. Neither Katz nor Admiral Simmons was in yet. A few sailors putted mindlessly between the cubicles, poking their heads up like prairie dogs. I logged into the computer and set about looking up Brown's email address. Without knowing his first name, the process became a fool's errand.

"Hey," I sniped one of the sailors trying to scurry to the safety of his cubicle.

"Yes sir?" He straightened up.

"Who is the assistant security manager?"

The sailor thought for a moment. "Pretty sure it's Commander Brown."

"No, he's the primary. Who's his backup?" I questioned.

"Oh yeah, well he was the secondary. We didn't have a security manager for a while because the old one retired in the middle of his tour. Brown was his backup and took on the position," the sailor recounted.

I clenched my jaw in frustration. "So, there's no assistant security manager?"

"Not that I know of," he scurried off to his desk.

There must be someone that I can talk to about my situation, I bargained.

Before I could plot my next move, Katz showed up wearing a sour expression. As she weaved between our desks to get to hers, I was revolted by the excessive perfume she had on. She plopped down, logged in, and scrawled something on a sticky note.

"Hey, can you add this to the calendar and then put this on his desk?" Katz turned to face me.

Why don't you do it? I thought.

I agreed and took the sticky note. It was bright yellow.

"He doesn't like the bright sticky notes," I corrected.

She opened her mouth slightly before replying, "I guess you'll need to copy it down then."

I gripped the note tightly in my hand and clenched my teeth. My cumulative lack of sleep and stress made keeping my cool nearly impossible. I eyed the stapler on my desk with violent intent. She turned away from me and typed on her computer. I stood up and slapped the note on her desk. The sound startled her and caused a few heads to perk up in the office. I pointed my finger directly at her face.

"Listen," I started, "I wear the same rank you do, and I think I've earned mine more than yours." Both my words and my volume outstripped my better judgment. "So next time you want me to copy a note for you, shove it up your—"

"LCDR Malden!" Admiral Simmons arrived on deck.

I turned my head, my finger still pointed in Katz's face.

"My office—now," he brushed past us.

I chastised myself for letting her get to me as I sulked to the admiral's office.

"Close the door," he instructed.

I began to sit in the chair in front of his desk.

"Stand at attention," Simmons corrected.

Once more, my anger boiled as I stood erect. I clenched my fists as hard as I could, and my nails dug deep into my palms.

"Jennifer Katz is a lieutenant commander in the United States Navy," he began his lecture. "You are also a lieutenant commander in the United States Navy. She deserves as much respect as you do. You, as a prospective senior officer, should know better than to . . ."

My mind went blank as I tuned out the admiral's words. Only a few days ago, this correction would have sent me spiraling. An admiral's rebuke would have collapsed my self-image and shaken my confidence. Now, all I could think of was my own survival—and my imprisonment.

"And this certainly will appear on your next performance report unless you seriously turn things around," Simmons concluded his tirade.

"Aye sir," I blankly replied.

He sighed. "Go ashore."

I drifted listlessly back to my desk. I glanced at my coworker expecting to see a coy grin. Instead, she was visibly shaken and averted eye contact. I noticed she was adding something to the admiral's calendar and copying the sticky note. One of the sailors walking by nodded at me with respect. It seemed as if I had impulsively expressed sentiments shared by the majority of the office.

The admiral left his chambers and informed us that he was headed to a meeting.

Waiting a short period, I asked Katz, "Who else is a security manager?"

My voice made her dart her eyes before sputtering a reply. "I think Colonel Avery handles the other side of the building."

Without asking, I got up to find him. I needed to get this sorted— I could not stomach one more night in that casket above the garage. I walked quickly in the hopes I could make it back to my desk before the admiral was done with his meeting. As I cut through the central courtyard, I observed a sailor wearing coveralls sitting with his back to me on a bench on the far side. He took a long drag on his cigarette and blew the cloud into the air. I did a double take. Before I could get a better look, a group of officers walked in front of my view. When they passed, he was gone.

Colonel Avery's office was on the inside ring on the third floor. I managed to catch him just as he was leaving.

"Sir!" I called after him.

The Marine officer craned his head to look at me.

"I know you're probably busy, but I have something very important to report." I stated quickly.

Avery looked at me silently and read my name tag. His austere gray eyes lifted to meet my own. I saw from his ribbon rack that he had earned the Purple Heart and Bronze Star with the combat "V."

"What is it?" his gaze dropped to my name tag again.

His voice sounded like the dying breath of a wounded animal. We entered his office and I relayed my predicament. Colonel Avery listened disinterestedly and periodically fiddled with his wedding ring. He began to stare blankly at a picture of his wife and children. Avery looked me directly in the eyes and interrupted my account.

"What's your first name?" he asked in a burdened tone.

"Richard," I replied.

"Richard, I don't want you to ever mention the name Jacob Green to me ever again," he began. Before I could protest, Avery continued, "This conversation never happened. We've never met. We never spoke. I have no idea who you are or what you do. Jacob Green is a name I've never heard before. You will never come by my office again. If you have to pass through this corridor, you take a different route," he emphasized each statement with a period of silence, "Now, you're going to stand up, turn around, and discreetly exit my office."

I sat back with a pleading look. "Something's got to give here!"

"Get out!" he leaned forward and aggressively pointed at the door.

I got up and stumbled over my chair on my way out. Avery aggressively closed the door behind me.

What does he know about Green? I stood in front of his door, awestruck.

Checking my watch, I forced myself to start walking back.

What is going on? I repeated in my head until my thoughts raced beyond my control.

I absentmindedly checked the bench where I had seen that sailor. He was gone, of course, but I couldn't shake the memory of him. Back at my desk, I was relieved to see that Admiral Simmons had not returned yet. Trying to get my mind off things, I fielded phone calls and answered emails. A piece of paper taped next to the phone dictated the mindless script I needed to repeat each time.

"Good afternoon, sir or ma'am, Office of the Chief of Naval Personnel, this is LCDR Malden speaking. How may I direct your call?"

"Mr. Malden, this is the admiral," he began. "I see you're settling in a little better now."

I affirmed.

"Clear my calendar for the rest of the day. Reschedule all of it. I'm needed at the meeting with the Joint Chiefs," Simmons commanded.

STIRRING IN THE EAST

We concluded our call, and I started re-arranging his calendar. I paused for a moment. An unexpected meeting of the Joint Chiefs of Staff, the heads of all the services, was certainly out of the ordinary. I opened up a new tab and looked at international news. In the aftermath of Taiwanese elections, China sortied a large fleet near the island. While ostensibly a pre-announced exercise, the presence of huge numbers of laden landing craft struck me as odd. Also in the lineup were three new full-sized aircraft carriers and ten light carriers. The article I read speculated that the fleet was unlikely to take any action beyond a soft blockade, selectively inhibiting or inspecting ships from certain countries.

The number of times in my life that war with China almost happened was more than I could count. I was entirely numb to the prospect and clicked away from the tab. The impromptu meeting of the chiefs indicated a heightened level of seriousness, but I brushed it off. I had bigger problems on my hands.

I frittered my morning away calling around to various departments to notify them of their rescheduled meeting. It was noon before I finished. I was thankful enough that my punitive second check-in was canceled for the time being. When Katz returned from her lunch break, I got up to head to the food court. The presence of a full selection of flagship fast food restaurants just off the central courtyard provided some much-needed situational comedic relief. I chose the fried chicken restaurant and sat down at a grubby table facing the window.

Pale autumn sunlight cast mournful shadows in the courtyard as the day grew shorter. I once more saw the sailor in coveralls at the far edge. His back remained turned against me as he smoked. The sailor sat hunched over as if carrying an unknowable burden. I had the urge to get up to investigate him, but I didn't want to waste the valuable minutes of leisure on my break. I thought it was quite odd that he was permitted to wear coveralls at all, a uniform reserved for shipboard wear. I finished eating and returned to the unflinching clutches of the basement.

Admiral Simmons was unexpectedly in his office upon my return. He beckoned me into his office when I approached.

"Let's knock out your check-in real quick," he heaved his flabby body around.

Katz regained some of her adversarial courage and glared at me.

"How are you settling in?" Simmons attempted to put on the facade of a caring commanding officer.

"Pretty good sir," I fibbed.

He nodded. "Do you feel confident with the calendar system?"

"Yes sir, I do."

"Good, good. Have you found a place to stay yet?" Simmons inquired.

I froze. The admiral didn't really care what my answer was. "Yes," I sputtered.

Simmons raised his eyebrows, "Well, here are my expectations for you going forward." He abruptly changed the subject.

I went through the motions of taking notes.

"And ensure we're using proper naval letter format according to the book. This is the office of the Chief of Naval Personnel. We have an image to uphold," Simmons muttered on.

I nodded and pretended to be engaged.

"And one more thing," he lowered his tone. "I know about the ongoing investigation with what happened on your last deployment."

In all honesty, Sloan's death had been the furthest thing from my mind.

"I've read the preliminary report," Simmons continued.

My pulse spiked. This report had not yet been released.

"I will reveal that it's looking good for you. Initial findings absolve you of wrongdoing," he stated with a large pause, "but I remain unconvinced."

"How so?" I asked.

Simmons went on to tell me that Commander Fowler, my former commanding officer, was one of his old friends. "She was one of our best division officers when I was a department head on that very ship."

I wondered what the real nature of their alleged friendship was.

"I acted in accordance with procedure," I informed him.

"In accordance with procedure," Simmons repeated in a lightly mocking tone. "Kate Fowler is a very special leader and an extraordinary woman. I am disappointed her career may be put in jeopardy over this."

"That's out of my control," I stated bluntly.

Simmons crossed his arms and nodded after a short period of silence. "Very well. Consider this check-in over. Return to your desk."

I got up to leave.

"And you finished rearranging my schedule for today?" He called out.

"Yes sir, all done." I replied.

"Good."

Simmons turned toward his computer once more.

When I returned to the partition, Katz quickly turned around. She had clearly been listening in on our conversation. I expected her expression to be saturated with schadenfreude at my increasingly rocky relationship with Admiral Simmons. On the contrary, she was brimming with jealousy.

The office phone rang.

"Get this one, will you?" I sat dejected in my chair.

Katz huffed, then begrudgingly consented. She was interrupted halfway through her script. "It's for you, Malden," she said in disgust.

My heart leapt. Perhaps Commander Brown had gotten back to me.

She transferred the call to my desk.

"This is LCDR Malden."

"Richard Malden," the woman stated, as if disappointed at how easy it was to reach me.

I tightened my jaw and looked around the office anxiously.

"Funny little trick with the quarterdeck number," she continued. "I recognized the number. It's actually quite easy to get transferred around the Pentagon when you sound confident."

I remained unable to speak.

"There's a party tonight at the mansion. Don't worry, you're not invited. What you must concern yourself with, however, is remaining in your quarters. Mr. Green instructed me to inform you that your presence is most prohibited. Lock your door, draw your curtains, and remain quiet. Is that clear?" the voice commanded.

"Yes," I croaked in a beleaguered tone.

"Mr. Green respects the privacy of his guests and compels you to do the same. Do you understand?" she warned.

"Yes," I agreed robotically.

She hung up.

In all reality, these expectations did not differ from my nightly routine. My hand drifted slowly to set the phone back on its receiver. The occurrence of this party was the only thing to alert me that it was Friday. The thought of a long weekend trapped in my loft apartment was enough to send me into fight-or-flight. I couldn't just sit there and rot all weekend; although something stirred in me that I may not be left idle.

I searched for a base directory on the Pentagon's intranet, hoping to find Commander Brown or at least the next level up the chain of command. My capacity for disappointment and dread had become so fatigued that Brown's complete absence from the directory made little impression. Colonel Avery appeared, but that was an obvious dead end. I took a deep breath and sought his superior. Air Force Brigadier General Darren Jones was in charge of counterintelligence for the whole Pentagon. My plan to meet him would come up against several roadblocks: Jones was sure to have a secretary like myself gatekeeping access to him. Second, I would be leaving a cyber trail if I got on his calendar. Finally, the whole exercise could be for naught if Jones gave me the same treatment as Colonel Avery.

Ultimately, I had no choice. After Admiral Simmons had left for the next session of the Joint Chiefs, I bided my time until Katz took a bathroom break. I didn't want to waste valuable time weaving through corridors and getting lost so I dialed the extension for Jones' office. The officer on the other end droned through a script that closely paralleled mine. He identified himself as Major Tyree Sievert. I recognized his thick Mississippi accent.

"Good afternoon, this is LCDR Malden with the Chief of Naval Personnel," I began. "Hey, didn't you do an exchange semester at the Naval Academy?"

"You know it," Sievert chuckled. "I was in Third Company that year."

I lightened up for a moment. "Man, that's a blast from the past. I was in Second Company. I remember when they glued your uniform to the Herndon Monument during Air Force Week."

He cracked up. "Those plebes were on restriction for months after that!"

We both took a moment to laugh. I couldn't remember the last time I smiled.

"What can I do for y'all?" Sievert asked after the memory subsided.

The immense seriousness of my situation spread like an unabated house fire, collapsing my transient happiness.

"I need to speak with General Jones," I said mournfully.

"Okay," he began typing on his computer. "What time is the admiral requesting?"

"No, no," I corrected. "It's me personally, not the admiral."

Sievert's voice changed tone "Oh. Well, he's looking pretty booked."

"That's fine," I attempted to move the process along.

"Let me get back to you," he abruptly ended the phone call.

Katz returned, and my chance was gone. I found myself slumping into a nihilistic depression for the rest of the afternoon. All I could do was sit helplessly at my desk, staring into the abyssal light show on my computer screen. The small peak of the comical memory only emphasized the deep trough I found myself in. I looked at my class ring and reflected on the course of my life. It all seemed so up and coming– until it wasn't.

Where did I go so wrong?

NO WAY OUT BUT THROUGH

The voice reiterated the instructions for the night when I returned to the gate. Surrender was beginning to creep into every crevice of my mind the whole drive to the mansion. I acknowledged my orders, and the gate opened. I had managed a small act of defiance, however. I rushed into a gas station somewhere along the Beltway and bought a few premade sandwiches, drinks, and a phone charging pack to hold me over the weekend. I took a deep breath at the threshold of my room and looked down at my key. I couldn't shake the feeling that I had seen that symbol before. I joked to myself that locking my door when I left in the morning was quite useless. I hoped to cultivate more humor in my situation, lest I go insane.

I entered the room and scrambled to get my affairs in order before the lights would rudely shut off. I became shrouded in darkness right in the middle of relieving myself. I forced myself to laugh at my plight. Doing my best not to soak the bathroom floor, I finished and went to the sink. Given the lack of ambient light, fumbling my way through the room became arduous. I settled in at the dining table in utter darkness. My phone showed that it was just before 2000. I did not know when the guests would arrive, but I figured it wouldn't be long. My curiosity at the nature of the party and its attendees got the better of me.

I cautiously separated the curtains just enough to peak at the gate. The mansion remained cloaked in its impenetrable haze of stifling inactivity. My pulse rose before I hurriedly closed the curtains. I wrestled with following my instructions in the name of safety. I couldn't ignore my humiliated state and felt an odd sense of duty to resist. I unwrapped one of the overpriced sandwiches and pulled a chair next to the window. I used my foot to move the curtain ever so slightly to observe the gate. Another half hour passed uneventfully. I grew bored of my defiance and wondered if the instructions were some kind of psychological warfare tactic to keep me in fear.

Perhaps there's no party at all, I wondered.

I pushed aside my half-eaten sandwich and decided to call it an early night; sleep was the only escape from the reality of my captivity. With the moon hidden behind clouds, the grotesque figure beside my bed finally vanished from sight, though I still felt the weight of its burning red eyes. I turned toward the painting—only to jolt upright as a sliver of silver light cut across the entryway. Through the curtains at the far window, a narrow blade of light stretched across the bed. I ducked low, heart pounding, and watched it crawl over the blankets before curiosity drove me to inch toward the window. A cold draft poured through a gap in the heavy curtains.

Like a carnival starting up for the weekend, the mansion was awash with light just as it had been when Green made his debut to me. The sculptures and fountains in the front plot cast long shadows resembling a Mayan priest's obsidian blade. I could barely see the tall man who surprised me in the Pentagon parking lot standing next to the bronze doors. The staircase was adorned with a blood red carpet. Next to him was a large coat rack already full of garments. I wondered if the guests were already here and were just now about to leave.

This speculation fell away when I observed the first car pull up to the gate. It was a British luxury sedan with a beautiful stainless-steel hood and cyan-blue bodywork. The driver approached the grand staircase and dropped off a passenger. The guest was exquisitely dressed in a fine tuxedo. The tall man recognized him. He handed the guest a garment from the rack and showed him inside.

Focusing my vision in the optic, I saw he took a robe the color of dried blood. It was simple and unadorned. The material looked to be some kind of felt or velvet. The other robes on the rack were all similar muted shades. Just before entering, the new arrival placed the clothing over his tuxedo and pulled its large hood over his head before entering the mansion.

I recoiled from the window. My face ran red, and my chest tightened. I felt a peculiar sense of shame as if I had just caught a close friend in an unspeakable act of impropriety. The scene, fast making a peculiar impression on my memory, burned in my mind like a wayward ember. My stomach turned, and I rushed to the bathroom. On my way over, I tripped over the couch and vomited on the polished marble floor.

My body shook like leaf as an unbearable heaviness permeated the air making it difficult to breathe. After regaining a small measure of composure, I managed to find some paper towels to clean up my mess. All the while, I heard more and more cars arriving while I dry heaved. Guests began laughing joyfully as they greeted each other on their way inside.

With the vomit cleaned up, I sat on the couch. The radiant beam of light penetrating the narrow gap in the curtains sat between my eyes, poised like an executioner's blade. My throat still burned from the acidic flow. I was caught between my morbid, magnetic curiosity and the sinking fear of looking again. I slid off the couch to the floor. My seabag sat in a shapeless pile at the corner of the room. I remembered a compact pair of binoculars sitting near the top.

My curiosity was overpowered by the unshakeable feeling of dread, but I felt a sense of obligation to peek through the curtain once more. Grabbing the binoculars, I observed a gloss-black German coupe pass through the gate. I saw that multiple rows of cars dotted the open space beside the garden, but most guests were dropped off by drivers. The coupe pulled into a spot at the far end of the first row. A heavyset man exited first, then did his best to scramble to the passenger side. A woman impatiently opened the door and stepped out. I could see that they exchanged some heated words as the man closed the door for her. As their faces turned to the light of the mansion's facade, I nearly dropped the binoculars. It was Admiral Simmons and Jennifer Katz. She was dressed in a lurid red dress, accentuated with a shining necklace. Simmons wore a standard tuxedo.

He offered his arm as they walked to the staircase, but Katz snubbed this gesture. Simmons let his arm fall flaccid to his elephantine torso in frustration. She struggled to walk quickly in high heels, desperately trying to outrun her escort. A few more guests arrived in limousines bearing small American flags. My focus, however, was on the unhappy couple. Katz arrived first and angrily took her robe. She attempted to rush in, but the tall man stopped her. They exchanged some words before she made a scene of putting on the robe. Following Katz, Simmons put on his garment and went inside.

I sat back as my body went limp. The binoculars weighed on my lap as if they were made of lead. I could not bring myself to look again as an untold number of guests passed through Jacob Green's mandible doors. After about a quarter of an hour, the raucous cheers and laughter on the mansion's grounds fell silent. I separated the curtain just in time to see the bronze doors shut with a tectonic thud. With this noise, the lights once more went out. An unknowable quiet returned as the house digested its visitors.

I jumped out of my seat as my cell phone rang. I scrambled to keep it silent. Though I was enclosed in the loft, I felt as if the sound of my ringtone would carry straight to Green's ears. When I found my phone, the caller ID again showed "Private Number." I silenced the ringer but debated what I should do about the call itself. My thumb hovered over the red "deny" button. Each passing vibration raised the stakes. In a panic, I accepted the call.

"Hello?" I whispered.

The caller said nothing for an eternity. I nearly hung up.

"You've been peeking," the woman said.

My adrenaline scrambled as I tried to come up with a plausible denial.

"Don't even try to deny it," she continued. "I saw you."

I made no reply.

"It's okay to be a little curious," the woman took on a conciliatory tone, "to wonder what takes place beyond the veil. So, what did you see?"

I struggled to piece together the words, "It—I, well…just random people arriving. I couldn't really see anything. The lights were too bright."

"So, you don't know Kevin Simmons or Jennifer Katz? That's a relief. I am glad you don't know those people," the voice cut with her words.

The phone began trembling in my hand.

"So, let me ask you again: What did you see?"

My voice quivered as I reluctantly told all that I saw. My soul felt tainted by the memories I recounted despite their surface level inanity. The voice took a voyeuristic pleasure in hearing the night's events retold.

"And did you see the robes?" she nearly giggled.

"Yes," I admitted.

"Excellent," she continued. "You've given me a lot of material."

Just when I thought the nature of my imprisonment could not get worse, it did.

"Information comes at a price. You've seen things that every desperate socialite would sacrifice their child to see," the voice described my situation. "You've been afforded an advance. A debt that must be repaid."

"I never wanted to see any of that," I protested.

The woman hissed, "No one made you crawl out of bed to look, did they?"

Words failed me. The fact she knew I had to get out of my bed revealed to me that there must be cameras in the room. I scolded myself for not assuming this from the beginning.

"Like it or not, Mr. Malden, you've crossed the threshold into a world beyond your comprehension. You've entered the arena to the jeers of an untold number of spectators who would love nothing more than to see your blood paint the sand."

I could not discern if the voice was one such bloodthirsty member of the audience.

"Now hush," she commanded. "Walk over to the door and embrace it."

I anxiously eyed the dark silhouette of the ancient portal leading to the garage. I found myself unwilling and unable to resist. Shuffling in the dark, I stood before it.

"Press your body up against it and listen carefully," the woman compelled.

I warily complied with my head turned sideways. She remained silent as I began to hear muffled voices in the garage below. They became clearer as a drunken argument augmented their volume.

"And if she's so great, maybe she should have been your date tonight!" a woman snapped.

A male voice fired back. "Get a grip. That was a million years ago."

She retorted. "Well, she was at the tip of your tongue when talking to Malden. Such a special leader and extraordinary woman!"

With this salvo, I realized that I was eavesdropping on Simmons and Katz.

"I was just putting him in his place," Simmons attempted to salvage the situation.

"So, the first thing you do is bring up an old flame?" she drunkenly screamed, throwing something that shattered against the wall.

His tone accelerated, "Where do you get off? You always fly off the handle about stuff like this!"

Katz sounded like she was in tears, "You keep your marriage for appearances, but I'm always available for a quick dalliance in your office, right?" she cursed him viciously. "I introduced you to Green. I think you've got the wrong idea about our arrangement. You'd be nothing without me!"

At this point, I heard the impact of a fist and a body falling to the ground. Silence once again assumed its regency after a rapid set of steps fled the scene.

"Did you hear that?" the woman intonated like a gossiping child. "Step back from the door. That's all you'll need."

"Need for what?" I asked in panicked exasperation.

"Remember what I've invested in you," the voice sidestepped my question. "And understand that nothing is free. The accumulation of interest has already begun."

I collapsed to the floor when she hung up. I could faintly hear sobbing in the garage below before the second individual left. The tightening bonds of servitude constricted my breathing. There was no way out but through.

OR ELSE

I woke up on the couch sometime in the late morning. The rain beat against the window of my loft apartment. DC had taken on a nightmarish character since my younger years in a way I never anticipated. I was enthralled to forces and people beyond my understanding, while my mental state declined. The rapidity of that deterioration sanded away my pride. I ate and drank very little for the rest of the weekend as I rotted in my cell. The fear of what I may witness or be made to pay for kept me rooted in place. I intermittently streamed shows on my phone and slept.

Another memory came to mind. It was a warm day in May. I was just a boy of twenty-one at the time. I flew Laura, my girlfriend, out to the East Coast for the Naval Academy's Ring Dance. I was set to receive my class ring, an important milestone to me. She was the most beautiful thing in the world. Her blonde hair lay like a bridal veil over angelic features.

The day before the dance, we took a trip out to DC to see the sights. The capital was just a short drive from Annapolis, and I had use of my buddy's car for the weekend. We walked tenderly with each other among the impressive monuments on the National Mall. In those days, DC was something aspirational and platonic. It would be the pinnacle of my future career. I had grand visions of admiralty, renown, and importance.

"You see the Pentagon over there?" I put my hand on the small of her back as we stood at the top of the Washington monument.

"I think so," she looked at me with a delicate smile.

"You can kind of see it," I shielded my eyes to shield the sun. "I am going to run that place someday."

She laughed and playfully pushed my shoulder. "Oh, so you're going to be the top general?"

"It's admirals in the Navy," I corrected, "and yes."

Laura turned to face me as we embraced. I was at the top of the world when we kissed up there. I snuck my phone out and took a picture of us together. That was the last photo as a couple I ever took. At Ring Dance the following night, I got uncontrollably drunk. Myriad lights strung in arches in Dahlgren Hall dazzled my vision. I stumbled out onto the dance floor while she went to use the bathroom. As I joked with my roommate, a female classmate of mine started dancing suggestively nearby. She made her way over to me and pressed her body against mine. I still look back on the moment I placed my hands on her hips with crushing regret. Laura came out of the bathroom and stood crestfallen. As was tradition, she was wearing my class ring around her neck on a ribbon. She looked as if I had taken our dearest hopes and aspirations together and sold them for a cheap thrill. Indeed, I had.

Laura placed a fragile hand over the ring hanging over her chest. She cherished it for a moment before tearing it away and throwing it on the floor. I swore and pushed away the girl I danced with and tried to rush over to her. The crowd on the dance floor shifted and formed an impenetrable human wall as my inebriation impeded my progress. I lost sight of her just before making it through the crowd. My second largest regret of that night was searching for my class ring over pursuing her. I crawled on the floor like a dog, clawing through discarded cups, spills, and under tables. When I found it, I tried to rush out to catch Laura. I just caught a glimpse of her ethereal, turquoise dress in the night as she exited the Barry Gate. She never spoke to me again.

Memories like these haunted the quiet times and the stillness. I scrolled through pictures on my phone the morning after the mansion party, trying to distract my harried mind. When I came upon that picture of Laura and I kissing at the top of the monument, I once more fell into a bleak despair. She was married to some stiff in the heartland somewhere with two beautiful children. My class ring sat in its case on the dining table, my only trophy of that night. I dated other girls since then, but they never measured up to my dear Laura. A part of my heart would always be adrift under the lights at Ring Dance in the precious, expiring moments before that needless catastrophe.

Before I knew it, Monday morning permitted me to change from my confinement at the mansion to the basement dungeon of the Pentagon. As I trudged lifelessly to my desk, I saw a substantial bruise on Katz's cheek bone poorly concealed by makeup. I settled into my chair as my sunken eyes looked aimlessly at the calendar.

"Good weekend?" I chided.

She put her hand to her face in a feeble attempt to cover the mark. "Yeah. You?"

I stared blankly for a moment. "Yeah."

Admiral Simmons emerged from his office with his right hand concealed in his jacket pocket. He coldly ignored Katz and turned to face me.

"I need you to clear my schedule today too," he instructed. "More sessions with the Joint Chiefs."

I sat frozen for a moment before nodding.

"Getting enough sleep, Malden?" Simmons prodded.

"Are you?" I lifted my hollow eyes to his.

He narrowed his vision. In my peripheral view, I saw Katz give a concerned look.

"Just enough," Simmons replied. "China's been keeping me up."

I twirled a pen in my hand. "I'm sure it has."

He frowned slightly and shuffled off to his meeting. I caught Katz broadcasting an anxious look to the admiral as he left. The dread I felt over my enslavement gave way to an anarchic, permeating bitterness.

"Where are you from originally?" I probed.

Katz looked at me with confusion. "What do you care?"

I rubbed my face. "Just because we got off to a rocky start doesn't mean it always has to be like that. We're going to be trapped together for a while."

"La Jolla, near San Diego," she replied after a moment of hesitation.

I nodded. "I know the place well. I did my first division officer tour in San Diego."

Katz acknowledged my statement impassively.

I wanted to know how she knew Green. "Any family in the area?"

She chafed at my questioning. "No, just a sister back in Cali."

I paused, waiting for her to tell me more. She took this as me inviting her to ask about my life.

"How about you?" Katz asked apathetically.

"I have two older sisters. I grew up in Wisconsin," I relayed. "Brand new to this area."

She acknowledged my reply, then swiveled away slightly in her chair.

I hadn't really thought of my family in a long time. I mostly lost touch as I clawed my way through my Navy career.

"Any relation to Vince Malden?" she asked.

I nodded. "My father."

My old man was in the heat of an election year. Having served on this board and that for decades, the RNC decided it was his turn to step into the breach. As his senatorial campaign wore on, our relationship grew increasingly strained. He too saw DC as something aspirational. The difference was, I supposed, that I worked to get there. I detested his enthrallment to those "calling the shots"—until I found myself no better. I returned to the conversation at hand.

"I hear Jacob Green is renting the loft above his garage," I said daringly, watching her reaction.

Katz did a double take. "What?"

I tapped my fingers on the desk. "I think I might go check it out. Do you know who that is?"

"No idea," she remarked quickly.

I stopped tapping. "Hmm. If you say so."

I turned to face my computer. I could feel her gaze like an open furnace door before she returned to her work. I wondered why the party necessitated such a high level of secrecy. I assumed the rich and powerful liked to make ostentatious displays of their social connections. What baffled me more was that Katz had some kind of access to Green while seemingly below his social strata.

My desk phone's ringing interrupted my speculation.

"This is the watch coordinator for E-Ring," the man introduced himself as Senior Chief Gander.

He informed me that I had duty today and would be in a duty status until the following morning.

"You'll just take a walk of the ring every two hours and make a phone report to the watch commander," he informed "Sorry for the short notice, but you never came by to tell me your schedule."

"Do I need to stay here all night?" I shook my head in disbelief.

"Yes sir. I will need you to swing by and grab the log, duty phone, and badge," Gander informed me of the location before hanging up.

Having a twenty-four-hour duty would've been enough to ruin my day in the best of circumstances. Now, adrenaline coursed through my veins as I tried to figure out a way to avoid my captors' ire. I made my way over to the Senior Chief's desk on the second floor. The first thing I noticed in his cubicle was a large cross and a few Bible verses hanging on his cubicle walls.

"Hey senior," I began. "I actually can't stand duty today. I have a prior appointment."

He looked at me with peaceful eyes. "Okay. Just find a replacement and I will get you on the schedule for another day."

I rolled my eyes. "Who can stand the watch?"

"O-4s and above," he informed me. "But good luck trying to find anyone. The whole Pentagon is rushing around today. Did you see what's been going on?"

"Just China doing drills," I shifted my weight to the other leg.

"They shot down a Taiwanese fighter jet last night that got too close to one of their ships," Gander recounted. "The pilot survived, but this might be the big time."

"I doubt it," I turned to leave.

I walked quickly to try and control the growing panic of trying to find someone willing to mindlessly shuffle around the Pentagon for twenty-four hours. Walking all five floors in addition to the basement and mezzanine levels of E-Ring would take a substantial portion of each two-hour reporting period. The only other O-4s I knew personally were Katz and Major Sievert. Sievert didn't even work in this ring and likely had his own watch schedule. Seeing as Katz would probably stab me if I asked, I wound my way over to General Jones' office bay. I could knock out two birds with one stone and see if I could talk to the general about my situation.

Sievert was on the phone when I arrived but smiled when he recognized me. After finishing his call, he greeted me.

"Hey man," I mustered the courage to ask my favor. "I got pulled for duty today and they only told me this morning."

His demeanor dropped as he perceived the reason for my visit.

"I could take your next duty day, if that works," I implored.

"Nah, man," Sievert chuckled. "My wife is scheduled to be induced tomorrow. And I already did my time last week."

"I'm really in a bind here."

His demeanor changed. "Did you not hear me? My wife's having a baby tomorrow."

"Okay, okay," I rubbed my face in frustration. "Did you ever see if I can talk to General Jones.

"He was booked solid before this stuff with China," Sievert shook his head. "Now he's never in his office."

I left in a fit of frustration. I resorted to stopping random O-4s in the halls trying to swap duty days with them. Without fail, they quickly refused. When I arrived back at my desk bearing the duty badge pinned on my breast pocket, Katz smirked.

"That sucks," she grinned.

"I don't suppose you—"

"Nope," Katz interrupted.

I sat dejectedly in my chair. I needed to notify the woman at the mansion somehow. Suddenly, I remembered that the number I first called about the listing was still in my call history. Stepping out of our office bay, I found it after scrolling for a few minutes.

"Mr. Malden," the voice answered, "I've been expecting a call from you."

The same mournful tone I heard in the first phone call returned.

I gripped the phone tightly. "Expecting my call?"

"You have duty today and can't get out of it," she recounted my situation.

"Well, yes. So, you know I won't be in tonight," I was surprised by her apparent understanding.

The voice cut in: "But you will. You are not permitted in the Pentagon tonight."

"Tonight?"

"Tonight," she repeated. "Ask Miss Katz to take your duty status."

I nearly laughed. "I already tried that."

"If you had really tried, we wouldn't be having this conversation. I was hoping you'd connect the dots on your own," the woman chastised.

"What do you mean?" I furrowed my brow as my chest tightened.

She lowered her tone. "She'll do whatever you say. So will Simmons."

I looked around nervously and whispered, "I'm not blackmailing an admiral."

"All you have to do is get Katz to take your duty status. You must not be in the Pentagon tonight!" The voice quivered with an almost undetectable panic.

"Why don't you just threaten the watch coordinator or something? It seems like you had some kind of advanced notice of me having duty today," I argued more courageously than I should have.

"You insignificant worm," she hissed at me. "You sniveling little child! You walk in the halls of power without the slightest idea of the sacred ground you trod. You know nothing. You are nothing. You will do as I say," the voice's tone took on an inhuman growl, "or else!"

MUNDANE DECEPTION

I slowly approached Katz's desk as if I had a gun concealed in my jacket. She noticed my approach and eyed me suspiciously. While I cared little what she thought of me, it was well outside my personality to deal in this way. Katz apparently intuited the threat even if she did not know what I intended to use against her.

"Hey, something came up. Family emergency," she darted up.

"You don't have family in the area." I stammered.

Katz gathered her things. "Make sure you tell the admiral."

"But–" I tried to argue with her, but she was out of the office before I could catch up to my thoughts.

I walked quickly to catch up with her. "Hey, who's going to cover the phones?"

Katz called over her shoulder, "LCDR McAllister is the alternate. She'll do it."

While I intensely disliked her, I had no will to utilize extortion.

Maybe I can pawn my duty off on McAllister, I reasoned.

I called her office phone after finding her number in the directory. She was upset at being pulled to cover for Katz but ultimately relented. When McAllister arrived at the desk, she heaved her overweight form into the chair.

"Hey," I began sheepishly, "I know you just got pulled to do this, but could I persuade you to trade duty days with me?"

She eyed my badge with derision. "You mean today? I don't think so."

"I really cannot stand duty today," I pleaded. "I have a very important prior engagement."

McAllister twirled one of her dreadlocks. "I'm exempt."

"Exempt?" I questioned. "What do you mean exempt?"

"I don't stand duty," she took out a piece of gum and began smacking it loudly.

I stood there for a moment. "Why not?"

McAllister turned her head to face me and gave a vicious look. "I'm pregnant!"

I had assumed she was just fat. My pulse rose as I scrambled to figure out what to do next. I thought about sprinting to catch Katz, but she was likely out of the building by now. I'd never find her even if I could bring myself to use my blackmail. I could continue to pester random officers in the halls, but I anticipated this to be a fruitless endeavor. It increasingly looked like I was trapped for the night. I could just leave in the middle of my duty, but I did not want to sink my career any more than I had to. I still held out a small hope of my imprisonment being temporary. Regardless, this ultimately became my only option.

As I completed my tours of E-Ring, I timed it so I would just be finishing one right before I left for the day. I planned to "gundeck" the remaining reports—a Navy term for falsely reporting something completed. It was risky, but I figured this was a silly watch anyway with little to go wrong. I still felt a twinge of guilt as I snuck away from the building. If anyone called the duty phone asking where I was, I had plausible deniability due to the large scale of the Pentagon. I doubted any intentions to track the duty phone's location. All I had to do was make my reports throughout the night.

I pulled up to the gate still wearing my silly badge. I yanked it off and threw it into the footwell as fast as I could.

"Information is more powerful than a gun to the head," the woman taught. "I'm glad you saw reason."

I nodded coolly as she opened the gate. Just as I passed, the duty phone rang. I nearly jumped out of my seat and pulled into the garage. I answered the phone.

"Good evening, this is the Officer of the Watch," the caller relayed. "One of the cleaning ladies told me she saw someone acting suspicious around E-Ring's basement. Go ahead and check it out for me."

"Acting suspicious? How so?" I tried to gather more information.

The officer of the watch sighed. "I don't know, we've had problems with this cleaning lady in the past. Very superstitious. Every once in a while, she claims to see things in the basement at night and won't stop calling the OOW until someone goes to look."

"So, do I have to check it out?" I asked, trying to get out of it.

"Normally I'd say no, but she seems really shaken up. Just go walk the deck with her and get her back to work. Make it part of your tour," he clarified.

He ended the call, leaving me in a large predicament. It would be easy enough to call in a half hour or so and claim I did it. However, the cleaning lady would likely keep badgering the OOW unless someone came to calm her down. I searched through the duty phone's contact list. I found the number for the poor wretch on duty for D-Ring.

"Hey, this the E-Ring rover," I opened. "I am drafting a situation report for the Chief of Naval Personnel, and I really need to get it done. Can you quick swing by the E-Ring basement and talk to the cleaning lady?"

"Oh, gosh," he huffed. "Is it Diana? She's always seeing things."

I was relieved to hear he was familiar with her antics. "Yeah, I think so."

"I got it, man," he agreed.

"Thanks, dude. I owe you one," I hung up the phone with relief.

I made my way up to my room and went through my ridiculous scramble with my limited light. Plugging in the duty phone to my portable charging block, I settled in for my night of mundane deception on the couch. I set an alarm for when I would need to make my next report and ate a paltry dinner. In short order, I was dozing off.

I jolted awake to the duty phone ringing again.

"Did you talk to the cleaning lady? She claims no one came to see her," the OOW asked impatiently.

"I don't know what to tell you sir. I made sure she went back to work," I carefully answered his question.

"Her shift's over, but she's refusing to leave unless someone checks out this suspicious person she claims to see. I know it's stupid, but let's both go down there and talk to her. I don't have the patience to call base security to kick her out," his tone was ragged with fatigue. "Meet down there when you get a second. I need to wrap some things up, and then I will head down there."

I swore after hanging up. I couldn't call in the other rover because the OOW specifically asked for me. If I didn't meet him there, he'd start asking questions about where I was. I did my best to look around the room in the darkness.

I don't see any cameras, I strained, but how did she know I was peeking that night? Or how did she know I had to get out of bed?

My mind raced through the possibilities.

Well, I wasn't nearly as subtle as I should've been. Maybe she saw a glint off the lens of my binoculars, I tried to think carefully, and saying I got out of bed was probably just a lucky guess.

I patrolled the room, feeling around corners, walls, and trim to try and find a camera. I checked under light fixtures, pieces of furniture, and in the cabinets. All my efforts came up dry. I scolded myself for not just blackmailing Katz into taking my duty. She deserved it after all.

Even if I make it out of the room, there's got to be cameras all over the grounds, I wrestled.

I speculated what sort of trouble I could actually get in for not being on watch when I said I was. In the worst-case scenario, I could be prosecuted for dereliction of duty under the Uniformed Code of Military Justice if this suspicious individual rooting around the Pentagon turned out to be real and malicious. This could land me with a dishonorable discharge.

Not much worse than where I am now, I joked.

Time slipped away as I pondered. I still hoped to someday escape the mansion's clutches and return to the career I worshiped so much. I decided to make an attempt at leaving the grounds or at least probe its perimeter.

After putting on my uniform again, I slunk over to the door and quietly slipped into the garage. On my personal phone, I ordered a ride on one of my apps so I did not need to drive through the gate. I set the pickup at just a few hundred feet down the road. I remembered how silently the garage door could open and used the remote to open it just enough to slide underneath. I closed the door and crouched close to the garage's profile. There was almost no ambient light at all, both helping and hindering my operation. I tried to follow the fence's silhouette with my eyes along its imposing path at the edge of the property. It was too tall to climb on its own. My gaze rested on a contorted oak tree at the far edge of what I could see in the blackness. There were enough low hanging branches to assist in vaulting the fence.

"It's possible," I whispered to myself.

Still, the immense likelihood of cameras made it a suicide mission. I checked my phone and saw that my ride was just five minutes away. I paused for a moment before realizing that, if there were cameras, they likely already captured me slipping out of the garage. I cursed myself for being so careless. The stress of my situation hampered my decision-making capabilities.

I'm already going to be screwed, I thought for a moment. Might as well do what I need to get done while I'm at it.

With this, I sprang from my crouched position and sprinted for the tree. I could see my ride's headlights pull up in the distance. At any moment, I expected the mansion's lights to flash and a squad of armed men to haul me in. Straining, I pulled myself up the tree's limbs and jumped to freedom below. Breathless, I ran to meet my ride down the road.

"You alright, man?" the driver asked in a thick Ethiopian accent.

"I'm good, just drive," I tiredly waved him on after settling into the back seat.

He muttered something in Amharic and drove off. I was surprised by my courage.

Why haven't I done this already and gone to the police? I questioned myself.

As the adrenaline subsided, a strange facsimile for guilt cropped up in my mind. Deep down, I knew that I had not escaped unnoticed. Worse still, there would be terrible consequences. After the hour-long drive, my ride dropped me off just outside the gate.

"Make sure you tip and leave good rating," the driver called out to me before I unceremoniously shut the door.

The duty phone rang again.

"Where are you?" the OOW scathed.

"I am on my way down," I tried to conceal my heavy breathing as I walked as fast as I could. "Just had to wrap some things up."

The OOW was skeptical but too fatigued and apathetic to care. "Just get down here."

I made it through the gate and finally entered the building. By the time I got to the basement of E-Ring, I was a sweaty mess. Thankfully, the low lighting of the Pentagon at night concealed my unprofessional appearance.

APPARITION

"And he just keeps walking around, going around corners, and taunting me!"

I could hear the cleaning lady's panicked tone as I descended the steps.

"Ma'am," the OOW tried to calm her down, "I don't see anyone. There's no one there."

I approached them and introduced myself. "Hey sir, I'm here."

He looked relieved to have some backup. "Okay, Mr. Malden is going to take it from here," the OOW motioned to me and pulled me aside. In a low tone he ordered, "Look, I don't want to hear another peep out of her tonight. This is your section to tour. I've been trying to get her to leave for a half hour. Get it done."

I nodded as he turned to leave.

"Ma'am," I began, "I think it's time for you to go."

She gripped her cart with white knuckles. "Why don't you guys ever listen? There is a man sneaking around the Pentagon!"

"He's probably just on watch like myself," I clarified. "Nothing to be alarmed about."

In the poor lighting, I could just barely see the fear in Diana's ice-blue eyes.

She put a hand on her hip. "Do you think I am stupid? I've been cleaning these halls for twenty years. I know what watch is."

I tried to get her moving so I could try and sneak back to the mansion. "Why don't you go home and I will make sure to talk to this guy?"

She shifted uncomfortably. "Let me just show you where I've been seeing him first."

I relented and walked with her around the corridor until we arrived at the hallway across from Admiral Simmons' office bay.

"He just paces back and forth here. Then he'll linger next to that closet," Diana gestured with a wrinkled hand.

I looked on with horror at the door she pointed to. "That closet?" I quivered.

"That's the one," she stated calmly.

My heart once again became laden with fear. The door radiated dread just as it had my first day at the Pentagon.

"He's probably just on watch, you need to leave," I felt as though we were trespassing in some wild predator's lair.

Diana became angry. "He's not on watch! What person on watch gets to smoke indoors and wear coveralls?"

I widened my eyes as her voice echoed down the intermittently lit hall. My feet became leaden as my breathing grew shallow.

"Please just go home," I began pleading. "I will handle it."

"Do you promise to look around?" she clutched at her necklace as the doorway to the closet sat like a gaping mouth a few feet away.

"Yes," I lied. "Let's get you home."

Diana finally relented and rolled her cart away. I followed her as far as the elevator and decided that was good enough. When the elevator doors closed, I was alone in the crushing silence of the empty corridor. I felt like any sound I made would alert the presence of some unknown pursuer.

There's nothing there, I sighed.

I turned toward the stairs to make the trek back outside. My hopes of returning to the mansion undetected were slim, but I was going to try regardless. The lit and unlit portions of the hallway washed over me like the pounding tide, eroding my ability to keep calm. When I reached the steps, I looked at the door again.

I forced myself to smile and said aloud, "Just a door."

A small red light pierced the morbid darkness at the other end of the hallway. The pin prick of illumination gained brightness for a second, then faded to a dim glow. It moved in slow, yet twitching motions. The light remained in a lower position for a few seconds before again cycling in a rhythmic fashion. It was unmistakably the ember of a cigarette.

Every fiber of my being screamed at me to flee. I felt dizzy and leaned against the railing of the stairway. The unknown figure took another drag as the ember's light seared my vision. I took a labored step away from the stairs back into the suffocating embrace of the corridor.

"Hey!" I called out.

I could not see any kind of outline—just the methodical smoking of the cigarette.

"Who are you?" My voice trembled.

I saw the light dart off to the side of the hallway as the unknown figure cast the smoke away. The squeaking of leather boots made plodding steps around the corner of the ring. The sound carried in my direction. I fumbled to pull out the duty phone but dropped it on its corner, shattering the screen. The sound halted the individual at the other end of the corridor.

I left the duty phone in place and took another step toward the abyssal blackness. "Who's there?" I called out again.

The void made no reply.

I grimaced as I once again trekked through the sandbars of light. I paused at each oasis and peered intently. Suddenly, the individual made a break for it around the corner. I inexplicably started running to catch him. When I reached the passageway, there was no one there. It was just more lights sitting astride long stripes of darkness. With shaking legs, I turned to where the cigarette had been cast away. I could still smell the smoke. Investigating, I found it where the floor met the wall. I knelt down to pick it up as the light behind me flickered.

I again called out into the void in the vain hope this person would show themselves. I waited for a moment to listen. Something moved behind me in the direction of the stairwell. I jolted around to see the dark silhouette of a man standing next to the closet in the somber region between two bars of light. He was smoking again.

We maintained a hair-raising standoff for nearly a minute. I thought about using my personal phone's flashlight but decided against it. I hoped the apparition would vanish on its own. The cigarette telegraphed his location with a sanguine rush of color. A shadowed arm extended to the closet's doorknob as he exhaled. The sound of his breathing made my blood run cold. His hand perched menacingly on the handle.

I slowly approached. An otherworldly percussion concert formed. Each step provided a cymbal crash in tandem with the pounding baseline of my heartbeat. As the ghastly tempo increased, a sudden tacet brought an end to the score. The silhouetted figure opened the closet. Dismay and horror poured from the opening like the first waves of cold from a long forgotten deep freezer.

The figure paused for a moment, flicked his second cigarette toward me, and entered the closet. The door shutting behind him caused me to flinch. I started walking again, acutely aware of the sound of my shoes on the tile. I looked around anxiously for backup I knew wasn't there. I turned to face the door. The silver handle loomed like a floating corpse in the ocean of darkness that surrounded me. I reached for it as a blacksmith would remove an iron from the fire. The cold surface of the doorknob sent an electric shiver through my arm. I gritted my teeth as I prepared to turn it in my hand. My legs shook and the air became dense with a chthonic terror. I turned my face while maintaining my gaze on the door to brace for what was inside.

At last, the door opened.

I jumped back for a moment anticipating the figure to lunge out at me. Instead, the space contained nothing but a few cleaning supplies. I stepped closer and peered inside. This brought further confirmation of my initial assessment.

I swore with relief although I could not explain what I had just seen. Just as I was about to close the closet, I noticed a symbol inscribed in black ink in the upper right of the closet's back wall. Due to the low light, I was surprised I could see it at all. I pulled my personal phone from my pocket and activated the flashlight. It was the same symbol on my apartment key. I hurriedly pulled it out to compare. Sure enough, I saw the same darting mix of angles and circles. The key trembled in my hand. I was just about to flee before I heard noises on the other side of the wall.

THE VISION

I pressed my ear against the back wall of the closet after turning off my flashlight. The cold surface sucked all the warmth from my body. The strange sound I heard rose and fell in a rhythmic fashion. There was a raspy, wheezing character to it. I could also faintly hear a low hum, perhaps from some kind of machine.

Air conditioning vents, I told myself.

I stood back and crossed my arms. The faint sound of respiration grated on my well-being as if a cosmic violinist was running his bow directly on my spinal cord. I simultaneously needed to get away from the noise and figure out how to stop it. With each rise and fall, my soul resonated with foreboding. I managed to break away from my fixation with the back wall and turn to leave the closet.

I halted in shock.

The same silhouette I had been chasing stood blocking my path. Once more, the dim light of his cigarette hovered ominously at his mouth. When he inhaled, the light grew brighter, and I could faintly see his face. I knew exactly who it was. Before I could cry out in terror, he shut the door and locked it. I rushed to the door like a rat caught in a trap, clawing and pounding at the small gaps in the frame.

"Let me out!" I screamed. "It wasn't my fault!"

I stepped back and attempted to heave my shoulder into the door.

After three futile tries, I returned to pleading. "I told her not to break away! I knew it wasn't right! You've got to believe me."

I had some vain hope of a miraculous act of forgiveness. Instead, all I received was the frigid, stony claustrophobia of the closet. Fear began to take over as I flailed helplessly against my confines. In a final attempt, I mustered all the momentum I could to hurl my body against the door. This succeeded only in badly bruising my shoulder and recoiling me further into the closet. I noticed I was significantly further back from the door than I used to be. Feeling with my hands, I found the rear wall completely absent. I began to shiver as icy, decomposing air filled the compartment.

With this development, I heard the squeaking of rubber boots as he mournfully trudged off. I made several more attempts at wrenching the handle but to no avail. I realized I had dropped my phone in the shuffle and began a panicked search. I did my best to keep away from the opening abyss at the other end of the closet. After failing to find it, I sat with my back against the door. I, a lieutenant commander in the US Navy, began sobbing with my head in my hands.

"There's nothing I could have done," I rocked back and forth. "That was her fault."

I took several whimpering breaths to try to calm down.

He's dead, Richard, I reassured myself. You're seeing things again.

In the stillness of the closet, the wheezing once again caught my attention. It was far more pronounced as if the wall separating me from it had been completely removed. I wiped my face and stood up to listen once again. My outstretched hands groped for the wall. My fingers felt like they had been frostbitten. To my horror, my right foot found nothing beneath it as I inched forward. This caused me to fall down a concealed flight of steps.

When I regained my balance, my body ached terribly from the fall. It was pitch black and I could see nothing at all. On my hands and knees, I shakily extended my hand. I found yet more steps extending into the abyss. The rasping was significantly louder. Thoroughly disoriented, I turned my head in the direction of the closet door. I slowly climbed the steps back to where I started. The frenzied escape attempts started again. I knew I would be forever marked if I went down the stairs. On the other hand, the closet door stood as an impenetrable rampart.

I ran my fingers through my hair and widened my eyes in the darkness. The respiration caused every one of my muscles to contract. I knew I would not be permitted to leave by the door.

"No way out but through," I whispered, as if in a dream state.

Gingerly, I crawled to the stairs and began descending one step at a time. My body still ached from my first tumble down the stairway. After twenty steps or so, I reached a landing. I fumbled around in the darkness to find the next course of stairs. All the while, the repeated rasping seeped from just below my feet. I discovered a narrow opening where the wall met the landing. I leaned down and found that the sound originated from this hole. When I peered into the gap, I saw a distant amber light at the end of a long crawlspace corridor. The sickly illumination reflected off several pipes that ran the length of the passageway. I continued to feel around the landing for some other route. I found nothing except the tunnel. The noise drew me in like an animal to its slaughter.

I got on my stomach and began the slow crawl toward the brilliance. There was only enough room to lift my head slightly. On a few occasions, I needed to turn my head completely sideways to slide under some horizontal pipes darting off into unknowable directions. The wheezing grew louder to an unbearable volume.

Suddenly, I heard a rush of fluid in the pipe above me. The respiration rapidly increased, and I heard what sounded like whimpering. I froze in place until the noise returned to normal. My neck ached as I strained to look at the amber light. I was about halfway through the corridor.

As I neared the end, the cold draft gave way to a smothering humidity. I took on a mindless, nihilistic character as I went deeper into the bowels of the Pentagon. I stopped looking toward the light and slid my body with closed eyes through the tunnel in tempo with the hellish breathing. By now, I had significant cuts and bruises from my fall down the stairs and my arduous slog in the low-lying concrete corridor.

With a large heave, I accidentally hit my head on the end of the space. Surprised and dazed, I opened my eyes. I was directly underneath the amber light. It was a solitary bulb encased in a metal cage. The wire conduit leading to it stretched to the right. To my immense dismay, I saw that the tunnel took a sharp 90-degree bend followed by another corner toward my initial direction of travel.

Panic took hold of my actions as my breathing grew shallow. I tried to turn around in the tunnel to return to the relative safety of the closet. Someone would eventually hear my pounding and let me out. However, the length of my body prevented me from going the other direction. I had no idea how long this tunnel stretched for and to what destination. I thrashed helplessly for a few seconds in frustration before closing my eyes in an attempt to regain my composure.

"No way out but through," I repeated.

I needed to contort my body in jagged forms to make it through the double corner. The heat rose considerably in the tunnel. I began to sweat profusely which aided my slithering through the obstacle. While I could not tell for certain, this new corridor appeared to have a gradual downward slope. My shoulders and arms were weak with fatigue when I made it to the end of the second leg. My uniform was torn to shreds as I lost all concept of space and time. In the end, I had no idea how many lumbering tunnels I crawled through. I simply kept slithering in the direction of the labored, hellish wheezing as the air became thick with heat.

I'm going to die down here! My mind raced with terror.

At last, the tunnel opened enough for me to crawl on my hands and knees. Instead of amber, the light at the end of this larger corridor was a pale green. It appeared to be coming from some kind of space above the tunnel. When I reached the source, I found a metal grate leading to a room. Looking upward, I observed harsh fluorescent lights reflecting off sage green tiles. I could acutely hear the breathing through the grate. Testing it with my finger, I was able to easily tilt the metal frame. I felt the rushing of air past my face as I carefully moved it away from its spot.

I broke the plane of the floor with my eyes. Green tile filled every space in the room, including the floor. There were two doors at either end. On one wall were several shower heads. I surmised the purpose of the pipes I had crawled under. Next to it were empty coat racks and towels. On the opposite wall were suits of hazmat gear. A bright red exit sign hit my eyes like a breath of fresh air over one of the doors. With considerable difficulty, I hoisted myself up into the room. I rushed to the exit door, but I froze when I touched the handle. That wheezing still bellowed from the opposite end of the room.

You must look, my conscience chided.

The heaviness emanating from the other door made it nearly impossible to breathe. My mind raced with thousands of questions.

What is this place? Who built it? What did I crawl through? What is on the other side of that door?

The labored respiration cycled through gravelly peaks and troughs. Despite its unbearable volume, it struck me as a miracle I heard the sound all the way in the closet. The room smelled heavily of bleach and cleaning products. Whatever was on the other side needed to be kept insulated from the outside world. I shuffled toward it. To my relief, the handle was locked. With that settled, I could follow the exit signs out of this horrific dungeon. Just as I turned to leave, I once more noticed a symbol located on the door frame. It was the same cryptogram as on my key. To the right of the door was a small plaque written in Hebrew.

❧

"And do you know what it said?" Edwards said in an indistinguishable tone.

"How should I know?" Malden challenged.

The captor sat forward and gripped the dirty folding table. "He saw He prevailed not against him," Edwards recited. "That's what it said."

Malden sat back and fiddled with his bonds. "How on earth could you know that?"

The man clenched his jaw. "Just what do you know about the war raging around us?"

Richard blinked several times. "Well, it's pretty much frozen in place."

"No," Edwards shook his head. "Closer to here."

"There's always domestic unrest," Malden recited mechanically.

"No!" the man exclaimed "All around us." He gestured as if pointing to a constellation of stars. He continued, "Do you have any idea the kind of forces you've been dealing with? What I've been fighting against? You clearly don't. I know that inscription because I know the people who put it there."

"Who put it there?" Richard asked hesitantly.

Edwards lowered his tone, "Not the individuals. "The people. The body. I know these people and their intentions. Jacob Green is just a cog in that machine. In the Name of the Lord, I will cast them down!"

The captive recognized the last line from the Temple of God manifesto parroted on all the major news stations. The group had been designated a terror organization amid the recent civil unrest.

"You're . . ."

"The same," Edwards smiled proudly.

Richard's breathing increased rapidly as he adjusted to this information.

"There's a spiritual war, far greater than the physical distractions all around us. It's been raging for thousands of years and you're late to the party. Green and his ilk are in their endgame," the guerrilla leader asserted, "I know what symbol is on that key and on that door. The so-called Tree of Life—Etz Chaim. A demonic sigil older than those who use it even know."

The captive nodded slowly, understanding even less than he did before.

Edwards continued, "What happened next?"

❧

I reached out to touch the inscription as the breathing behind the door slowed. A coursing of energy like an electric current shook my arm. With this gesture, I heard the door unlock. The sound spiked my adrenaline. I extended a shaking hand to the handle. My soul cried, "No! No! No!"

What unfolded before me as the door swung open will forever haunt my every waking moment. The room was dimly lit by a low-hanging spotlight under which was a hospital bed. Beside the bed were all manner of machines, each closely monitoring some specific aspect of what was going on in the space. The monitors for these implements were the main source of light. The scene was cloaked in sickly blues, greens, and reds from charts closely reporting vital signs. The room smelled like rotting flesh and urine. On the bed itself was the worst thing I have ever seen or ever will see.

His form looked to be human but there was nothing of humanity left. He was no more than four feet tall and was completely naked apart from the dozens, perhaps hundreds, of wires and tubes interconnecting like a spider's web. A panoply of IV bags hung like icons in a temple apse above his head. His arms and legs were bound loosely with straps. The bed itself had no sheets and more resembled a grated metal shelf propping up his wretched form. The figure's rib cage protruded above a sunken stomach which had a large, sutured gash. Each one of his ribs could clearly be seen and resembled courses of piano strings. The flesh hung like melting suet over his skeletal frame. His skin was an ashy gray, pockmarked by millions of indiscernible red dots. As my eyes drifted up his torso, I saw his jaw hanging open to reveal a total lack of teeth. A shriveled tongue twitched slightly, the only indication to me that he was still alive besides the appalling sound of his breathing. The almost completely absent nose sat astride prominent cheekbones and hollow cheeks. He was mostly bald apart from a scattering of wispy blond hairs toward the back of his skull.

What struck me most of all, however, were his eyes. When I noticed he was looking directly into mine, I jumped. He was giving me a wretched, pleading look through pallid blue points of tortured light. He communicated more with this gaze than any author could in a thousand books. He moved his focus back and forth between my two eyes with fear, hatred, confusion, agony, and torment. Foremost of all, there was boundless and eternal sadness. I had never seen such a look of anguish in all my life. Contained in those peerless points of blue was enough grief to break the soul of even the bravest warrior.

I was filled with such incalculable horror I was unable to move or speak. He began twitching his fingers and grasping at the grates in the bed. A speaker started to play some kind of recording. Judging by the sound quality, it seemed to be quite old. It was a simple loop of a woman gently saying something in German I couldn't understand.

The recording distressed him even more as his eyes darted all around the room. At once, thousands upon thousands of needles rose from inside the bed and started to methodically lance him all over his body. He flailed and contorted as much as he could in his deteriorated state. I had seen far too much. My stomach churned. I could not even manage a scream. His breathing rapidly increased as I covered my eyes and stumbled back. As I did so, my foot caught on a cord. I stumbled to the side into one of the monitors and knocked it over. I heard an indiscernible vocalization from the figure. At last, I regained control of my actions and turned to sprint out of the room just as an alarm started sounding throughout the space.

My legs quaked as I frantically tried to open the opposite door. I could faintly hear a noise far worse than screaming behind me. When I at last controlled my hands long enough to articulate the handle, I sprinted away from what I had witnessed. I felt that if I lingered a second longer, I would be taking his place. On the other side of the door was a long, well-lit hallway. I picked up speed as I tried to escape the infernal noises pursuing me. Amber sirens lined the hallway and whistled out a mournful tune.

I feared being caught by some unknown entity at any moment. I peeked behind me to see the lights behind me shutting off in quick succession. The darkness rapidly overtook me. The siren lights turned off but the terrible din of their alarm remained. Rapid footsteps swarmed my location. I writhed and struggled with all of my might as a multitude of hands restrained me. At last, I was able to scream—and scream I did. The sound carried in every direction as the morbidity of night consumed me.

ȣ

"The engine room," Edwards let a small tremble modulate his voice.

Malden stared blankly while the tears flowed. "That's what they call it."

"Were you ever able to return?"

The captive sobbed and strained at his bonds. "Who is he? Why is he there?"

Edwards took compassion on the wretch before him. "Steady. I will tell you the story soon. Right now, I need more details," he said.

Richard wavered and looked up at the solitary lightbulb in agony. "I wish you would just kill me. Those eyes. Those eyes! That's the only thing I will ever see when I close my own. I can't go on. I just can't seem to die. The sight of him…" he cried.

The guerrilla leader crossed his fingers and rested his chin on his hands.

"The Lord lift up his countenance upon thee and give you peace," Edwards recited.

Richard's tired eyes fell from the lightbulb to his captor's gaze like an autumn leaf sloughing off a tree. "Please, Richard. If you ever want to see him free, you need to tell me what happened next."

DECADES HAPPENED

I awoke in the sitting area of the loft in a blind terror. I jumped from the couch and ran all through the apartment, nearly jumping out the window. Every ounce of blood had been replaced with adrenaline. I went through several cycles of yelping and retching before I understood where I was. I shook uncontrollably on the floor, intermittently sobbing. My anguish was only interrupted by a phone ringing.

"Why haven't you made your report yet?" the OOW barked.

I could not speak for an uncomfortable period of time.

"You there?" he repeated impatiently.

"Yes," I squeaked.

"Okay. You complete your tour?"

"Yes," I sounded unhinged.

The OOW prodded, presumably due to my tone, "See anything out of the ordinary?"

I trembled as I grappled with what I experienced. I didn't know whether to mention anything I witnessed or to what degree.

At last, I forced out a single word: "No."

"Very well," he replied. "Don't forget your next report."

He hung up. I looked at the duty phone. The damage I remembered was gone. My uniform was draped neatly on the chair next to the table, just where I had left it. Even in the darkness, however, I could still see the cuts and bruises on my arms.

I investigated my khaki uniform. It appeared untouched and unmolested. The tears and wrinkles were all gone. I strained my eyes in the darkness to see if my initials were still written in black marker on the tag. Sure enough, the writing was still there in my handwriting. I checked the garment bag I had hanging in the bedroom closet and found I was not missing a shirt. Returning to the kitchen, I took the uniform and laid it out on the table. At first glance, all was correct and in place.

"Name tag on the right, ribbon rack and warfare device on the left…" I recited methodically.

In my fatigued state, it took me a moment to realize the insignia were flipped. The name tag was indeed on the right but from my perspective as the viewer. The name tag needed to be on the right side of my body. The uniform was rigged incorrectly in a mirrored fashion. I was always meticulous about my professional appearance and never would have made this mistake. From this error, I deduced two things. I knew what I saw—and I would never forget it. And Green and the mansion staff knew it too, though they intended for me to dismiss it as a dream. It seemed as though the night had gone out of control for both sides. I was never supposed to be there.

Why don't they just kill me? I darkly contemplated.

Green, by this point, had ample opportunity to snuff me out. I began wondering if my misfortune en route to DC was part of this effort. I ultimately disregarded this explanation.

There's no way they could have coordinated all that; I regained some of my composure.

Still, I deduced that I was being kept alive for a specific reason. At least, Green was not permitted to harm me. I was still shaking from the memory of what I had seen, but a small wellspring of confidence formed.

If they're not allowed to harm me, what can they really do? Has it all been empty threats? A myriad of defiant plans formed in my mind.

This rising tide of assurance hit a ceiling.

They may only be prohibited from killing me for now, my pulse rose again, and by whose authority?

The notion of Green being part of a broader hierarchy was somehow more terrifying than thinking of him as a lone wolf. If he were acting alone, that would be as far as the rot went. I remembered him mentioning his resentment of following orders. Given Green's already lofty status, I shuddered to think of who could have authority over him. I recalled the host of high-end vehicles parked in front of the mansion for the party. Each car or limousine represented a piece of the mosaic making up a close-knit group of elites.

I shuffled over to the large window and peaked through the curtains. The mansion's grounds appeared frozen in shock. I wondered who would hang for failing to keep me from the Pentagon and what I'd hear about it. I fully expected a call from the woman detailing some medieval, torturous punishment for my misdeed. Instead, all I received was silence—the frigid, unwavering silence that forced me to think about what I had seen.

His face hovered before my gaze no matter where I looked. He was there when I closed my eyes. He was there when I buried my face in the pillow. The soul crushing agony of his countenance left a permanent stain on my own. With a chance to reflect, I tried to recount everything I had seen. My memory retold the visual to me, but it was like listening to a homeless schizophrenic yelling in your ear at a bus stop. I couldn't trust it even if I wanted to. The horror I had witnessed shattered every conception I had of humanity. I, of course, paid lip service to the depravity of man and his capability for atrocity. Yet, the cruel fate of this wretch below the Pentagon surpassed any sensationalized account of human barbarism in history.

Perhaps he was some kind of medical patient, I attempted to find a more mundane explanation.

I simply could not fathom that the sole purpose of his existence was to be tortured. I recalled his appearance once more. His small stature stood out to me. Despite his wrinkled appearance, there was an element of boyhood to his structure. He did not appear to be a dwarf or have some other genetic malady. Instead, he had the presentation of youth held in place by straining cosmic cables while time itself sought to sever the bond—a peculiar, appalling intersection of young and old.

I came to refer to him in my mind as the boy. The label felt right in my soul.

"The boy," I repeated aloud.

When I did so, my heart grew heavy. Speaking this into the abyss caused the air to shift noticeably as if I had trespassed into the forbidden court of a foreign temple and spoken aloud the name of its god. I felt quite observed. My eyes darted around the room to search for cameras again. Unsurprisingly, I found nothing. I looked out the window once more, anxiously searching for a concealed observer. I elected to not speak the title aloud again. I shook my head incredulously. The events of the past week had evolved me into a raving lunatic.

Unable to sleep, I sat dead-eyed on the couch until the first sorties of daylight brimmed over the horizon. I soullessly donned my uniform after fixing the misplaced insignia.

I know what I saw, I repeated. I know what I saw.

I nearly spoke this truth aloud but decided against it. When I pulled up to the gate, I braced for what the voice would say.

"You did not do as I said," she criticized. "You did not use the tools I provided."

Her tone was more like a coach after a lost football game.

"I stayed here all night," I lied to perpetuate their deception.

"You're a doormat, Mr. Malden," the woman said in a low snarl.

The gate opened and I was on my way. I surmised that feigning ignorance would be the best option to buy me time. Time for what, I had no idea. As I concluded earlier, Green needed me alive for something. However, I was certain that there were limits to his patience. Whether I expended this patience through my continued existence or by acts of defiance, I felt a pressing sense of urgency.

I had several close calls with drivers on the infernal Beltway. The only sleep I had in the past twenty-four hours was the cat nap on the couch before the OOW called me. I must've looked like a prisoner of war when I showed up to my desk. To my surprise, the Pentagon was in a flurry of activity. Everyone in the corridors had concerned looks and rushed around like headless chickens.

I saw Admiral Simmons pacing uselessly in his office through a small crack in the door. Katz looked at me with wide eyes.

"What's going on?" I rasped.

She struggled to articulate her thoughts.

A chief walking by simply stated, "War with China. They just sank a destroyer."

"A Taiwanese destroyer?" I wheeled around.

The chief stopped and his face dropped. "One of ours, sir. Taken out by a submarine. It's really happening."

I stumbled forward as the cumulative lack of food and sleep added to my confusion. I steadied myself on the corner of the desk as he walked away. I could hear panicked whispers sprouting throughout the office. In my own mind, a seedling of fear over China suffocated in the waterlogged soil of last night's experience. I felt a mixture of detachment and shock.

I could hear Admiral Simmons muttering to himself through the crack in his door. "This could not have happened! This could not have happened!"

I almost took a vague sense of pleasure at seeing everyone else in a similar state of anguish as myself. This was rapidly extinguished by the fast-setting reality of being a member of the armed services during a time of high intensity conflict. Formerly, I would have stormed into the admiral's office and demanded a seagoing billet. I used to long for the chance to cut my teeth in combat. Now, I sat impotently on the sidelines, paralyzed from any action.

I looked at the news headlines. No declaration of war had yet been formalized, but American and Chinese vessels were trading blows in the South China Sea. I was certain I knew people in the combat zone. A few articles made limp-wristed appeals to democratic ideals while pining for a nice ceasefire. As I already knew, the US military establishment was purposed for everything except warfare.

Overall, the information making its way across the Pacific was scant. I recognized the name of the ship sunk. One of my friends from the academy was finishing up his department head tour aboard her. I went to his wedding. He had three children. The division chief from my very first tour was the command master chief on that ship.

"You'll make a fine officer one day," he chided me years ago.

On my last day I retorted, "And one day you'll make a fine chief."

He was notorious for soliciting androgynous company during port visits in East Asia. I couldn't look his wife in the eyes when we would return to San Diego.

My head began spinning with the news. I wondered how many other friends or acquaintances had already perished or would be caught in the meat grinder. It was a small Navy, after all. Rising above all the chaos, however, was the churning memory of what I had witnessed the previous night.

What is happening right now?

I clenched my teeth as more news rolled in.

The Chinese had begun their pummeling of Taiwanese coastal defenses. Land-based batteries were exchanging salvos while the air war was in full swing. The Russian foreign ministry expressed strict neutrality, but announced another large exercise in Eastern Europe. Reports rumbled of North Korean troop movements on the DMZ. Iran seized several commercial ships in the Straits of Hormuz and threatened to close the waterway. Various paramilitary groups amped up their shelling of Israeli settlements. Across the whole world, resistance to American hegemony found its voice. The regional scuffle over Taiwan threatened to become a global conflict. As Lenin once quipped, decades were happening.

Admiral Simmons at last emerged from his hideout. He was sweating profusely and his shirt was badly stained with ketchup. He smelled terrible as he waddled past.

"Good morning, sir," I greeted instinctually.

Simmons turned to me with a deranged look before continuing to some meeting. The president was expected to address the nation at any moment. Curiously, the only thing broadcasted from the White House was imperiled silence. There wasn't even a tin facade of patriotic fervor. The public received nothing except the rolling reports of haphazard exchanges on the high seas. I got the impression that the whole affair had been a tremendous accident. Some Chinese sources were claiming the American destroyer was launching anti-submarine missiles long before it was struck, implying the destroyer fired first. The engagement would likely sink into the mire of history with the true story never being told.

The admiral slunk in and out of his office in increasing states of disarray and sweat all day. I heard the word draft thrown around in the phone calls I eavesdropped on several times. From initial reports, the losses were staggering. Many of the forward-deployed naval forces had either taken damage or were presently engaged. The Seventh Fleet carrier strike group waffled outside the second island chain like a wallflower at a school dance, unable or unwilling to commit to the fight. The country was bucking and heaving like a poorly laid foundation in an earthquake. While the whole world caught flame, I could only focus on the abomination beneath my feet.

THE REPLACEMENT

While the admiral was constantly in and out of meetings over the next several days, I found myself mostly forgotten about. As long as I effectively de-conflicted his schedule and answered phone calls professionally, I was left to my own devices. Every night, I was tormented by nightmares of what I had witnessed. The growing conflict with China occupied much of everyone's attention, but not mine. It felt like the whole Pentagon got on a train, and I was left at the station. Every so often, I would get up to walk by the closet door. I would check its handle and look around pensively. It was always locked. I never saw anyone access it or pay much attention to it.

I was brought back down to earth by a text from my friend, Ben Conger.

"Hey man, we need to hang out this weekend." he said.

I hesitated to reply. "I don't think I'll be able to."

"I know you're probably tied up doing the admiral's laundry, but I really need this."

"What do you mean?" I inquired.

After several minutes, he replied, "Off to see the fireworks soon."

My heart ached. Ben was an attached helicopter pilot for a destroyer in Norfolk. If sent into the theater, he would be flying dangerous aerial reconnaissance for the ship and possibly have to engage Chinese vessels with onboard weaponry. The aging helicopters the Navy had left for its pilots had enough trouble staying in the air during peacetime.

"Sorry man," I texted, "but there's just a lot going on right now."

I desperately wanted to give him a proper send off. He had been one of my closest friends. However, I figured leaving the area was out of the question. I could tell by his reply that Ben was deeply disappointed.

"Alright, another time," he messaged back.

I couldn't bring myself to reply to this text at first. I was almost certain there would not be another time.

He texted again. "Can't you can get away for a day or two even with everything going on?"

I thought of the perilous possibility of asking my captors for any kind of favor. A feeling of blind terror toward what I had seen the previous night overcame this sentiment.

Conger sent this grave text in closing: "It's this weekend or never."

I put away the phone and leaned against the wall across from the closet door. My hands covered my face as the fatigue overtook me. Personnel washed around me like an aimless mountain stream on its way toward a suicide over a raging waterfall. The hellish screams of several individuals receiving orders of reassignment to the Western Pacific pierced my contemplation. No military in history was fuller of clock-watchers and paper-pushers. To my own dismay, I had become one of them, paralyzed with fear and misgiving. I hurried back to my desk to find a stapled and stamped packet.

Katz shot me a concerned look as she curiously eyed the paperwork. "ADM Simmons dropped those off. They're for you," she pretended to turn away while watching with her peripherals.

I stood a short distance from the papers and observed them upside down at first. I moved my leaden feet across the tile floor by an unnatural effort. Trembling, I picked up the packet. I had to sift through nearly a page of headings, date-time groups, address lines, copy lines, and half a dozen other silly headings so common on naval messages before I got to the actual content.

"TAD orders to the school house in Norfolk?" I read aloud.

Katz shot a confused look. "School house? You're a SWO—why aren't they sending you to WestPac right now?"

I glared at her. "Don't get too antsy."

She started to compulsively bite her lower lip. I supposed she felt one of the two of us would be sent to a watery grave. My new orders appeared to her to be my exemption letter and her death sentence.

"Relax," I gripped the orders tightly. "Simmons still needs his phones answered."

Katz huffed and adjusted her jacket. The phone rang, and I gestured for her to answer it. I read my orders in more detail. My check in date was no later than this weekend.

Simmons returned with a calm look on his face. "Mr. Malden, I see you've found your orders," he trumpeted.

I pursed my lips and nodded.

"Don't get too comfortable," Simmons knocked his fist on my desk. "After the school house, you're going to sea."

"To sea?" I repeated.

The admiral shook his head with widened eyes. "Are you that clueless? The final orders haven't been cut yet, but you're getting an early command. You'll be in Norfolk for three weeks for a ship handling and command refresher course, then it's off to LCS-109 USS Peoria. I guess you're lucky that they made LCSs an O-4 command last year. I pulled a few strings for you to get this billet. You'll be XO for a little bit then CO. Congratulations, captain."

After this remark, Simmons retreated into his office and shut the door. My jaw hung agape. Given that he was the Chief of Naval Personnel, the alleged strings could not have been more effort that the shoelaces Simmons strained to reach every morning.

Suddenly, cheers broke out in one of the cubicles. I hurried over to see what was happening. A few sailors were huddled around a computer screen. Some nameless Chinese cruiser of an indiscernible class had allegedly been sunk by F-35s near Guam. The picture on the article showed the outline of a ship I knew wasn't Chinese.

"It's fake," I mistakenly said aloud.

The sailors turned around to give me a perplexed look. I stumbled back and returned to my desk without saying anything further.

"So, when do you leave for Norfolk?" Katz could barely contain her excitement.

I glared at her with what little willpower I had left. "Not soon enough."

I settled into my desk while ignoring every last call. She could handle that. I had bigger fish to fry.

It looks like Green is getting rid of me after all, I thought. Why would they not just shoot me in the back of the head on the Beltway somewhere?

Senior Chief Gander, the watch coordinator, stopped by and broke my contemplation. "Hey sir," he bore a sullen look.

I looked up from my computer screen and rudely gestured for him to speak.

"I saw your orders in message traffic. I've taken you off the watch list, if it's any consolation," Gander managed a wry smile.

"Word travels quick, I guess," I clenched my teeth.

The senior chief hesitated for a moment, then ventured, "Do you believe in God's Will?"

"Sure, I believe in God," I frowned.

Gander continued more confidently. "That's not what I asked. Do you believe there's a plan for each of us?"

I thought of the boy writhing in unspeakable agony just below us. "He must be a wicked sadist if there is."

The senior chief nodded empathetically. "Sir, I understand you're under a lot of pressure right now. God told me there was a burden on you when you came by to get off the watch calendar."

"Yet you added another one," I intimated, belying the true weight behind my words.

Gander smiled slightly. "You know, there was a civilian, I think a contractor, who came in and told me to take you off the watch rotation for that day. He was really adamant about that and was making everyone uncomfortable. He kept looking at the cross on my cubicle wall. I am a stickler for policy, so I kept you on."

I wondered if this was one of Green's men.

The senior chief continued. "I'm getting sidetracked. What I came by to tell you is that God's hand is on you in one form or another. There's a plan, sir. I don't know you very well, but it's been on my heart to pray for you. Now I know why." He began glancing at my orders.

"Trust me, you don't know the half of it," I widened my eyes.

As I sat at my desk, I lifted my feet off the ground slightly as if to create a degree of separation from what I had seen.

"I'm praying for you and your safe return home," Gander stated quietly while fumbling with his wedding ring. "Only the Lord knows if I will be joining you soon."

I nodded slowly as he left the office. I got up from my desk to find a computer rated for secret clearance. I found a terminal tucked away in a small SCIF at the far corner of the office. Logging my use of the computer in the binder, I put "admiral's business" in the reason field.

I hoped to see if there was any message traffic from LCS-109. I already knew the ship was home-ported in San Diego. My heart sank when I saw a message to the parent command detailing a suicide onboard. The rank of the individual was O-4—undoubtedly the captain I was going to replace.

ZENITH

"Hello?" I had just called my father on my drive back from the Pentagon.

"Son, I am so glad you called. This campaign is really heating up. And those Democrats want to just throw in the towel to China! Can you believe it? And only a short while before the election. We're going to take this country—"

"I'm going," I interrupted.

"Going where?" he stumbled.

"I have orders. I am going."

A grave silence captured the line for a moment.

My father swore. "I can't believe that. You just got off your sea tour, right?"

I gave no reply.

He continued. "This is an injustice. It's that liberal-Marxist secretary of defense who can't muster the cojones to institute a draft. Instead, they're putting heroes like you in harm's way." He concealed a growing sense of panic.

"Believe it or not, I think it's for the best," I said resignedly.

I could faintly hear my mother sobbing in the background.

"I'll tell you what, Rich, I know some people. The same people I've got endorsing me. Let me make a few calls."

I hung up the phone. Over the course of my enslavement at the mansion, I noticed an increasing resemblance to my father's enthrallment to his new masters. I wanted no favors from them any more than from Green.

When I returned to the mansion that night, the prospect of being sent to the front in an unwinnable war grew favorable in my mind. Each time I pulled up to the gate, I felt complicit in my own spiritual murder.

"Good evening, Mr. Malden," the woman greeted as she did every night.

"I won't be—" I began.

"You'll be having dinner with Mr. Green tonight," she interrupted.

My heart sank.

"I am going to be leaving soon," I feebly protested.

She gave no reply and instead opened the gate. As I pulled up the driveway, the mansion once more flashed its lights. The ostentatious display—a defiance of the natural darkness of night—peaked with the opening of the bronze doors. When I exited the car, there was no one to greet me at the top of the steps. I wavered at the foot of the stairs and kneeled for a moment. I hadn't had a good night's sleep or a square meal in days. Bit by bit, I was being consumed like a burn victim too weak to swat away a growing swarm of flies.

I nearly fainted at the threshold of the door after a slow, beleaguered climb. Only a short time ago, my mind would have been filled with silly plans to escape or kill Green. The dim nihilism that arrived early in my imprisonment had germinated into full hatred of my choices or ability to make them. I wheezed for a moment, weak from the stress and the anxiety. I halted my breathing for its passing resemblance to the boy's.

While it appeared that I was unsupervised in Green's home, I knew this not to be the case. Perhaps the most effective means of control are those which the captive feels are omniscient. I stumbled to the doors with the blue and white columns on an assumption Green would hold his dinner there.

"Mr. Malden," a voice I recognized called from behind me.

I wheeled around to see the source of the disembodied female voice that had been assisting in my torment. The first thing I noticed was her smile. More desires and intentions were wrapped up in that expression than could ever be retold or understood. In the lower part of my vision,

I could see she was dressed in an elaborate black evening gown. I dared not look at her body as her eyes pierced my own. Her sable, bobbed hair contrasted starkly with her sharp white skin so as to give the impression she made up one space on a chessboard. Given her demeanor, the woman estimated her own status in the game as the queen.

I stood dumb and mute. She was beautiful like a Venus fly trap consuming an insect—complex and intriguing, yet maintaining an element of the repulsive; something you would never want to touch.

"Mr. Malden," she repeated. "Don't you recognize my voice?"

"I . . ."

She put on a mocking expression as she walked closer, "Then there's the interview," the woman repeated in a completely believable, mournful tone before letting out a scornful chuckle.

The sound of her heels on the polished floor reverberated until she was only a foot away from my face. "Have you been getting enough sleep?"

She oscillated her gaze quickly between my right and left eyes, as if trying to hypnotize me.

At this distance, I noticed her eyes were two different colors. In her left, a dazzling blue sky. In the other, an impenetrable green swamp.

"You know, I've grown to look forward to our little chats every evening." The woman placed a clawed hand on my chest directly over my heart.

I assumed she meant our curt conversations at the gate.

"I must confess that I made up some of that paperwork I had you do. It's a shame you're leaving so soon," the woman continued, "being with Green is such an honor."

"You know about my orders?" I managed my first complete sentence of the conversation.

The woman made no reply, except a bizarre raising of her carefully trimmed eyebrows. Her fingers lingered on one of the buttons on my khaki shirt before she turned away abruptly. I stood as an awkward statue as this feminine apparition toyed with me. She made a coy glance over her shoulder before setting the same hand on the door to the great hall.

"I will go in first," she instructed. "Then you follow a little after. Mr. Green gets jealous."

I nodded meekly as she slithered into room like a snake finding an opening in a house's foundation. The whole interaction left me feeling violated. Not for a moment did I think she was genuinely trying to seduce me. Her gestures and tone indicated a posture not of lust, but of a ravenous intention to devour.

A short while later, I walked over to the door like a bovine in a chute. My hand trembled on the handle while I took a series of labored breaths. When I entered the great hall, I observed several figures leaving through a door at the other end. Green was silhouetted by the fire at the head of the table, while the woman sat to his right. I halted as the door closed behind me.

"Approach," Green commanded.

The room was as dark as the first night, yet the enormous paintings on the wall appeared more vivid. I passed panel after panel of unspeakable images. Protruding ribs, looks of anguish, and sunken eyes observed my progress along the table until I reached the seat opposite the woman.

"Sit," the man compelled.

The table was already set with a broad array of foods and culinary delights. A roasted turkey was the centerpiece. Despite the smell, I had no appetite at all. We all sat in silence for what passed like an eternity. Green stared blankly at the far end of the room while the woman looked at him dotingly. The fire behind him caused his face to be encapsulated in an unknowable shadow until he abruptly turned to me. The left side of his visage glowed red as it caught the rays of the fireplace.

"You're going away," Green stated.

I nodded silently.

"But you'll be back."

My eyes widened.

"It's a silly little attempt," Green began serving food onto his plate. "Don't they know the kind of things around you?"

I rubbed my face as if to wake up from a dream.

"It's best if I can keep him here," he turned toward the woman, yet his eyes looked past her. "Sending him off to the Pacific is a fool's errand."

I mustered the courage to speak. "What do you mean?"

Green angrily set down a serving spoon on his plate and turned toward me like a scolding parent interrupted by a petulant child. Instead of replying, he gestured at the woman. At this signal, she grasped the roasted turkey with her bare hands and pulled it to her plate. The woman tore at the meat and bones, making a horrendous racket. Any beauty she had sank into the depths of her repugnant consumption.

Green turned to me and began speaking as if the woman's behavior was normal and expected. "She's going to be punished," he intimated.

The woman gave a brief, fearful glance at Green before returning to her feast.

"She was supposed to keep you out of the Pentagon that night," Green recounted. "But it seems the nice little God of the Christians was very keen to keep you there."

I was utterly bewildered.

"I see from the look on your face you remember everything," he continued. "Down to the last detail."

The squelching and breaking of bones across from me made my stomach turn.

"Now tell me," Green used a fork and knife to politely eat his meal, "what did you see?"

Remembering his imperative to keep my mouth shut, I replied, "Nothing."

He smiled imperceptibly and took a sip of wine.

"Nothing? Good. I am glad you saw nothing at all," Green set his glass down.

He got up and picked up the poker for the fire. He stoked it several times and looked back at me.

He sighed. "I knew this would happen. I can't be too upset with the girl, after all. I've been warning everyone the tide is turning. At the very zenith of our power, the foundation is already crumbling. They don't believe me. They consider themselves invincible."

I hadn't the slightest idea what he was talking about—or to whom.

"This scuffle with the Chinese," Green set the poker down, satisfied he had kept the fire alive, "may yet break our backs. But I have other plans. I will find a replacement. His energy is running out. I warned them. They said it would go on forever. Every time he nearly expired, new technology emerged to keep the cycle going. Now, everyone has blind faith in some far-off scientific achievement leaping from the pages of textbooks yet to be written to save the day. I am going to put a stop to this. If we are to survive, our salvation will leap from the pages of another tradition, one passed from long ago."

I nodded along cluelessly.

"I can't be too upset with you either, despite your trespass in the engine room. Your upset to him only showed how fragile and declining this all is." Green sat down and carefully gauged my reaction. "We nearly lost him because of you. In a short while, it won't matter, though. His replacement is nearly ready. I would have preferred to keep you under close observation. Others wanted to get you as far away from the Pentagon as possible. Don't worry, though. I will make sure a watchful eye is kept."

I shivered in my seat despite the warmth of the fire. "Replacement?" I ventured.

Green gave me a venomous look for interrupting his monologue. He continued without answering my question. "Unfortunately for both of us, you'll survive this little war. It will all be wrapped up soon and forgotten. Our campaign in Syria will continue, however. One small benefit to this charade."

I wracked my brain for any involvement the US had in Syria. To my knowledge, only a few forward deployed special operations forces were left. Israel, on the other hand, was engaged in a punitive bombing campaign from the Golan Heights while the world was distracted elsewhere.

"It will surely yield a strong field of candidates," Green assured. "Our enemies have a long history in that land."

When he said "our," his tone indicated I was not in the group.

"It's a miracle he came out of the Germans of all people," Green shrugged. "Such a short yet punctuated history with us. I am returning to a much more reliable pool. A whole sea of people, ripe for the harvest."

He took a perverse pleasure in speaking riddles and code to me. At last, Green relented.

"Eat something, Mr. Malden. I do not offer my table in vain."

I looked with disgust at the remaining scraps while the woman gave me a wild look, her mouth dripping with grease and suspicion.

ALL THOSE YEARS AGO

"I have no idea what any of it meant. Not the slightest idea," Richard Malden recounted to Edwards.

He had regained his composure after retelling his account of the boy, but the pain of that memory still sent courses of agony through his body.

The guerrilla leader nodded along silently. When Richard's voice trailed off, he got up from the table without a word.

"Where are you going? Are you just going to leave me here?" Richard called out.

Edwards returned from the darkness with a black backpack. He advanced slowly and set it next to his seat before resuming his position. The zipper reverberated in the dark warehouse.

"It's just as I've known all along," the man had a dour expression on his face.

He took a spiral bound book from the pack and threw it on the table. Taking a knife, he traversed around the table to cut his captive loose. Richard winced at the sight of the blade but kept his cool.

"That document," Edwards began, "was not easy to come by. I saw some things in Iraq that didn't seem quite right."

Malden at last could move his arms freely. He brought them to his lap and rolled his shoulders. "You were in Iraq?"

The man froze for a moment and stared far off. "Iraq, Afghanistan, Yemen, Syria, any other hellhole you can think of."

Richard deduced he must have been some form of special forces.

"But Iraq," Edwards returned to his seat with a deep breath, "that's where I saw . . . and did things that shook me to my core—more than all the others."

Malden eyed the dossier on the table curiously. He knew better than to ask about his captor's time in the sandbox.

"I am going to ask you a question I already know the answer to," the guerrilla leader placed a hand on the document. "Have you ever heard of Stimulosis?"

"Stimulosis?" his captive repeated.

Edwards clenched his jaw and spun the dossier around on the table passively with his finger. "It's a compound word between the Latin stimulus and the Greek suffix –osis. Stimulus, in its origin, described an ox goad or a pointed stick. In its metaphorical use, it was used to describe a sting of torment. Osis means a state or abnormal condition. Together, the word 'Stimulosis' means the use of torment by pricking to maintain an unnatural state. It's a little modification to the scientific name for a genus of a stinging nettle native to Florida; those strange little flowers you saw lining Green's driveway blooming so unnaturally late in the year." The man leaned forward and lowered his tone. "Do you understand where I am going with this?"

Richard realized he had been scratching his bare leg compulsively at this point. His breathing was shallow and his adrenaline coursed out of control.

"I—" he stammered. "Does this mean . . ."

Edwards nodded slightly and opened the spiral bound book and slid it toward his captive.

"Let me tell you a story from Iraq, all those years ago. We were assigned to kidnapping children. Dozens upon dozens of kids snatched up and sent off to who-knows-where." The guerrilla rubbed his right hand, which trembled almost imperceptibly. "We were told the parents were militants, and we were relocating the kids to safe houses." After nine or ten houses of not finding any weapons, ammunition, or anything to suggest ill intent of the parents, I realized what we were really doing. Every time we returned to base with the children, a spook was there to meet us. They loaded them up in a van or a helicopter, and none of us ever saw them again."

"Why were they making you do that?" Richard ventured.

"I will get to that," Edwards looked down for a moment before resuming piercing eye contact. "One night, I decided to get blackout drunk at the Green Zone Café. I had had enough of my so-called job. This was in my pre-conversion days." He turned his gaze to heaven briefly, "God willed it that two spooks sat a few spaces away from me at the bar. They were pretty good and drunk too. Eventually, one of them bumps into one of my teammates. I guess my buddy also was getting fed up with doing the spooks' bidding. A fight broke out. I came to the aid of my friend without question. All the pent-up hatred of what we were doing got taken out on those two wicked men. We dragged them outside and beat them both senseless. One of the spooks had a coded briefcase chained to his wrist. In the scuffle, one of us had stepped on it pretty good and the cover sheet of a document poked out just a tiny bit. My judgment heavily impaired, I decided to tug at that piece of paper. My buddy looked on curiously. It tore a little as I fed it through the crack, but I got about three-quarters of it out. That was all I needed. Do you know what the title of that report was?"

Richard shook his head.

"'Stimulosis Candidates in Suburban Baghdad: June–September.' A title so mundane and meaningless, my inebriated mind almost didn't give it a second thought. But God told me to sear that cover sheet into my mind. Every last detail of that paper sunk into the deepest recesses of my soul before my friend told me base police were on their way. We high-tailed it out of there, the sheet still where I found it." Edwards shared. "The cover sheet had emblems of both the CIA and the Mossad."

The man placed his hand on the document again, flat and fully stretched out. Richard got the sense the man was itching to give it to him but couldn't bring himself to do it.

"What's that dossier?" Malden spoke sheepishly.

Edwards pulled the document closer to himself. "I will let you read it soon enough. I held on to that word Stimulosis through several more tours in messed up country after messed up country. I was without conscience then. I just followed orders and got over it. But what we did in Iraq will haunt me to my grave. Sometimes I wonder if even Christ himself could forgive me." He paused to pray shortly, then continued, "My friend and I never talked about what we saw on the cover sheet, not that we really knew what it meant. He was killed in Yemen several years later. RPG right to the gut," Edwards trailed off, "but I held on. God brought me through. When I got out, I got hooked on opioids. I was homeless, wandering the streets of Virginia Beach trying to drown out the memory of everything I knew and took part in. One night I walked to the end of a fishing pier and stared deeply into the water. I climbed up on the railing and prepared to jump in. Suddenly, I heard a voice call out my name. The word Stimulosis repeated in my head over and over until I stumbled back from the railing. As I laid on my back on that pier, my vision blacked out. That's when I saw it."

"Saw what?" Richard asked after a period of silence.

"What you saw," Edwards said matter-of-factly. "God showed it to me."

"He showed you the boy?"

The man's eyes welled slightly. "He showed me. He showed me every last detail. Just as you described."

Richard challenged, "But you were on drugs, right? You clearly weren't in you right frame of mind."

The guerrilla grew incensed. "How dare you question what the Lord revealed to me!" He slammed his fist onto the table. "Wise in your own eyes! How is it then that I already knew what you were going to tell me about the boy? Just pure chance?"

The captive shrunk back, "I have no idea. I just . . ."

"You're struggling to grapple with things beyond explanation, just as I was," Edwards took an empathetic tack and lowered his voice. "Remember that spiritual war I told you about? Like it or not, you've been pressed into service, just as I was. As you said in the depths of the Pentagon, 'The only way out is through.'"

Richard sat back in his chair, his body limp.

The guerrilla continued, "If I hadn't already been at rock bottom, what God showed me would've sent me there. All I had was a word and a vision. Nothing else. Nothing else besides a gnawing desire to find out more. I got clean off drugs. An old operator friend hooked me up with a contracting deal in DC. We were auxiliaries to the Secret Service— protection details and the like. All the while, the vision haunted my nightmares even more than my time in Iraq. Then came the party."

His captive shifted in his chair.

Edwards nodded. "You know what I'm talking about. I was driving an armored limousine for Senator Bradley of New Mexico. All I knew was that he needed to be driven from his residence in Georgetown to some place southwest of DC. When I pulled up, there were dozens of opulent vehicles and guests filing their way into the mansion. Nothing too out of the ordinary, right? That's when I noticed the robes. I dropped off the senator and parked the car. He instructed me to keep the vehicle running as he wouldn't be long. I strategically parked where I could observe his entrance to the mansion. Bradley received a robe just like everyone else. As the bronze doors shut behind the last guest, I saw just the last glimpse of a child being led by the hand. From what little I saw, I knew the kid was gagged and bound. This set off all kinds of alarm bells. I leapt out of the car and briskly walked to the bronze doors. They were locked of course. I walked the perimeter of the structure until I could just barely see inside through a crack in drawn curtains."

"What were they doing in there?" Richard asked impatiently.

The man leaned back and stared off into space. "Eating."

"Eating? That's it?"

Edwards widened his eyes and shook his head slowly. "No, Richard. That table. That huge table you saw and sat at? From one end to the other, it was covered in the bodies of children! Babies, toddlers, some as old as eleven or twelve. All the while, these horrible people were laughing, drinking, and most revoltingly, eating. Others were doing unspeakable acts with each other in full view of everyone."

The captive's stomach turned and he leaned over in his chair to retch.

"You listen good!" Edwards pointed aggressively. "This is who we're dealing with. These are the ones who rule us! You were shown a little, but God chose me to see worse!"

"What is even the point of these parties?" Richard managed to regain his composure.

The guerrilla answered, "Call it whatever you want. Blackmail, extortion, initiation, the price of doing business."

"Does everyone in power have to do this?"

"Have to?" Edwards contemplated the question, "No. But you'll find most are willing to do just about anything to ingratiate themselves with the power structure. After a while they start to enjoy it. It's certainly required to be allowed near any real power. If I told you the names of some of the people I saw . . ."

Richard waffled, "It's so much worse than I thought."

The guerrilla remained silent for a short period. "If your father stays on this path, I wouldn't be surprised if he got an invite sometime."

Malden opened his mouth to speak but remained silent.

"There were a few there who looked revolted at everything going on. Eventually peer pressure got the better of them, and they took a small taste—just like Adam and Eve in the garden," the man concluded.

The captive rubbed his face. "Okay, but what does this story have to do with Stimulosis?"

"After I drove the senator home, I got a text the next day from my supervisor saying I was fired. No warning, no reason, just canned. In any other world, I could have sued. But I didn't care anymore. I wanted nothing more to do with protecting these people. What that party taught me was that these people are evil to the core. It's not just a few bad apples. It wasn't just the spooks in Iraq. The whole power structure needed to go. That's what brought me to my status as an enemy of the state. I needed to find what kept this horrific system lurching forward despite all forces to the contrary. I knew the vision had something to do with it," Edwards leaned forward and spoke in a hoarse, low tone. "To figure out how to destroy something, you need to find out how it works first; what drives it."

"The engine room . . ." Richard's heart sank.

SELF-DESTRUCTION

"How did the dinner end?" Edwards inquired.

„

I sat in silence while that woman kept gorging herself. Every time I thought she was done, she would take a deep breath and continue.

"Eat something," Green commanded.

I politely refused, "I am not hungry."

"You insult me," my host tightened his fist around his knife.

At last, I relented and brought a small helping of some dish I didn't recognize. Green sat back in his chair and watched keenly as I brought the food to my mouth.

"You were only with us a short while, but you'll be back. I wanted to give you two things: a proper sendoff and a warning," he said cooly. "As I am sure you've deduced at this point, there's little I can do to physically harm you at this point. The nice little God of the Christians won't permit it. But you listen closely." The blasphemer rose from his chair and loomed large over me. The woman stopped eating for a moment and shrunk back in her chair.

"I can make your life hell. Nowhere is beyond my reach. I see everything. I know everything. The nice little God of the Christians wrestled with Jacob once before and saw He prevailed not against him!"

I did my best to remain calm and unfazed. In reality, Jacob Green had already made life hell.

My tormentor continued after sitting down, "You will tell no one about what you've seen. You would do well to heed my instruction. If you do, things may go very well for you. This regrettable lump of clay unceremoniously dumped on my wheel may yet be molded into something useful." Green paused then turned to me, "Do you understand?"

Something in the way he asked me gave rise to such indignation as I had never felt before. The way he talked to me made me believe he really did view me as something less than human.

In no position to bargain, however, I meekly replied, "Yes."

The woman resumed her repulsive consumption.

Green got up from his chair and faced the fire. "You have thirty minutes to grab what you need from the loft. I will be keeping the rest of your items for when you return. Leave the key on the table."

I sat dumbfounded for a moment.

"Does he have to go so soon?" the female asked in the same mournful tone she used in the first phone call.

The master of the house ignored her and continued to stare deeply into the fire. After a minute, he stated, "The clock is ticking, Mr. Malden."

With this invitation to leave, I sprang from my chair and hastily made my way out of the house. Green was a man of precision. I knew there would horrible consequences if I took even a second too long.

When I got up to the loft, I grabbed my seabag and haphazardly shoveled items in. The time crunch gave way to a small inkling of optimism in my mind that I was going to be leaving my prison cell, even if it was only a temporary parole. My seabag full of everything I could think to bring on deployment, I hoisted the heavy sack on my shoulders. As I walked out of the door, it closed automatically behind me. I turned to view the infernal chamber and caught a glimpse of the painting for what I hoped to be the last time, eyes ablaze.

My legs felt shaky and limp as I trundled down the stairs. I threw the seabag in the backseat and started my car. Tears began streaming down my face as I set a heading for the gate. As I drove anxiously down the driveway, Green stood as a black silhouette in the open doorway of the mansion. The woman stood a few feet behind him still in the light of the foyer. She concealed a curt wave at me before I turned my head toward the road running parallel to the grounds. The gate was already open, and I sped off into the night.

I laughed, I cried, I screamed. At last, I was, in some sense, free. I didn't know whether to trust Green's prediction that I would survive the war. I rather welcomed the prospect of death. Being killed in action was a far more preferable outcome than returning to that den of torment above the garage.

I didn't have any destination in mind. I just drove. The streetlights passed above me like waves beating against the keel of a great warship. I was caught up in the moment of freedom, however transient and fleeting it was. Green, the loft, and the boy were unceremoniously escorted into the deepest recesses of my brain to be repressed and forgotten.

I stopped by a liquor store and got a bottle of the cheapest whiskey I could find and a generic soda. I finally parked somewhere just outside the Pentagon and drank my fill. As I grew more and more intoxicated, I stepped out of the car into the cool, autumn night air and hurled curses and obscene gestures at the building, all while still in my uniform from the workday. This display continued until I observed a dark SUV at the other end of the parking lot. In my spirit, I knew it was the calavera adorned enforcer. I gave him the finger before returning to the inside of my car. The small dose of liberty appeared beyond what I could handle. I slumped into the backseat and slept free of nightmares for the first time in too long.

I at least had the wherewithal to set my alarm. I awoke hungover and stiff the next day to the clanging of an artificial bell. I swore bitterly as I rubbed my face. The memory of the previous night returned after a brief moment of ignorance. I sat up and looked at myself in the rearview mirror. It was the first time I had really examined my appearance since being incarcerated at Green's mansion. My hairline was receding faster than the tide. Deep wrinkles cut their way through my forehead like furrows left in the wake of agony's plowshare. My eyes sat atop horrific dark circles. At least with the war going on, few looked much better.

After shaving painfully with a cheap razor and no water, I made my way to the Pentagon and returned to my fleeting post as the admiral's secretary. When he arrived, I requested to speak with him in his office.

"Come in," Simmons beckoned.

The admiral looked even more stressed and disgusting than his usual.

"If this is about your orders, don't even try to get out of them. Do you have any idea how many strings I pulled to get you early command despite this investigation going on?"

"I'd like to leave today," I interrupted him.

My report date wasn't until the following Monday.

"Today?" he stumbled.

I nodded without a word.

"That excited, hm? Well, Peoria will be glad to have you as soon as possible. They'll be in the thick of it soon."

I stood with a blank expression.

"Well," Simmons shuffled some papers on his desk, "I suppose you're off. Katz will man the phones like she did before you got here."

Before he was finished with his sentence, I was out the door.

Katz gave me smug expression as I gathered my things from the desk. "Off to WestPac?"

I glared at her. "You'll get your turn soon enough."

The sailors in their cubicles gave me dour looks as I shuffled out of the office and grabbed my official orders. It took all of my willpower to ignore the closet door and keep the lid firmly on that memory. Once out of the Pentagon complex, I changed into civilian clothes and mounted the Beltway to head to Norfolk. Once I got on I-95, I left that rotten city in my rearview mirror. Green's warning that I would return hung at the back of my mind like a feral pursuer. Some power greater than him had decided to send me off to the war to die. I hoped they would be successful.

I dialed my friend Ben Conger.

"Hey," he replied in a far more subdued tone than what I was used to.

"Guess who's on his way to Norfolk."

Ben's tone lightened. "No way. They let you have some leave? What I'd do for some leave right now."

I half chuckled. "Nope. No leave. Schoolhouse."

He understood what this meant. "Shoot man. We'll be going together."

"What are you doing tonight?" I asked after a period of silence.

Ben sighed. "Contemplating life."

"Want to get hammered?" I interjected, my head still pounding from the previous night.

"On a Thursday?"

"On a Thursday." I repeated.

Ben was quiet for nearly a minute. "Screw it. This is my last weekday to get trashed before I ship out. Why not?" he replied. "Meet me at my place when you get here."

Ben told me his address and we ended the call. To be honest, the last thing I wanted was alcohol. I just wanted to be numb.

I arrived at his house about four hours later. He was sitting in a folding chair sipping a beer on the front porch next to a cooler.

"Whaddup," Ben raised the bottle to greet me.

When I emerged from the car, his expression changed.

"Geez dude, you look terrible," he started. "I thought the stress was getting to me. Is giving the admiral massages really that hard?"

I just shrugged nihilistically and fished a beer out of the cooler. "It's not just that," I said before taking a drink.

Ben nodded and sipped his own beer. "Yeah. I get that."

We drank in silence until we both finished our bottles.

"I'm out of here on Monday," he piped up. "It's looking pretty rough out there for helos right now."

"Let's not talk shop," I diverted the conversation. "What do you say we hit the scene early?"

Ben laughed. "Look at you raring to go. It's not even 1600 yet!"

I looked out into the preened suburban neighborhood and all the silly American flags everyone was flying. I saw dozen of "Give 'em all you got" and "God Bless the USA" bumper stickers on my drive down. A few banners had been hung on overpasses, impelling passersby to "pray for our troops." I was disgusted by all of it. This was some small measure of solidarity the apathetic public could muster before the squeeze of losing access to cheap Chinese goods could sap their patriotic fervor.

I pulled up a chair next to his and cracked open another beer.

"How's the morale in your squadron?" I asked.

"In the toilet," Ben rubbed his face. "No, flushed down the toilet. In the sewer. Washed out to sea."

"The Pentagon was awash with paper pushers getting the letter of doom to go fight the Chinese," I chuckled sadistically.

"Like you?" he prodded with his elbow.

"Just like me."

Ben scrolled on his phone for a few minutes while I did the same. Laura was pregnant again. Her beautiful family sat as a mockery of everything that should've been in my life. I was filled to the brim with resentment, anger, fear, and loathing. My self-destructive bent beckoned me to spend as much money on losing control of my faculties as quickly as possible.

"Did you see the carrier USS Adams took a hit? Nothing serious, but those destroyer captains in the screen are all going to hang," Ben interrupted my dark contemplation.

"No, they won't," I flicked the cap of my bottle into his yard. "The Navy's far too desperate for warm bodies. They'll shuffle every last paper pusher, delinquent, and incompetent to the front before instituting a draft. They know that'll kill the war effort."

My friend watched the cap land next to a disheveled bush.

"You're probably right," he tossed his bottle cap too.

His landed in the street, bounced a few times, and rolled into a storm grate.

"Let's get out of here," I implored again.

Ben finished his beer and sat for a moment. "You know what? Time's a-wasting. Let's go," he acquiesced.

"I'll drive," I informed.

Ben grabbed my arm on the way to the car, "Dude no. If you intend on getting as wasted as I do, you'll be in no condition to drive."

I brushed his hand away. "Who cares? Warm bodies, remember?"

I could see the degree of my self-destruction worried him, but he ultimately relented. The nihilism was setting in for him too. We shuffled into the car.

"Let's make it a night to remember," he looked mournfully out the window as I started the engine.

A NIGHT TO REMEMBER

We hit an Irish pub somewhere in downtown Norfolk overlooking the Elizabeth River. A mass of potential energy saturated the air as we both anticipated the night's course. Conversation bounced from past girlfriends to academy memories.

"Do you remember that trip to Dallas?" Ben asked.

"I remember having to catch your vomit with my hands so we wouldn't get the cops called on us," I laughed while ordering another drink.

"Oh yeah," he put a hand to his head. "I am going to have to trust you on that one. I don't remember much from that night."

"How's it going with Alyssa?" I asked.

Ben pursed his lips. "It's not going anymore."

"I'm sorry to hear that," I shook my head. "To be honest with you, I never liked her."

He threw his head back. "Neither did I. Drove me nuts most of the time."

We both shared a stress-relieving laugh. All the while, a TV showed a news broadcast of updates on the war. An older gentleman noticed us and walked over. He wore a Vietnam veteran hat and sported a grey beard.

"You fellas military?" he asked.

Ben and I exchanged uncomfortable looks.

"Yeah," my friend admitted.

The veteran looked at the TV then back at us.

"Your war will be nothing like mine," he rested his hands on his belt. "Nothing at all."

With this cryptic comment, he left. I gave a confused expression to Ben. We both came out to the bars to forget what was going on, not to receive bizarre editorials.

"C'mon, let's ditch this place," I advocated.

Ben reluctantly agreed. "Yeah, that news broadcast is bringing me down. It's too bad. This place reminds me a lot of Bay's Castle in Annapolis."

Bay's Castle was an Irish pub where our friend group at the academy hung out almost every weekend once we hit drinking age. Danny was off in a submarine somewhere, that is if he was still alive. John got hit with a medical discharge shortly after graduating.

"You remember John?" I asked after we paid our bills.

"Lucky guy. I hate to say it kind of makes me loathe him right now, sitting pretty at home while we go off," Ben led the way out into the street.

I took a deep breath of the evening air. The sky was starting to turn a pale orange as the day retreated. It was one of those pleasant afterglows of summer where the temperature still hovered at comfortable levels.

"I can't hold it against him," I shrugged. "It's all random. He gets the golden ticket; we get the shaft."

My friend bit his lower lip. "Can we go a minute without talking about the war? Let's get it going tonight. I know just the place to take our minds off it."

We walked casually to the next spot while Ben ripped a cigarette. Just like at the academy, he only smoked when he drank. I decided there wasn't much harm in joining him. When we arrived at a dive bar off the main drag, it was nearly dark. I checked my watch to find several hours had passed since we left his house like the fleeting vestiges of summer vacation before a dreaded school year.

Inside, Ben recognized a few people he knew from the squadron.

"I see we're not the only degenerates on a Thursday night," he greeted them and introduced me.

I awkwardly said hello and joined them all at the table. At first, I kept up with the conversation, adding funny anecdotes or silly stories.

Gradually, my focus drifted to whatever was in the glass in front of me. By now, I had quite the buzz going. Not since my academy days did I drink so diligently and persistently.

"Really putting 'em away, huh?" the guy next to me nudged with his elbow.

I looked at him bleary-eyed. "What do you care?"

He raised his eyebrows and went back to the conversation. The less I joined in, the deeper I sank into my thoughts and the booze. Finally, all I could think about was the boy. I closed my eyes vigorously several times trying to snuff out the ghastly vision, but to no avail.

"Richard."

I rubbed my face and ordered another whiskey.

"Richard!" Ben tapped me on the shoulder. "You good?"

The look I gave in return must have shaken his confidence in how the evening was going.

"Let's maybe call it a night. I'll call a ride," he pulled out his phone and opened an app.

My hand struck like a cobra as I slapped it down. "Put that thing away!"

My outburst caused most of the bar to look my way. Ben's phone laid on the ground with a shattered screen.

"It's all good everybody," Ben reassured the other patrons. "It's all good."

He picked up the phone while everyone else went back to their drinks.

"What on earth is going on with you?" Ben pressed quietly after taking me aside.

I stumbled for a moment before he sat me down in a chair at an empty table.

"Look, I know this deployment thing is putting a damper on everything, but we're here to forget all that. Drinking seems like it's just making it worse for you." Ben said.

"You don't get it," I slurred. "You just don't get it."

"What don't I get?"

I looked into his face and saw a childlike innocence.

"You don't get it," I repeated. "I saw . . ."

"What did you see?" Ben asked ignorantly.

The horror I witnessed in the Pentagon emerged from the pits of my stomach and regurgitate into my mouth. I placed my hand across my face to try to stem the flow.

"Are you good?" he put a hand on my shoulder.

"I'm good." I managed to keep the unpleasant memory down.

I persuaded him to let me rejoin the table instead of going home. Later, a woman entered the bar alone. From what little I could perceive, she was quite beautiful. A rather plain-looking woman in Ben's friend group seemed annoyed that she caught my eye.

"So, you were stationed at the Pentagon before you got orders?" she made an attempt at conversation.

"Yeah," I bluntly replied while staring uncomfortably at the girl at the bar.

"Oh yeah, I remember visiting there one time. . . ."

I swallowed the rest of my whiskey with a wince. I got up in the middle of her story and made uneasy locomotion to the bar. The woman noticed me approaching and grew uncomfortable but remained in place.

"Hey, how's it going?" I opened the conversation. "My name's Richard."

She gave a disinterested smile and turned her back.

"Hey, I was talking to you."

Anger started to build. I pestered her a few more times before I felt a hand on my shoulder.

"Ok you're done," Ben pulled me away from the bar.

I made a haphazard attempt at punching him. At this point, the bartender called over the bouncer to have me thrown out. Ben sat me down and talked it over with him. The plain looking girl shot me a disgusted look. After a short while, he returned.

"Hey, let's go. I paid your tab," Ben tried to lift me up.

I was too hammered to resist much. Instead, I began babbling about how I didn't want to go home. My friend managed to get me outside with some considerable embarrassment. He pulled out two cigarettes and handed one to me.

"Take it," he ordered.

We stood outside with the other smokers sanding away their lives in the cool fall darkness. A single streetlamp next to the bar marked the territory of what could be seen.

"Seriously man, there's something deeper than going to Seventh Fleet with you right now. You're doing a crap job of hiding it," Ben lit his cigarette before lighting mine.

I inhaled deeply before sitting on the curb. My friend joined me shortly after.

"I saw things," every fiber of my better judgment strained against my loose, drunken tongue—"down there."

"Down where?" Ben asked. "In the Pentagon?"

I nodded slowly as some ash fell from my smoke.

"What do you mean you saw something?"

The liquor caused my mouth to outrun my inhibitions. "Nothing you'd ever believe. There's a boy down there."

This last statement caused a number of the other smokers to recede into the darkness, leaving only small puffs of smoke, little piles of ash, and discarded cigarette butts. It was as if everyone knew exactly what they shouldn't learn.

Ben looked noticeably uncomfortable but pressed on. "A boy? Like someone's kid was in the Pentagon?"

"I don't even know how to describe it," my vision careened out of control. "They're torturing a boy in the basement."

"What the . . ." he took on a wild expression.

"I was staying at a loft in a big mansion. Some guy named Jacob Green," I rambled incoherently.

Ben shook his head.

"Needles, Ben," I dropped my cigarette and grabbed both of his arms. "They just stuck him with millions of little needles over and over again! I can't get him out of my head!"

"Calm down dude," he looked around anxiously. "The stress is probably just getting to you."

"The eyes! Those piercing eyes!" I shouted and slumped back onto the sidewalk in tears.

Ben picked me up in a fireman's carry and started his way back to my car. The whole time, new aspects of the memory I had repressed came erupting to the surface.

"He's just down there. Writhing in agony. You can almost feel him down in that basement," I exclaimed in a tortured whisper.

Ben resorted to just ignoring my ramblings.

"Do you think you can walk?" he asked, breathless.

I agreed. He set me down on a grimy sidewalk. I stumbled for a moment before vomiting into the gutter. Ben was fed up with my antics.

"C'mon man, this night's over. I am calling a ride." He pulled out his phone again. "On my broken screen," he cursed.

We waited in silence for about a quarter of an hour before a black sedan pulled up. When the driver rolled the window down to call to us, his face was obscured by shadows. On his arms however, the sickly amber streetlights cast their rays on calaveras like a lighthouse warning of shoal water.

"We're not taking this one," I haphazardly grabbed Ben's shirt.

He grew frustrated. "Shut up! It's done. We're going home."

"Not in that car!" I cautioned in a slurred tone.

Ben cussed me out before dragging me into the back seat. The driver's black eyes met mine in the rearview mirror. He shook his head slowly, maintaining deathly eye contact. His expression communicated an unspeakable impending punishment.

My friend buckled me in and whispered harshly to me, "If you throw up in here, you're paying for it."

The fear of the man sobered me up quickly as the car pulled away from the curb. Periodically, the driver checked on me in the mirror.

I leaned over to Ben and tried to say in a hushed tone, "We've got to get out of this car."

He looked at me with a confused, contemptuous look as we whispered. "What's the big problem?"

I waited for a moment while the man checked on me before answering. "I know him. He works for Jacob Green."

The driver's eyes shot to the mirror once again and widened slightly.

"I have no idea who that is," my friend shook his head and looked out at the city scape as it passed by.

I reached a hand slowly to be seatbelt to unbuckle it as quietly as I could. Ben noticed what I was doing.

"Dude you're acting crazy," he said at an uncomfortable volume.

With this interruption, the driver had had enough. He pulled off rapidly onto a side street, slammed on the breaks, turned off the headlights. I tried unlocking the door and yanking at the handle but the child locks were enabled. The man pulled what looked like a suppressed pistol from under the seat and shot Ben in the chest. I looked wide-eyed at my friend to find a strange dart protruding from his body. Before I could turn to face the man again, a sharp hiss put an end to my night to remember.

KOMPROMAT

I awoke the next morning in a seedy motel. The first thing I noticed was the odd mix of smells. Stale cigarettes, dirty laundry, and mold intermingled freely in my nostrils. It took me several minutes to fully regain consciousness. I was caught in a thick haze from the night before and whatever I was injected with. My head felt as if it were stuffed with cotton wool.

Suddenly, I sat up to the sound of a camera shutter clicking. The dark man lowered a camera from his face. I stood up in panic when I saw what was lying next to me in the bed. It was the woman I had approached in the bar with a knife plunged in her chest. I looked down at my hands and saw they were covered in dried blood.

"Good morning, Mr. Malden," the man said, putting the camera back in its case. "I see you had a good night."

I stumbled back in horror as I tried to make sense of the situation.

"I didn't do it!" I pleaded, "I didn't do that!"

He put the case's strap over his shoulder after putting on his jacket.

"I never accused you of anything. Guilty conscience?" the man chuckled.

"Where's my friend?"

He headed to the door in silence.

"Hey!" I called after him. "What are you doing with those photos?"

"I wouldn't stick around here, Mr. Malden," he informed me. "I'm not doing anything with these pictures. That'll be up to Mr. Green. Maybe next time you'll keep your mouth shut."

The man left the room and partially closed the door leaving a piercing strip of light to cut across the room to the dead woman. I did not even know her name. Her lifeless eyes stared blankly at the ceiling. I put my hands to my face before I realized I was smearing her blood all over me. I rushed to the sink behind the partition and tried to wash it off. Though I scrubbed considerably, it stuck to my skin like glue. I swore over and over as my mind raced. For the most part, my thinking was still heavily clouded by the cocktail of drugs and my hangover.

"I know I didn't do that!" I assured myself.

I looked over my shoulder at the bed. I could just see her feet poking out from behind the wall. I was filled with intense sadness and regret that she had been caught up in all of this. I finished washing the best I could and returned to her bedside

"Why did they do this to you?" I covered my mouth in panic.

I knew I had to get out of there as soon as possible, but my legs refused to move. I crumpled to the floor and pulled at my hair. I heavily contemplated taking the knife out of her chest and ending it all. I was in too deep. I was filled with so much regret, angst, and fear that I was paralyzed from any further action. My dark disposition only sank further when I thought of Ben and what terrible consequences my drunken rant may have caused him. I wondered whether my phone was bugged and chastised myself for not assuming so already. At the bottom of my downward spiral, appalling memories of the boy waited for me.

I began to feel the urge to vomit. I rushed over to the toilet and emptied what was left of the night into the scummy water. The bile and acid burned my parched throat as I gripped the bowl. I at least had the wherewithal to clean up my mess and flush the toilet. When the sound dissipated into the stagnant air of the motel room, I began to feel as though I was trapped in a tomb with the dead woman.

My mind raced over what to do. I couldn't go on the run as a fugitive. That would just make me look guilty. I couldn't report Green's henchman to the police due to the incriminating photos he possessed and the leverage they yielded. If I left the motel and tried to go about my daily life, there was a strong chance the police would track me down as a suspect. My DNA was everywhere in that room and witnesses saw me harassing her in the bar. I was at a complete loss. Just then, Green's man stepped back inside with a large duffel bag.

"Are you coming out yet?" he scolded.

I stood wide-eyed in silence.

"Get out of there. I need to clean up."

"What do you mean clean up?" I asked with a quiver.

"I've got what I need. Get out." He commanded again.

Bewildered, I hugged the wall as I walked out of the door. I took one last glance at the woman before stepping out onto the sidewalk.

"You're not going to let the police find this?" I inquired with hesitation.

The man rolled his eyes and chuckled. "The police will find it if they need to." he entered the room, "You just keep your mouth shut," the thug said as he closed the door and locking it behind him.

I grasped the true intention of the whole exercise. It was not to land me in prison. Far worse, it was the purchase of a premium insurance policy. I found myself further enslaved to Green, even though I was no longer living in the mansion. When I turned to the parking lot, I saw that my car had been courteously delivered to the scene of the crime. In reality, I knew the man did this only so there would be further record of me being there. I surmised he used my card to pay for the room. If they wanted to turn me in, I'd be dead to rights. I contemplated for a moment why they didn't just have me locked up and throw away the key as I walked with trembling legs to the car. The analogy Green used of the clay on the potter's wheel returned to my mind.

I stopped dead in my tracks. "He doesn't want to get rid of me. He wants to use me," I whispered.

The latter proposition was far worse than any other outcome I could imagine. Where fear and intimidation formerly gotten me to follow Green's direction, the blackmail would be far more effective.

I floated on my trembling legs to the seat of my car. It was unlocked with the keys in the ignition. I rested my head on the steering wheel, reeling from the slew of disasters only in the distant past. I hoped Ben was alright. I felt intense guilt and self-loathing for getting the woman killed. Suicide had never really crossed my mind before, and only briefly at this juncture. Even in my depleted state, I still looked down on the act. Ironically, I would be pursuing an end to my own life with a few extra steps. I hoped to be sent to the Pacific as soon as possible. That would be the capstone of my defiance to Green: putting an end to my usefulness.

I started the car with a heavy hand. Not sure of where to go, I decided to check on Ben's residence.

Maybe they just dropped him off after giving him some memory loss drug, I childishly speculated.

When I tried to pull up his address, my navigation app refused to work. I closed and reopened the program several times before trying the nav system on my car. The car's screen rudely informed me that it had no signal and my subscription had expired. I decided to just get on the road and put some serious distance between me and the tragedy in the motel room.

All the other drivers seemed to be in a panic. Once I had gotten far enough away, I noticed I was low on fuel. I stopped at a gas station to fill up and was shocked at the prices which doubled overnight. I peeked at the window of a rusty newspaper stand to see grim images of the war at sea. The card reader wouldn't take my payment, so I went inside the grubby structure.

"Hey, can I get fifty bucks on pump four?"

The darkly complexioned attendant tapped a poorly written sign which stated that payment processors were out across the country due to a cyberattack. The ancient TV on the wall added that civilian GPS systems were experiencing an unprecedented outage. In short, the war was coming home even if only in silly inconveniences.

"I have cash," I informed him.

He shuffled over to the register and took the money. The sky clouded over in the time I was inside and began to rain. After taking my receipt, I stepped out into the cold precipitation. The rain soaked me almost immediately but could not wash away any of the disgrace or remorse. I hovered just outside the door drinking in the negative stimuli as a petty means of self-punishment.

I didn't feel much of a need to rush to check on Ben. He was either alive or he wasn't. Speeding through the teeming masses of directionless drivers wasn't going to change his fate one bit. Regardless, I did my best to remember the way to his house. I passed many cars on the side of the road with their emergency flashers on in bleak surrender to their own inability to find their way. In many ways, I resembled them.

By some stroke of luck, I found Ben's house tucked away in a nameless suburb. I peered through windows, knocked on the door, and ultimately sat dejected next to the front door. It was no surprise he wasn't there. With my head on my knees, I mourned my friend. Though I already knew it, Ben's absence from the house confirmed to me what I already suspected. This hit me harder than the woman's death. By this point in my journey, the stigma of crying had all but evaporated. I shed tears for Ben like I had never before, not just because he was gone. Rather, I had killed him with my inability to shut up. All he was trying to do was help a friend in deep turmoil—and got killed for his trouble.

TOP DEAD CENTER

"How did you know for sure he was dead?" Edwards asked.

Richard's voice faltered. "I saw his family post on social media the week after. They said he was killed in action. His squadron went to the Pacific that Monday and took staggering losses. There probably wasn't anyone left to tell his folks he wasn't even there. I don't suppose grieving families look too closely at things like that."

The guerrilla agreed and crossed his arms. "I don't know how many times I had to lie to families about their son's death," he gestured skyward. "He died gallantly in the line of battle, defending our country and sacrificing for his comrades," he parroted. "That sounds better than, 'Your son died trafficking children for the Stimulosis Program.'"

"You still haven't explained what that is yet."

The dossier still sat menacingly on the table open to a blank inside page.

Edwards clenched his teeth. "I don't think you're in a mental state to handle that."

"Then what's the point of all this? Dredging up all my worst memories when I could just rot in ignorant silence at Walter Reed!" Richard said bitterly.

"In all my research and operations, you're the only person I've known who has gotten this close," he replied.

"Close to what?" the captive countered.

Edwards took a deep breath. "Close to ending it all. Do you have any idea how close to the brink you brought the whole rotten edifice?"

"I have no idea what you mean," Richard shook his head.

"This war with China. The success of the operations of my organization. The sheer chaos at every level of this country can all be traced back to that night in the Pentagon." the guerrilla posited

Malden slumped back in his chair and exclaimed, "I'm already responsible for the death of that woman, Ben, and more. Now you want to pin all of that on me too?"

"Indeed," Edwards fiddled with the spine of the spiral bound book. "But that's quite alright. I will show you why what's happening is a good thing. But time is running out before they get everything back up and running again."

"I am tired of you dancing around the subject." The captive leaned forward and rubbed his face. "What does any of this mean? I've answered all your questions and told you everything I know. Can't you tell me what's going on?"

The lightbulb above them swayed slightly.

Edwards remained silent for a minute, staring into his captive's eyes with a searching look. "Do you think you can handle it?"

The captive had serious doubts. After all, he was already at his mental and emotional limit.

"Tell me," Richard resolved.

The guerrilla closed his eyes for a moment, as if the man across from him had just requested a firing squad.

"Water Bottle," Edwards began, as he took the document to his lap and flipped through the pages, "That's the first reference to it I found. The British were working on a project codenamed 'Water Bottle' while Europe burned in 1940. How long it had been going before this point, I couldn't tell you. That was until I found information on a little-known biochemist in Germany named Chaim Sachsenhauser. He made a bizarre discovery about the unassuming Florida Cnidoscolus stimulosus stinging nettle in the thirties. Rats on the verge of death could be kept alive indefinitely by the repeated lancing of key nerve centers. The electric impulses of the extreme, rhythmic pain acted as continual jump-starts to the rats' nervous systems. Well, when the National Socialists took power, they didn't look too kindly on individuals like Mr. Sachsenhauser. He fled the country and landed in the UK. He was quickly recruited by the British government to pursue his studies under their funding. As war loomed with Germany, the crown looked desperately for scientific projects that would give them an edge. The British Ministry of Defense thought the technique could be used in the field to save the lives of the severely wounded in transit. That was 'Water Bottle.' Sachsenhauser coined the term 'Stimulosis' during this time. The MoD eventually considered the effort too costly and the benefit too low. In a bloody total war, they simply didn't have the time or the resources to save the lives of a few extra men."

Richard lowered his brow. "How do you know any of this?"

Edwards appeared agitated at the interruption. "When I got fired from the security gig, I went dark—dropped off the map, so to speak. I knew whoever made the call to give me the boot would be coming to snuff me out next. What I am presenting to you is the result of years of research, interviews, stolen documents, data leaks, hacks, and more than a few close brushes with death. Stimulosis became something of an obsession. Every time I tried to turn away, God picked me up and set me back on this path. I founded my organization, the Temple of God, when I gathered a few like-minded men to myself. Stopping the Stimulosis Project is a means to an end— cutting the vital jugular pumping lifeblood into the beast system."

The captive nodded.

"Now can I continue?" the guerrilla gave a displeased look. "Where was I?"

"The British had lost interest."

"Yes," Edwards continued, "While the British had given up on his discovery, Chaim Sachsenhauser never did. He believed the process could yield far more than what the Brits ever imagined. The record goes dark on him until he shows back up in 1941 in the US. A White House visitor's log shows that he was granted an audience with then Secretary of the Treasury Henry Morgenthau. What the Secretary of the Treasury had to do with a crackpot scientist is anyone's guess. We know from history that Morgenthau's ambitions extended well beyond his department. Sachsenhauser came into quite a bit of funding shortly after. Seemingly out of nowhere, he found himself the head of a major research team out in New Mexico. I found documents listing membership of the unassumingly named 'Botanical Research Group.' A number of prominent rabbis including Stephen Wise were curiously listed there as research fellows."

"What did religious leaders have to do with scientific research?" the captive asked.

The guerrilla answered, "That will become abundantly clear. A former NSA employee—someone who knew about the Stimulosis Project and was disgusted by it—gave me the diary of one of the researchers he had come across. I learned the BRG dabbled in all kinds of apparently non-scientific research like the performance of rituals in the desert and attempting to summon entities."

"Entities?"

Edwards gave a stern look as if Richard should know better. He continued without clarification.

"One particular entry, dated April 15th, 1941, caught my attention. The writer described the detailed ritual sacrifice of a boy from a nearby Indian reservation. I suppose they assumed correctly that the government wouldn't care if a few natives went missing. This all occurred over the Passover holiday. The boy was apparently even a Christian. Where they differed, however, was the use of needles to prolong his death. The writer noted, the slower the death, the more powerful the ritual. They managed to keep him on the threshold of life and death for four agonizing days. When the boy finally flatlined, the writer recorded a curious phenomenon. Normally, the body would be exsanguinated and disposed of. Not this poor wretch. When one of the scientists went to draw the blood, a rabbi in attendance grabbed his arm and commanded him to stop. He pointed to an electro magnet sitting idle on a table nearby that had curiously brought several metal objects to itself. He compelled the researchers to lance the boy again while he drew a sigil over his chest."

"The Tree of Life?" Richard sat wide eyed.

Edwards gave a stern nod, then continued. "They managed to get his heart going for another thirty seconds. One of the scientists brought the electromagnet over his chest and observed a strong impulse through it when the boy's heart stopped again. They had discovered something incredible. At the intersection of science and ritual, the BRG learned that the energy of the soul leaving and reentering the body could be harnessed and harvested like an appalling reciprocating engine.

Stimulosis would be the spark at top dead center. They attempted to recreate their findings the following year on April 1st. They lined up 100 different candidates of varying age, ethnicity, religious background, sex, and states of health over the previous twelve months. While they were able to generate enormous quantities of energy for short periods of time, they were not able to achieve a continuous cycle with any of the candidates. The BRG did find, however, that some victims lasted longer than others. The data showed youth was the most important factor. None of the candidates over the age of twelve lasted more than one cycle. Secondly, the adrenaline of mortality made a large difference. In the victims they sedated beforehand, results were far less promising. For some unknowable reason, boys managed more cycles on average than girls. Christian children, especially of some ethnic background that had a history of conflict with these people, also yielded more mileage. The candidate that showed the most promise was almost never in the data field. On the way into the lab, one of the researchers hit a small boy that ran out into the road with his car in the early morning. An enterprising scientist, he scooped up the child and rushed him to the lab to make him candidate 101. The mortal wounds inflicted from the accident heightened the receptivity to Stimulosis. According to the diary, this phenomenon was never fully explained. Regardless, the boy yielded an astonishing forty-three cycles before giving out—far outstripping the next best candidate."

Richard's soul contorted under the heaviness of Edwards' tale. The sheer amount of information and its shocking implications sent his head spinning. Through it all, he started to gain a small amount of clarity of what he had witnessed in the Pentagon.

"The scientists were astonished at their progress, but the central conclusion was that they needed more data. This is when Sachsenhauser returned with his findings to Morgenthau in the middle of 1942. That's where I hit a dead end in my investigation. All of the easy trails to follow dried up. The diary entries stopped around the same time the Stimulosis Project became shrouded in the highest levels of secrecy. I grew disillusioned. I couldn't understand why the government would be interested in such an inefficient energy production source. I gave up on my research for nearly a year and retreated into the woods."

"Did you ever find out anything more?" Richard prodded.

"Remember that NSA employee? He continued digging long after I gave up. Instead of seeking US sources, he discovered the Stimulosis process had been leaked to the Soviets. With a whole new avenue to explore, he managed to put together the final pieces. The Reds ran a parallel program deep in Siberia. Rabbis and scientists in danger of being purged found an agreeable respite from Stalin's ire. Within a year of the leak, they had recreated most of the American team's findings. This was 1943. They achieved a remarkable 102 cycles with a farmer's child. What was most intriguing, though, was that the Soviet team seemed entirely uninterested in harvesting electricity. Mention of conventional power was wholly absent from the documents my friend translated and provided to me. In its place were cryptic references to someone or something codenamed 'Z.' As the reports went on, the language surrounding 'Z' grew more and more anthropomorphic. The literature goes on to describe it assisting in finding new candidates and giving suggestions to the researchers. As they succeeded in performing more cycles, the data field shifted to military victories."

"How does that correlate?"

Edwards widened his eyes slightly. "It's one of humanity's oldest technologies: human sacrifice. The ritual killing of people for the purpose of currying favor with the gods has given rise to civilization after civilization. Only recently has it fallen out of fashion. The Stimulosis Project is the industrialization and resurrection of this ancient practice."

Richard shook his head. "What do you mean, gods?"

"Demons, of course. I thought that much was obvious. The arrangement is mutually beneficial. The humans gain favor and earthly success while the demons feast on the energy of the sacrifice. As the foul beings feed more and more, their strength grows in kind. Consequently, they are able to grant more and better favors to their faithful servants." Edwards recounted in a blunt monotone.

"But if that's true, wouldn't we see a total dominance of human-sacrifice centered societies?" the captive challenged.

"Richard," the guerrilla leader leaned forward and interlocked his fingers on the table. "Is any of this really that unbelievable? We kill a million babies a year as a matter of so-called healthcare, and you question that human sacrifice is still around?"

Richard tilted his head. "Abortion is one thing. I am talking about the human sacrifice you're depicting in your account. If it were really so powerful, wouldn't the civilizations that practiced it be the dominant forces of history?"

Edwards smiled slightly. "That would be the case, wouldn't it? However, there is something far more powerful: the Holy Blood of Christ."

The captive was taken aback.

"When Christian armies landed in the New World, they came across the most appalling and universal systems of human sacrifice ever recorded. Do you know what happened? God used us to wipe them out," the man let a smile curl on his lips.

"So, the human sacrifice of Christ trumps other human sacrifices?"

At this comment, Edwards lunged at Malden and struck him viciously across the face. The captive fell over in his chair.

"Don't you dare blaspheme the Passion of Christ! Not a mere human sacrifice! The death, burial, and resurrection of God Himself!" he proclaimed into the dark, echoing chamber of the warehouse.

Richard got up slowly and righted his chair before collapsing into it, too weak to fight back.

"That's why the Temple of God is destined to put an end to this nightmare," Edwards pointed before taking his seat also.

The captive's face ached terribly as the flesh over his cheekbone began to swell.

"I've given you enough background for now," the guerrilla calmed "But I need more information from you."

"What else is there to tell?" Richard hung his head, surrendered to the constant pain permeating his physical and spiritual self.

"What about the rest of your time in Norfolk and your journey to San Diego?"

GOOD EVENING, CAPTAIN

I spent the next three weeks in the on-base hotel. Normally, the class was three months. I was saved from that lengthy sentence by the expedience of wartime manpower shortages. I seldom ate and even more rarely slept.

As part of the command preparation portion, they would call us in the middle of the night and quiz us on shipboard procedures. This didn't bother me much. I was rarely asleep anyway. The phone rang one night as it always did.

"Good evening, captain," a female caller greeted.

I was in the middle of my nightly ritual of staring where the corner of the walls met the ceiling.

"Good evening," I played along. "What is it?"

"How are you holding up?"

Expecting to be asked about oil pressures or hazards to navigation, I was taken aback. "How am I holding up?" I repeated.

A sultry giggle came from the other line. I at once realized who was calling.

"I have something I need you to do," the woman instructed.

I made no reply as my heart sank in my chest.

"I hope it's not too late," she teased. "I know you're used to lights out at sunset."

"What is it?" I interrupted.

The woman sighed. "Drive your car to the main gate on Admiral Taussig Boulevard and park outside the base at the exchange. A man will get in the trunk of your car. Drive him to Pier 11. He will get out and be back in fifteen minutes. Once he is back inside your trunk, you'll drop him off in the same location you picked him up."

"I am not doing that," I insisted.

"She was very pretty," she stated. "Her family is very curious about what happened to her. Such a shame. The police chief knows not to investigate you at the moment, but things can change very quickly."

I gripped the phone tightly. "Then what? I just go to prison, right? Who cares?"

"You'll be arrested, certainly," the woman recounted with a chuckle. "After that? I have absolutely no idea what would happen."

"What does that mean?"

"How do you feel about needles, Mr. Malden?"

I could almost feel her devilish smile through the phone. My skin crawled as if the tormenting lances hovered just millimeters away, spring-loaded with a hair trigger.

I acquiesced and hung up the phone. Shuffling through the dead hallways of the hotel, I made it to my car and drove through the gate. I parked in a space at the unlit back portion of the lot and popped the trunk. Sure enough, I felt the jostling of the suspension shortly after. The man closed the lid and tapped the inside wall of the trunk. I had no fear of getting caught at the gate. Base security had always been abysmal. They seldom even checked the ID cards of visible passengers in the vehicle. Whatever consequences the Navy could mete out were eclipsed by my fear of what Green could do to me—fates far worse than death.

I drove carefully up to the gate and filed into the one remaining open lane. I rolled down my window as cool ocean air poured in. There were two cars ahead of me, each passing through without incident. I pulled up to the guard with my ID already in my hand.

"How's it going?" I casually greeted.

The sailor took the card from me and scanned it. He appeared to be no more than eighteen years old. Normally the process took less than a few seconds for the information to pull up. I kept my eyes planted in front of me in anxious anticipation of my task. The second beep of the scanner caused me to snap my glance to the gate guard. He had a confused look on his face as he scanned it another time.

"You're not coming up," he informed me.

I replied with a twinge of fear in my voice. "What do you mean I am not coming up?"

The guard leaned down to look at me. My wild-eyed appearance and tone must have set off alarm bells for him.

"You're not in the system. What command are you with?"

I rubbed my face as my pulse rose. "NETC. I'm in the LCS command and ship handling refresher course. I probably haven't been gained to the command in the system yet."

"That's weird," he looked closely at the ID. "You should be coming up."

I realized I must've looked quite different than my ID picture. It was taken at a time of silly ignorance and blind faith in my own meteoric rise. Nothing about me resembled that haughty social climber in either appearance or mental state.

"You'll have to pull over to the ID card hut and work it out with them," the guard told me, gesturing at the small structure to his right.

With no choice, I reluctantly complied. The young sailor motioned to the other guard on duty. The pair escorted my vehicle through the gate, around the guard house, and out the other side. A pang of anxiety shot through my body when I felt a shuffle in the trunk. I quickly pulled into the parking lot of the ID card hut and went inside, leaving the engine running to mask any potential noises.

A sailor sat apathetically on her phone at the desk.

"The gate guard said my card isn't working," I reported briskly, casting a nervous glance out of the window at my vehicle.

She took the ID from me and tried to scan it herself. After going through this process an additional three times, the sailor handed it back to me through the gap in the window separating us.

"You ain't coming up," she went back to her phone.

I stared angrily at the top of her slouched head. "I know that!" I snapped.

She looked up at me with a severely offended expression.

"That's why they sent me here," my hands began trembling.

I placed them behind my back and clasped tightly, trying to hide them. With every minute that passed, I felt the ethereal needles getting closer.

She took the card from me once more and slid it through another gadget on her desk. Her dark eyes glazed over as she periodically checked her phone. A cheerful tone indicated the machine had done its work.

"You should be good now," the sailor shoved the ID through the partition and got up to leave.

"What was wrong with it?" I called to her.

Just before she entered the bathroom at the end of the hallway, she shot a hateful glare in my direction. "I dunno? I put a temporary pass on it."

I rolled my eyes and decided this was good enough. I rushed back to my car and clambered inside. I took a nervous look at the backseat of my car as if to check on the unknown individual in the trunk.

"It's ok," I managed in a shaky voice. "We'll get through the gate now."

The infiltrator hit the wall of trunk rapidly, as if to say hurry up.

I wheeled the car around and pulled up to the gate once again. The sailor scanned my ID, then saluted.

"Sorry about the trouble, sir. They're getting on us for base security real bad right now," he muttered, waving me through.

I nervously watched the gate guard shrink in my rearview mirror. The base was lifeless and dark, apart from a few individuals on duty. An oppressive veil of fearful anticipation blanketed the whole facility. Weaving my way through a series of stop signs and crosswalks, I pulled up to Pier 11. The nuclear carrier USS Buchanan floated motionlessly as it imperceptibly tugged at its mooring lines.

I stopped on H Street, turned off the car, and informed my cargo we were as close as we were going to get. I released the trunk latch and observed a shadowy figure exit quickly and shut the lid. He darted off beyond my line of sight.

"What am I doing?" I rested my head on the steering wheel.

In the twenty minutes it took for the infiltrator to get back, my mind raced through the regrettable course of events that led me to that moment. I looked back on my drive up to the Pentagon.

What an idiot, I chastised my former self.

Suddenly, a knock came on my window to shock me out of my grim contemplation.

A base policeman shined his flashlight directly into my face. I rolled down the window with a terribly shaking finger.

"Can I see some ID?" he extended his hand.

I unsuccessfully tried to keep my arm steady as I gave him the card. The man examined it briefly.

"What are you doing out here in the middle of the night, sir?"

I started to bite my lower lip nervously. "Just wanted to get out of the hotel for a minute." I managed.

I could see nothing of the MP's face behind the piercing rays of the flashlight.

"You headed to WestPac?" he took on a quieter tone.

I nodded silently. He lowered the light and turned it off.

"I get you're under stress, but you're not allowed to park here. The base McDonald's is just up there." He pointed into the darkness, "If you're looking for somewhere to sit."

I sat motionless, paralyzed by indecision.

"I get you're under stress, but—"

A shadow came up behind him and broke his neck. I jolted back from the chaos and looked on in horror.

"Open the trunk!" a heavily accented voice commanded.

The MP went limp as the man dragged him to the rear of the car.

"Open the trunk!" he repeated impatiently.

My breathing—rapid and tortured—hastened as I fumbled for the release lever. The sharp sound of the release bore a terrible resemblance to the fatal adjustment to the man's spine. The suspension shifted as the infiltrator loaded a seabag, his kill, and finally himself into the trunk.

"Drive," his muffled voice emerged from the rear of the car.

I dropped the keys several times trying to find the ignition switch. At last, I got the vehicle moving. I couldn't keep my foot steady and struggled to maintain a constant speed on the slow base roads. The sound of the MP's neck played on repeat as I dug a fingernail nervously into my hand under the steering wheel.

I stole a glance at the gate guard as I left the base. He noticed my fear-stricken countenance but became distracted by another car pulling up to the gate. Eventually, I made it to the parking spot at the exchange where my night had taken such a horrible turn. A dark van sat parked next to it. I winced at the sound of the trunk lid once more. The sliding door of the van opened in kind.

A few shapeless figures inside awaited my cargo. I overheard them chattering in what sounded like Hebrew. The infiltrator dragged the lifeless body of the MP inside the van then retrieved his bag. He didn't bother closing my trunk this time. Once the sliding door of the vehicle was closed, they sped off into the night. I sat dead-eyed in the crushing silence of my car's cabin, awash with shame and guilt.

Suddenly, my phone rang. I scrambled to pick it up and answer.

"Hello?" I whispered.

"Good evening captain," a voice began. "We have a break-bulk freighter bearing two hundred fifty relative, and a car carrier bearing 010 degrees true. We are traveling in the northbound leg in a traffic separation scheme. Course is 015. Speed is twelve knots. Who has the right of way according to the rules of the road?"

I sat back in my seat and lowered the phone, staring skyward in agony.

SUNRISE

My tormentors left me alone for the remainder of my course in Norfolk. The class had a haphazard graduation ceremony where an admiral who was supposed to be the keynote speaker never showed. There were roughly 300 of us in that batch of disposable leaders.

By the end of my course, I looked like a skeleton. I performed well enough in the classroom. The instructors didn't care much if I did regardless. They were under orders to ramrod as many of us through to get COs and XOs ready for the harsh attrition in the Pacific. The last unit, which lasted all of one day, was a "Mental Health Preparedness" module. It talked about the stresses of combat and the toll it would take on all of us.

I sat blankly somewhere in the middle of the classroom with hollow eyes. I was sure I had seen worse than anything I'd witness out there. The memory of Ben and the woman festered with the comorbidity of that wretch deep below in my beleaguered soul.

I got my orders stamped at the admin office and got ready to go to San Diego.

I left Norfolk with a trail of destruction, death, and compromise in my wake. Even though GPS service was still unreliable, I elected to drive across the country with some leave en route instead of taking a flight. Most of the flights were grounded due to the ongoing cyberattacks, parts shortages, and supply issues anyway. I wanted to swing by my home town and see my parents before getting shipped off to an unknown fate. The more I heard about the scale of the casualties and attrition over there, the more it made Green's prediction of a safe return seem unlikely. I hoped to take comfort in the solace of the road, far from Green's prying eyes and the Navy. The faster I drove, the more I could outrun my thoughts.

I had a week and a half to get from Virginia to California. While I couldn't dawdle excessively, I had plenty of time and see whatever I wanted to. I pulled into my parents' driveway at the end of day two. Though it was long after sunset, I knew the location well. I had managed my way across the country the old-fashioned way—with atlases and maps I once thought were silly markers of the geriatric.

My parents' home sat atop a bluff overlooking the Mississippi River in the upper west part of Wisconsin. A welcoming light flickered gently on the porch. I pulled up the half-circle driveway and parked behind my dad's SUV. When I shut off the car, I sat in silence for a moment. The son they were about to see was vastly different than the one they proudly sent out into the world. I hadn't seen either of them since my deployment. Sloan, the boy, the woman, Ben, the MP. All these deaths haunted me and taxed my mental state daily. The horror of Sloan's death at least was eclipsed by worse memories, something I never thought possible.

The opening of the front door broke my train of thought. I emerged from the vehicle and prepared myself for my parents' shocked reaction at my appearance.

"Hey Rich!" my father called out. "Dina, get down here. Rich is here!"

I walked up to the porch still concealed in darkness.

My mother came down the steps and joined my dad just as I entered the glow of the porch light.

"Hey, mom. Hey, dad," I said, greeting them calmly.

My mother concealed a gasp before coming in to hug me. My father joined soon after.

"You're all skin and bones!" she cried. "Have they not been feeding you?"

I looked at her with hollow eyes. "I am alright, ma."

"Give him a break, Dina. He's under a lot of stress—can't you see that?"

My mom ran her fingers through her gray hair. "Oh Vince, I'll always be his mother. I am allowed to worry about him."

They brought me inside, into the brighter lights of the foyer. With the added lamination, both of them saw the toll that had been taken on me.

"You do look rough," my father ribbed, slapping me on the back. "Long drive?"

I nodded silently and drifted to the couch. He joined me after grabbing a tray of snacks.

"We have a bottle of wine open, if you want any," my mom called from the kitchen.

"No thanks," I replied, my voice cracking slightly.

The thought of alcohol now repulsed me.

She returned to the living room with a full glass and sat next to my dad.

"How's the campaign going?" I tried to make conversation.

"It's heating up for sure," the old man launched into an animated monologue. "You just would not want to believe what the Democrats are wanting to do with China! Sanders, my opponent, would rather just give them Taiwan for free. We've already lost too many good American men and women," he emphasized the latter, "to just roll over! I remember when we told Saddam what for. He couldn't stand up to the full might of our military. We need to let our troops take the gloves off, right?"

He waited expectantly for a reply. To be honest, my mind had long since started to wander.

"Oh yeah, for sure," I halfheartedly agreed.

"And that's another thing Sanders gets wrong. . . ."

As he rambled on and on about the superiority of the GOP platform, my eyes drifted to a picture on the mantle. My parents had printed out and framed the photo taken of Laura and I dipping my class ring into the bowl of water from the seven seas at Ring Dance. My past-self shined brightly with confidence and vigor. To my left was the love of my life, gently holding the other side of the ribbon. My gaze landed on a picture taken a year later at my commissioning. My mentor at the time, Captain Rausch, pinned on one shoulder board while my dad pinned on the other. At that time, he had just won his election to be county commissioner the previous year. Oh, how up and coming we all seemed then.

The sound of my father's rant faded back in.

"And can you believe it? What kind of Middle East policy is that? Our greatest ally, and Sanders won't lift a finger."

I blinked several times. "Oh . . . um."

"Stop pestering him," my mother chimed in. "He's had a long drive."

"Alright, alright," he assented. "I just get fired up. This campaign has me really amped."

My mother turned to me. "Are you feeling pretty tired, Rich?"

I rubbed my face and let the cumulative fatigue of recent events spill into my curt reply: "I am really exhausted."

My parents exchanged a worried look.

"Let's get you to bed," my mother advised.

Before I was up the stairs, I heard the sound of the TV come on. Some pundit was droning on about shortages, the war with China, and all the "real issues."

"Just ridiculous," my dad muttered.

All of those little problems were totally inconsequential to the growing list of burdens on my soul.

In my childhood room, I managed to steal a few hours of decent sleep from my harried mind. I awoke before sunrise and went outside behind the house. As I looked west, I imagined what laid beyond the dark horizon. Just out of sight was a blazing inferno on the water. Multitudes of dead and dying were being carried away by the cold waters of the Pacific at that very moment, I was sure. Between that hell and my own were thousands of miles of roads, mountains, deserts, and the ocean itself. It was all so peaceful as the gentle Mississippi lumbered on its path to the sea. Just like the river, I felt as though my journey to the ocean was as scripted as the landscape.

The sun began to pierce the early morning darkness behind me. I started to shiver in the crisp dawn atmosphere. It was the first moment of tranquility I had managed since before I could remember. I found a lawn chair and sat high up on the bluff, the wind giving me the sensation of flying over the great expanse of troubles in the world.

"Early start?" my father placed a hand on my shoulder.

The gesture caused me to nearly jump out of my chair.

"A little jumpy, are you?"

I nodded without a word and returned my gaze to the river.

"Beautiful, isn't it?"

I took a deep breath through my nose. "Sure is."

All the while, the sun's light grew brighter. The blissful, liminal period between the torment of night and the crushing responsibility of day was over. The sojourning rays revealed the world in all its little details—devil and all.

"I love coming out here to watch the sunrise and sunset," my father put his hands on his hips. "I'm sure you remember that from when you were a kid."

We sat in silence until the sun had fully risen.

"C'mon, let's see if your mom made breakfast," he gestured to the house.

I followed him as far as the glass door on the patio.

"So, how long are you in town for?" my dad asked passively as he opened the door.

A horrible sinking feeling emerged as if a deeply repressed memory managed to slip to the surface. An insatiable curiosity scratched at the inside of my skull. There was something in the way he moved at the entrance to the house that caused an intruding hand to rummage through my memories at the mansion.

"Dad," I began.

He stopped and turned his head.

"Have you been to DC recently?"

My father's brow lowered, and I noticed him grip the handle tighter.

"Well, uh, why do you ask?" his eyes darted around the patio furniture like a squirrel trapped inside a house.

"Have you?" My gaze must have felt like the searchlight of a prison camp.

"C'mon, let's go inside," my dad motioned again.

I approached him rapidly. "Just please answer the question." Tears began to well up in my eyes.

His countenance was overtaken by the creeping vines of unbearable shame.

"Look, Richard," my father started.

I slowly shook my head and widened my eyes. "What was going on in there?" I demanded.

"Now hold on," he slipped into politician mode. "Just what exactly are you referring to?"

I pushed past him and started to grab my things. My mother was making pancakes in the kitchen.

"Now wait just a minute, Rich!" he called after me.

"Vince, what's going on?" she followed her husband.

I grabbed the change of clothes I wore the previous day and shoved them into my seabag.

My dad stood at the front door. "Are you really leaving right now? Dina, try to talk some sense into him."

My mother gave me a concerned look. "Rich, what's the matter?"

"Just ask him about his DC trip," I hoisted the bag onto my shoulder and pushed past him on my way out to the car.

As I started the engine, I heard sounds of arguing. "What trip to DC? You said you were in Memphis!"

I rolled down the windows to let in the fresh morning air and sped away, setting my heading toward the west and my tumultuous future.

IT'S YOUR PROBLEM NOW

"I knew it!" I hit the steering wheel in blind anger and betrayal. "I knew it! I knew what I saw."

That darkened silhouette that received the robe. The feeling of deep shame I felt. It all made horrible, disgusting sense. So much for the nobility of truth. That shining city on a hill is really just the tallest zit on the rump of cruel fate.

I grabbed at the passenger sun visor and twisted it until the plastic snapped. I tossed the piece into the footwell with a summary scream. At that point, I hadn't the slightest idea of how bad it really was, but I knew whatever happened in that mansion was beyond recoverable. Anyone who knowingly associated with Green was nothing short of a monster. Then again, I found myself in the unfortunate service of that same individual.

I sped recklessly as I maneuvered onto I-90. Slipping through traffic, I cared little whether I had close calls or posed a danger to the other drivers. All the pent-up impotence of my inability to change my circumstances found its expression in a reckless fit of speed and chirping tires. Just as I passed over the Mississippi, the loudest sound I had ever heard erupted behind me.

I strained my neck to look over my shoulder. To my shock, a cloud of dust and flames grew where the bridge formerly was. I had only just made it over the expanse when the explosion happened. I pulled over as fast as I could, exited my car, and ran toward the scene. A shapeless mass of concrete, steel, rebar, and cars full of passengers were consumed by the Mississippi's churning, brown waters. One SUV bobbed precariously on surface of the river before submerging forever. The strained palms and fists of its passengers battered on the surface of its windows before disappearing into the murky depths.

I looked in vain for signs of saboteurs. The acrid smell of explosives and burning gasoline filled my nostrils. I looked across the expanse to see a number of other horrified observers on the other side. As sirens began to approach, I felt a bizarre sense of guilt as if I were the one to press the detonator. I fled the gruesome scene and got back in my vehicle. I turned my rearview mirror away so I wouldn't have to look at the rising column of smoke.

After a half hour of driving, my news aggregator app sounded a chime. The notification said there were multiple reports of bridges up and down the Mississippi collapsing. Some sources claimed explosions, others stated the reason was seismic activity. The country cleaved in two as if a zipper running the length of the river was pulled down, taking more than a few hapless travelers with it.

I got a call from my father.

"I'm alive," was the terse reply I gave before hanging up the phone.

If I hadn't driven so recklessly, I would've likely been caught up in the explosion. I pulled off into a gas station to gather my thoughts and grab something to eat. I regretted still being alive as Green's prediction of my survival returned to my memory. Everyone around the station was glued to their phones or whatever screen they could find in blind shock at the attack. The exorbitant prices on the sign would have made an impression if it weren't for the recent chaos. Some were tearfully recounting how they were just on that bridge less than an hour ago. I shuffled past these fear-stricken individuals, completely disinterested in their world coming down. The repeated traumatic experiences eventually numbed my brain's capacity for grief or shock.

After buying some bland processed food from the counter, I got back on the road hoping I would get caught in the next explosion. As I drove, the news app chimed incessantly. Updates were rolling in every few minutes. The Department of Homeland Security flitted between neurotic accusations of domestic sabotage, White supremacists, Chinese special forces, and even Islamic terrorism. In reality, the state had accumulated so many enemies—real or imagined—that the "usual suspect" list was already a mile long. Later, I heard strange conspiracy theories that the Mossad had blown the bridges in an attempt to curry separate favor with the Chinese. In my mind, the Chinese themselves were obviously at fault, though they denied responsibility.

In the coming days, American forces made a few abortive, effete attempts at blowing the Three Gorges Dam. All this accomplished was a few shot-down aircraft, millions of dollars' worth of missiles lost, and a few more flag covered caskets making the return journey over the Pacific. All the posturing and joking about destroying the barrier pre-war amounted to nothing more than damaged national prestige. With these assaults, China announced that it considered domestic American infrastructure targets fair game. Whether the Mississippi bridge attacks were truly attributable to the Chinese was irrelevant. Now the war had been brought to the American people in more kinetic ways than simply losing GPS.

I pulled in that night at a hotel in Kearney, Nebraska. I had long since deleted the news app and silenced my phone. The attendant tried to make small talk about the attacks, but I brushed it off. She pulled out a crude map of the hotel and drew the route I would have to drive around the parking lot to get to my room with a dying highlighter. I thanklessly took the map and left the lobby.

The weather had turned unseasonably and bitterly cold as the winds swept in along the plains. A few snow flurries dusted the dark parking lot as I followed the haphazard map to the back of the building. When I parked outside the room, the power went out. It made little difference to me if the outage was due to more attacks or crumbling infrastructure. Luckily, the rooms were still operated by a physical key. I entered the dark room to the smell of cigarettes and ozone. Using my phone's flashlight, I discovered the room had both an exterior and interior door, presumably leading to the central courtyard. Exhausted from the day's events, I collapsed on the bed.

A rude knock came from the interior door several minutes later. I jumped down from the bed and sat crouched on the floor for a moment. The knock came again. I quietly shuffled over to the door and looked through the peephole. In the sickly glow of the emergency exit light, I saw the attendant stood with her arms crossed.

I opened the door. "What is it?"

"Hey our power is out," she informed.

If there was more light, the woman would've seen an exaggerated eye roll.

"Yup," I answered.

"You can't stay here anymore. It's a local ordinance," she said in a monotone, "You'll get a refund. If you had been here longer, we could've let you stay, but since you just checked in."

I closed the door in her face. Any tact or social graces I had were shed a long time ago. I went back to the bed and crumpled once more. She didn't seem too invested in evicting me and left me alone.

Around 0300, there was another knock. I was already awake, having just suffered a nightmare. Angrily, I rushed to the door.

"Look, I paid for the room. . . ."

There was no one on the other side. The exit sign cast an otherworldly orange hue on the hallway. I peeked my head out of the doorway and stared intently in either direction. The darkness of the corridor yawned a consuming blackness, apart from another emergency exit sign at the far end to my right. Another light pierced my vision where the hallway made a ninety-degree bend to the courtyard—a glowing cigarette.

"No!" I cried in a rasping whisper.

The light made the same cycle of glowing, dying, lowering, flicking, raising, and repeating as it did in the basement of the Pentagon. The smell of the tobacco smoke advanced up the hallway until it briskly grabbed me by the throat.

"What are you doing here?" I trembled.

The light froze for a moment before making a circuitous path to the adjacent wall. A shower of embers falling to the carpet and dissipating indicated the snuffing out of the cigarette. Labored steps retreated down the hallway. I clenched the door handle tightly in my hand. I wanted nothing more than to slam it shut and sprint to my car. My feet remained cemented in place. The steps halted for a moment, then approached my direction again.

"You're dead!" I called out. "You're not real!"

"Then you have nothing to be afraid of," a cool, low voice replied from the abyssal hallway.

I shrunk back and shook terribly.

"Sloan," I began with hesitation, "why are you here?"

"You killed me," he took a few steps forward, stopping beyond the glow of the sign's light. "You killed me." he repeated in a disgusted whisper.

I clenched the door handle tighter. "You killed yourself!" I challenged.

As soon as the words crossed my lips, I regretted them. He made an abrupt about-face and walked rapidly down the hallway.

"Sloan?" I stepped out of the doorway.

The corridor returned once more to silence. Against my better judgment, I pursued him. The hallway made a ninety-degree turn before opening up to the courtyard. An emergency floodlight hovered like a latter-day sun above the surreal, artificial landscape. A pagoda shaped tower stood at the corner of the expansive space under a ceiling of glass panels. An empty pool still gave off the strong smell of chlorine. Artificial turf carpeted the whole courtyard except for a faux brick pathway meandering through the space. Every feature of the second-rate water park cast ghastly shadows from the flood light. My eyes darted throughout the space searching for a silhouette I wasn't sure would be visible.

Huge sweeping black shapes passed over the courtyard. I ducked as one of them swept over head. I remained in a crouched position until I saw that the shadows were being cast by a large moth pestering the floodlight. The bizarre light show continued as I stood up and resumed my search. At last, my eyes rested on the dark outline of a man standing next to a door in the pagoda.

My pulse rose as I cautiously approached. The silhouette reached over to the handle and opened the door. He paused and turned to me while motioning with his other hand for me to step inside.

"I'm not going in there." I halted.

The silhouette dropped his shoulders.

"Don't you want to see it again?"

My blood ran cold. "See what?" I asked a pointless question.

The figure crossed his arms and leaned against the frame of the door. "Have you already forgotten? That's no surprise seeing how quickly you forgot all about me."

I shook my head as the moth's shadow passed over me again. "I never forgot you," I assured.

A chuckle echoed in the courtyard. "Only because of me. If I hadn't showed up, you'd be riding high on your precious career."

I took a short step back while clenching my fists to prevent my hands from shaking. I knew he was right.

"I saw it first. I know everyone thought I did it because of the divorce, but that's not true. I told her to initiate that," he lit another cigarette.

"Then what was the reason?" I tried to stay calm.

"Down in that engine room," he sputtered. "I saw it in the engine room. The night after I killed that civilian on accident. I bumped into him when I was plastered and he went careening into traffic."

I furrowed my brow while the moth's silhouette hovered for a moment over top of me. "The engine room of the ship?"

The figure took a long drag and exhaled, "There too."

I hesitated before asking, "What do you mean?"

"It's not so much a physical place. I was just lucky enough to come across the engine room, I guess," he lamented.

"Did you tell anyone about what you saw?"

Sloan shook with an otherworldly laughter, "Who would I tell? What would I tell them? A junior sailor with a story is the least reliable source in the Navy."

I nodded slowly and clenched my jaw as the moth grew bored of the light and ceased its passes back and forth.

"What I saw ripped me to shreds," he ashed the cigarette to emphasize his point. "Couldn't take it anymore. My family life was a mess. The investigation was going to end my career. Nobody missed me. Who even really cared?"

The figure took another drag as the ember reddened and intensified.

I recalled all the times I passed him in the ship's passageways. His thick glasses and perpetually greasy hair were always overshadowed by his permeating look of despair. His department head would constantly complain about how he was messing things up. I shamefully joined in the disparagement without the slightest idea of what was brewing beneath the surface.

"I'm sorry, Sloan," I managed. "I am so sorry."

The light of the cigarette jostled back and forth as the silhouette shook his head in disapproval. "You could have told Captain Wonder Woman to pound sand. There was still a chance to save me if you didn't let her do that emergency breakaway," he informed with contempt.

I shifted my weight uncomfortably. "You were hanging by your neck. It was over for you by that point."

"That's not the way I see it," Sloan replied, ashing his smoke once more. "You just threw up your hands and said, 'You have the deck.' All for your precious career. I'm glad it's come through so unscathed."

"Is that why you're doing this?" I raised my volume. "To get back at me? To ruin my life?"

He remained silent for a moment.

The moth returned to the light and resumed casting hellish shadows on the space.

"It's your problem now," the figure replied cryptically.

He retreated into the recesses of the pagoda and shut the door. I ran after him and yanked on the locked handle.

"Come back here!" I commanded with the full knowledge he would return at some point in the future.

The power suddenly returned to the hotel as the moth's shadow passed overhead once more.

THE FIFTY THOUSAND

I sat sleeplessly in my room for about an hour before deciding to just get back on the road again. I knew I wasn't going to get any rest—that night or ever again. I returned the key to the front desk to the immense displeasure of the receptionist.

"So, you're going to leave now that the power is back on?" she took the key with disgust.

When her eyes raised to meet mine, she shrank back. My dead, hollow sockets were portals to a world of torment. I almost relished her fear. I exited without saying a word and drove into the frigid night. By now, the early snowfall coated nearly everything in sight. A Wisconsin native, this didn't slow me down one bit. As the wipers oscillated smoothly on the windshield, my thoughts wandered to Ben.

It hit me like a ton of bricks when I realized I never even tried to attend his funeral. Formerly critical inflection points in my life were ironed out by the crushing steamroller of anxiety. As the miles passed under me, I could almost hear my mental state declining. I turned on the radio to drown out my thoughts. I picked up a talk radio station in the early hours of the morning.

"Thanks for joining 101.5 Prairie Radio. It's the top of the hour and snow is still coming down. . . ." the voice droned on.

The pleasantries of local media were soothing. For almost five minutes, they mentioned nothing of the Mississippi River, China, the war, or cyberattacks—the endless drumbeat of catastrophe that had come to dominate the airwaves.

". . . for the last time this week. For your extended weekend forecast—"

The host broke off mid-sentence.

"Folks, I am getting some breaking news here. I apologize while I take a minute to read this."

The station cut to a commercial break as the anticipation grew. The silly advertisements danced from my speakers like relics of the time before the Pentagon. They were campy, local ads for towing shops, restaurants, and the like. I let myself get lost in their cheesy jingles and forced catchphrases.

"Welcome back, everybody. This is 101.5 Prairie Radio. It's 5:07 a.m., and I have a breaking story to deliver to you guys. We just got an email from the governor's office sent out to all local media. I don't want to mince the governor's words, so I am just going to read it to you. It says the following," the host prepared to read the communique with trepidation.

"Given the present state of crisis, the need for personnel has outstripped the available pool of volunteers. It is with a heavy heart that I relay the dire manpower situation our armed forces find themselves in amidst the fight for freedom. Following a closed session meeting with the Joint Chiefs of Staff, the President of the United States issued a letter to each governor of the fifty states and overseas territories. Our chief executive stated that, if the country does not provide fifty thousand volunteers by the weekend, the federal government would be forced to activate the Selective Service System. Consequently, I have authorized $3 million in emergency funding to set up impromptu recruiting stations. . . ."

The governor's statement sounded like he wrote it with a gun to his head. I listened in dim realization of the full gravity of the situation.

"A draft . . ." The words left my mouth like cloud of blue smoke from an unhealthy engine's exhaust. "They don't dare."

It wasn't that I particularly cared if random guys got pressed into service. After all, I stepped up. Why shouldn't they? Nevertheless, I knew the political ramifications were unthinkable. This all was in an election year, no less. Politicians' careers would be made or destroyed over the coming few days. The fact the president couldn't delay the decision until after the election was proof just how dire the manpower situation had become. The silly little trick of neurotically demanding fifty thousand volunteers like it's 1863 made the whole affair clownish and out of touch.

No doubt, the ploy was to see which governors played ball and which could be scapegoated as "unpatriotic." Once the number was inevitably missed, the commander in chief could blame the shortfall and ultimately the draft on his political opponents. If by some miracle the fifty thousand materialized out of thin air, the President and the Republican Party could ride a wave of patriotic fervor through the midterms when the fifty thousand dupes would be used up. It was a surprisingly erudite political maneuver by the Republicans. I would've admired it had it not been so grim.

I shut off the radio as my eyes grew leaden. Convinced I would be able to sleep regardless of my racing mind, I pulled off into a rest stop parking lot as the snow continued to blanket the plains.

I awoke the next morning in the peculiar blue light that managed to penetrate the coating of frozen precipitation obscuring my windows. I pried open the driver's side door and got showered with snow. Brushing it off, I stumbled into the rest stop building to find the bathroom. To my immense astonishment, a little folding table with a haphazard sign reading "armed forces recruitment center" hovered next to the men's restroom of all places. A rotund state employee, probably pulled from the DMV, sat anxiously with a clipboard.

I told him exactly where he could shove his forms when he tried approaching me on my way to relieve myself. While I was already in Uncle Sam's thrall, I imagined the makeshift recruiter was getting similar responses from everybody. He comically refused eye-contact on my way out.

In my shorts and T-shirt, I removed the snow and ice from my windshield with the ice scraper I had kept under the seat even in Florida. Just as I returned to the cabin, my phone rang. My soul shriveled when I saw that it was a private number.

"I wish you were still here," the woman said wistfully. "I do miss you."

I felt like I was going to throw up. "What do I need to do?"

She giggled. "I am glad that you're coming around to this whole arrangement. Mr. Green will look favorably on that."

What little capacity I had left for sorrow wracked my body.

"The next major city is Denver," the woman noted accurately. "You'll pick up a bag and bring it to San Diego with you. Simple and easy."

I listened in a detached despair to the details of where and when I needed to be.

"Stay safe out there, Mr. Malden," she appeared to say with some measure of true feeling.

I swore bitterly as I started the car. I remembered when I first got my license. It was like being sprung from jail after sixteen years of incarceration. The freedom of movement caused me to get on the road for every excuse. I would sneak out of my parents' home just to sit in the driver's seat of my first car. The ecstatic rush lasted until I got into an accident only a month later. It was all my fault, and my beautiful car was carted off to be crushed along with what felt like part of my soul. I, of course, was being dramatic at the time. I saved up enough working at the farm supply store to buy an old beater the following year, but the charm was long gone.

Now in my sleek import sedan with the vast expanse of the nation's roads, I was more chained and restricted than ever before. The compromising material and the threat of torture was enough to break any last vestiges of free will I had left. Reluctantly but inevitably, I set my course west toward Denver.

When I pulled off the interstate at the exit the woman told me to, the city was in mass chaos. The snow had all melted, and a feverish warmth returned to the air. Protestors had blocked off entire sections of downtown over the potential draft. I nervously covered anything in the car that could give away my status as military in the off chance someone would think I was a recruiter. I spotted the parking garage next to a city park just as she described it. The only problem was that the park and surrounding area was saturated with rioters and police.

I parked a few blocks away and walked up to the chaos. A loud bang caused me to flinch. The police started to deploy rubber bullets and tear gas. I was approaching the mobile mass of people from the side of the protestors. Instead of pressing through the scrum, I managed to find a path around the pocket of unrest to the parking garage. To get to the pedestrian entrance however, I had to walk within a stone's throw of the police cordon. A riot cop eyed me suspiciously as I walked briskly to the structure. He gestured to one of his buddies, and the pair started to approach rapidly. I noticed their advance when I was only ten yards away from the entrance.

My judgment clouded by cumulative fatigue and paranoia, I made a break for the door. The riot cops broke into a sprint as well. They shouted after me as my mind became soaked with panic. When I entered the parking garage, I saw a group of five or six rioters had already made it inside and were preparing to scale the stairs. The gathering startled at my loud entrance and turned hostile when they saw the riot cops hot on my tail. They began lobbing Molotov cocktails indiscriminately in my direction irrespective of their intent to hit me or the police. One caught fire on a parked van only a foot to my right. The cops wavered for a moment then retreated to grab backup.

"You screwed it up for us!" One of the rioters rushed over to me with a knife drawn, "We were gonna drop hellfire on those pigs from the top of this building, but now they know we're here!"

I put up my hands defensively, "I wasn't trying to bring them in! I didn't know you guys were in here!"

When he got closer, I saw he was wearing red bandanas and anarchy symbols. His friends caught up to him and told him it was time to go. They climbed up the ledge of the first level and jumped to the street below. Acutely aware the cops would rush the structure at any moment, I sprinted away from the burning car's pouring smoke and breathlessly climbed the stairs to the fourth level. I found the bag underneath the blue sports coupe with Illinois plates, per the instructions. It was an enormous duffel bag, larger than my seabag. When I tried to lift it, I was surprised by the weight. Curiosity got the better of me and I peeked inside.

The yawning opening of a gun barrel pointed at my face. Opening the bag further, I found twelve rifles, six pistols, and dozens of magazines for each.

"You've gotta be kidding me," I swore in shock.

The sinking realization I would have to transport eighteen illicit, probably loaded firearms on foot through a state of civil unrest filled me with dread. I didn't fear the police. I feared failing Green's mission and the terrible consequences that would follow. The sound of the riot police rushing the first floor snapped me back to reality. I zipped up the bag in panic while my eyes searched wildly for an exit. I heard the clambering of personnel up the stairwell I had just come up. Unsure of what to do, I rushed over to the other stairwell heavily encumbered by the duffel bag. Sure enough, I heard police rushing up this corridor as well. I could feel the net closing in around me while the horrific memory of the boy's torture played over in my mind. I decided to toss the bag underneath a low-lying sedan and scraped my face along the concrete to hide underneath another. To my immense discomfort, the engine of this vehicle was still warm. I sat cooking under the heat when the police burst onto the level.

ARRIVAL

About ten riot cops searched the level. Some were checking under cars, others weren't. One of the more motivated police officers started searching down my row. He was only a few vehicles away when the sounds of breaking glass and screaming erupted from the streets below. One of the officers ordered the rest to return to the ground level. I surmised the anarchists began heaving their payloads from another vantage point.

I rested my head on the concrete, drenched in sweat, partially from the hot engine above me. The lion's share of the perspiration came from my close brush with unthinkable torture. I waited for a few minutes to make sure the police were really gone.

Really, I was already in a state of torture. I had been built up as a promising officer and given the pedigree to boot. Now I was an emotional wreck, in servitude to a devil, and on my way to fight an unwinnable war.

I slid out from under the car with the duffel bag in tow. I managed to get the heavy load on my shoulders before waddling to the nearest elevator. The sounds of the erupting city below were snuffed out for a brief ride to the bottom level. When the elevator doors made a cheerful chime, the incensed masses made their voices heard in my ears once again.

"NO, no, we won't go!" they chanted.

"Not our shops, not our fight!" others moaned.

Someone's sign read, "got $50,000 in debt, not 50,000 volunteers."

The crowd had been pushed back several blocks by successive barrages of tear gas canisters and baton strikes. Several cars were on fire, contributing to the load of an increasingly absent fire department. The duffel bag's strap dug into my withering body like a slave master's whip. When I made it to my sedan, I found it had been defaced with all manner of graffiti and the passenger side mirror was missing.

"Animals," I muttered to myself.

With a great deal of sweat and grunting, I heaved the illicit cargo into the trunk. I shuddered when I saw its cavernous opening that had callously swallowed up the MP. Just then, my phone screeched an emergency alert tone. The city of Denver was going to shut down all exits to the highway in thirty minutes due to the influx of rioters.

I scrambled into the driver's seat and started the car. Much to my chagrin, I discovered the vandals siphoned out most of my gas too, probably to make more Molotovs. The needle hovered a hair's breadth above empty. With no expectation of success, I tried looking up the nearest gas station on my phone. Of course, GPS was down. A growing sense of anxiety set in at the prospect of getting trapped in the city with the rioters. Struggling to get my bearings, I tried to retrace my steps to the interstate. When I found the road leading to the interchange, I found National Guard troops blocking the road. I pulled up next to one of the Humvees and rolled down my window.

"The exits aren't supposed to be closed for another thirty minutes!" I sputtered.

An overweight female sergeant huffed as she dismounted the vehicle. "The exit's closed until further notice," she informed.

I lowered my brow and pulled out my military ID. "I have orders to be in San Diego. Let me through," I said rudely.

She narrowed her eyes and looked at the card. Her demeanor changed when she read that I was an O-4. "My apologies, sir," the sergeant motioned to the others to let me through.

"Can you guys spare any gas? The rioters siphoned most of mine."

A large explosion sent a cloud of smoke rocketing into the air a few blocks away.

"No chance sir," the woman rubbed sweat from underneath her helmet. "We barely had enough to get here."

I pursed my lips and passed through the checkpoint unhindered. When I ascended the ramp to the interstate overpass, I got a bird's-eye view of the unfolding bedlam. I mostly had the route to myself apart from a few overtasked emergency vehicles. Plumes of smoke arose throughout the city while a police helicopter made passes overhead. Laughs, jeers, screams, and cries burst from the urban landscape like fireworks.

It was as if all the bottled-up tensions and hatreds of the past decade were unleashed. Black, White, Hispanic, Asian—it didn't matter. Everyone came out to participate in the melee. They fought the cops, they fought each other, they fought anybody at all. The city was awash with blind violence and carnal impulsivity. After the state-enforced softening of skulls and gratification of the flesh, what else could the government expect when they called upon civic virtues long since dead and buried?

A group of motorcyclists that had run the barricade zipped past me to do speed runs on the empty ring road. One of them gave me the finger while he did a wheelie. These were the same young men that would soon be sent off to die in the name of "our values," whatever that meant. I couldn't help but cheer them on as they outran the sheer insanity that leeched into everyone's minds.

A sleeping demon, bound for centuries by better caretakers of our prosperity, had escaped its confines to loot the masses of any peace they had left. By the way everyone acted, we could all sense it too.

I managed to find a gas station still open at the outskirts of Denver. The employees were hurriedly putting up plywood on the windows. My fuel gauge showed I was well past empty and running on fumes.

The swarthy cashier informed me the new price was $15 per gallon. Shaking my head in disbelief, I handed him a $100 bill.

"I want that receipt," I informed him.

In the unlikely event I survived the whole ordeal I found myself in, I was in for an enormous travel expense claim. When I finished pumping gas, the meter informed me I had purchased 6.66 gallons. I shrugged at the number.

Can't have any more bad luck than what I already have, I thought to myself.

With that, I continued on toward San Diego. As I left the fevered city, the power went out in tandem with the setting sun. The artificial light of street lamps was replaced with a turbid glow of burning buildings and burning souls.

It would be useless to recount the whole of the journey. I was ordered to make more pickups in location after location. All the while, the country was in the pangs of labor, set to birth a new era of despair and suffering. I stopped checking what each duffel bag was somewhere in Utah. I knew what it all was.

The only city that was utterly unchanged from its pre-war character was Las Vegas. I arrived just after sunset on the Sunday of the fifty thousand-volunteer deadline. I filled up the car miles ahead just in case of civil unrest but was shocked at how unaffected the decadent metropolis was.

No, not unaffected. Las Vegas was magnified. All the casino lights were on. The interstate was bumper to bumper with revelers. Some even got out of their cars and danced in the traffic. Women debased themselves publicly to the honks of passing vehicles.

The interstate had devolved into an inching block party of the damned. Underpinning the debauchery was a thinly concealed sense of dread. The celebration of carnality was devoid of any limp-wristed patriotic fervor. None of the partiers even sported flag attire. They had all made their pilgrimage to the Mecca of a dying version of the American dream—one that could still endlessly and thanklessly vomit hedonic slop into their herpes-ridden mouths.

Even the policemen on the road joined in the festivities. As with the rest of the country, the revelers knew this time was soon passing away. It would be replaced by the cold austerity of privation, but not that night. For just one more rotation of the earth, the pleasure-seekers could gratify every last desire. I pulled out of Vegas into the moonscape beyond after spending hours stuck in traffic.

After spending the night in a scummy roadside motel, I checked the news to see if the governors had pulled fifty thousand unwitting rabbits out of the hat. To my immense surprise, I saw a White House press conference video clip announcing the goal had been exceeded by over 5,000. Given what I had seen over the past few days of resistance and chaos, I was convinced they were lying. I figured they were quietly sweeping the idea of a draft under the rug as a direct result of what I had witnessed.

However, I found something interesting buried deep in one of the articles. Some states had resorted to pressing police and first responders into service. Surprisingly, California and New York had supplied the bulk of the recruits. When I read further, I discovered the two states accomplished this feat by simply offering amnesty to any physically capable individual in their sprawling prison complexes. Only about 10,000 actual volunteers nationwide had answered the call. The rest of the ranks would be filled in with murderers, rapists, child molesters, and thieves.

I was nearly to LA when I was told by the woman to reroute south around Joshua Tree National Park. She instructed me to make the drop at a town called Borrego Springs somewhere in the desert east of San Diego. I marked the location on my map and trundled through the empty waste. On one of the rare occasions I let myself acknowledge my hunger, I stopped to grab some food at a local restaurant as the sun went down. I couldn't remember the last time I had eaten. My body felt depleted of all resources—physical, emotional, and spiritual.

After a quick meal, I stepped out into the cold desert night. I noticed every last light in the town had been extinguished. What little illumination was left cowered behind thick curtains. I had been instructed to meet my contact by what she described as a "metal sea monster." I hadn't the slightest idea of what she meant, but I was not inclined to prolong the conversation. Wandering through the town, I found she had given quite a literal description.

With all forms of artificial light extinguished, the moon shined brightly once it rose beyond the distant mountains. Its pale, silvery glaze backlit a roadside art attraction depicting a sea serpent poking its head and several loops of its body out of the sand. I pulled off the road and approached the beast. When I shut off the car, I observed a shadow shift in the moonlight from under one of the serpent's loops. I exited the vehicle and waited for the figure to approach. Headlights from a van I hadn't even seen turned on, silhouetting the man as he approached and blinding my vision.

I started to pull the multitude of bags out of my car when he finally arrived. As my eyes adjusted to the bright headlights, I saw the man had black eyes and the same sort of tattoos Green's man in DC. I speculated the enforcer at the mansion and this individual were members of the same gang or cartel. The man took the bags without a word and loaded them into the van. In less than five minutes, the whole deal was completed.

Where are all those weapons headed? I wondered.

The van started up and briskly joined the road. The driver had face tattoos which gave him the appearance of one of the calaveras on his accomplice's arms.

That was the last mission I received on my way to San Diego. At long last, I returned to where my naval career began as a bright-eyed division officer. This time, I sported an extra few ranks, wrinkles, and pangs of self-loathing.

I pulled into the 32nd Street Base with red eyes and a broken soul. I decided to take a walk to see my new command, something I formerly always dreamed of. USS Peoria, a single-hull variant LCS, sat idly on the pier. A solitary sailor smoked silently on the fantail.

COMMAND

Intense lights rose out of the sea to the west. It was as if every star in heaven were instead shooting up from the ocean. I realized what it was as the first otherworldly thunderbolt landed several hundred yards from where I was standing. A fiery explosion lit up the adjacent building. Missiles from an unknown source were pummeling the base. I surmised it to be a ballistic missile submarine making a surprise visit. No other Chinese asset could have gotten this close. I lay prostrate next to my car as the ground shook with repeated impacts. I saw a destroyer take a direct hit to its superstructure. The mast, cut in half, fell to the forecastle fully ablaze. Dark figures started to dart to and fro on the decks of the ships. One cruiser managed to get its CIWS deployed. The multi-barreled gun sent a bright stream of bullets to intercept one of the incoming missiles.

In all reality, the attack lasted only thirty seconds or so. The submarine needed to evacuate the area if the crew ever hoped to see dry land again. No doubt, one of the destroyers was preparing to get underway at that very moment. A P-8 aircraft passed over the base in the direction of the barrage. In the peacetime Navy, someone would've hung for this brief but punctuated attack. As with the rest of the military, no one could be spared for such frivolous things as fault or justice. Several fire trucks started to blare their sirens as firefighting efforts got underway both on ship and shore.

I stumbled to my feet and brushed myself off. From the cyberattacks to the Mississippi bridge explosions, nothing quite brought the reality of the war to the forefront of my mind like this strike. In the grand course of the conflict, I doubt it would even be worth mentioning. Maybe a few sailors were dead. The damage, besides the one destroyer's mast, appeared to be superficial. Nevertheless, the Chinese had shown up unannounced at our doorstep where we had never thought possible. The whole affair was to prove a point and shake the resolve of American leadership and the broader populace. From where I stood, cloaked in the horrid glow of burning missile debris, it worked.

I decided to take a jog over to my ship. I was surely bucking procedure showing up in a T-shirt and shorts, but I doubted they would care. The sailor on the fantail was gone. The crew were in the middle of preparations to retract the gangway when I clambered up. The sailor on duty bristled at my approach until I identified myself.

"LCDR Malden," I breathlessly held up my ID. "Permission to come aboard?"

He haphazardly saluted. "Come aboard."

"Where's the acting CO?" I asked.

The sailor gave me a blank expression. "Ain't you him?"

Brushing this off, I took a moment to catch my breath. I weaved my way through the narrow passageways and up the ladder wells to the bridge. It seemed as though the sailor on duty was the only personnel on the ship.

I lifted the lever on the door to the pilothouse. Inside, I saw a man and a woman in various stages of undress scrambling to put their uniforms back on. When the male got his blouse back on, I saw he was an O-4 like myself. The woman was an undesignated seaman, straight out of bootcamp. She shamefully slipped past me while avoiding eye contact.

"What the . . ." I rubbed my eyes as if I were seeing another vision.

The other LCDR stood stone-faced. I was overcome with rage. While the Chinese had just pulled off a daring trans-Pacific raid, this acting captain had been caught quite literally with his pants down.

I lunged at him with reckless abandon. My movement surprised the man before I knocked him the ground. I got on top of him and just started swinging. I was caught up in a rabid sense of rage, at whom I wasn't quite sure. Regardless, this nameless officer was the recipient of all my stifled sense of action.

"Stop, please!" he cried out.

I was about to unload another salvo before I got ahold of myself. I could barely see his dark, pleading eyes in the dim light of the pilothouse.

"Get off my ship," I ordered.

As he wordlessly shuffled off the bridge, I rubbed my face on my way to the captain's chair. I sat limp as I viewed the churning ocean beyond the pier from my petty throne. Command had arrived when I least expected it and under circumstances I never anticipated. I later learned his name was Jones or something. I never saw him again. Maybe he jumped off the Coronado Bridge in shame. Maybe he begged to be transferred to another ship. Whatever his ignominious fate, I was now master and commander of what I would later find to be the worst ship in the Navy. A pale glow from the fires danced in mocking forms across the deck of Peoria for the rest of the night.

I made the trek to the LCS squadron command headquarters to check in with the commodore the following morning. The base was still covered in smoke and debris from the previous night. I was greeted with a familiar face, who beckoned me into the office.

"LCDR Malden, we meet again," my former commanding officer, Kate Fowler, said with contempt.

She bore two eagles on her lapels, marking her promotion to O-6. Her desk was strewn in disarray with several unfinished cups of coffee sitting atop misplaced documents. Her walls were hung with various newspaper clippings and magazine articles about herself.

"Good morning, ma'am," I robotically replied while trying to conceal my cut and bruised knuckles.

She scowled at me before motioning for me to sit. "Admiral Simmons warned me you were coming my way," Fowler adjusted her unkempt hair. "He asked if it would be too much. I told him to bring it on."

Her look, only describable as spited girl-boss, made my stomach churn. I wondered how she picked up captain with the ongoing investigation. The crashing understanding of the dire personnel situation clicked the pieces together.

"I've only been in this seat for a week," she informed. "Normally I would've served a year as the deputy commodore before taking the reins, but we're all being flexible, aren't we?"

I nodded silently.

"The report is out. The Navy absolved us both of wrongdoing," Fowler fondled the eagle on her collar. "But . . . I don't agree."

"Ma'am?"

She scoffed. "Telling the quartermaster to log your objection? Really? That kind of insubordination is crazy."

I just sat there and ate the criticism.

"I expect you to play as a team here in LCSRON 12," Fowler raised her eyebrows. "And you'll need to. Peoria needs to get underway in a week. You're going to Hawaii, then off to WestPac."

"A week?" I exclaimed.

"What's the status of your manning?" she grilled. "Maintenance reports? Fuel stores?"

I didn't have the answers to any of her questions. In reality, she should've already known the answers from her staff. I wondered if she was asking just to grill me or if she genuinely had no idea.

"You don't know?" Fowler chastised, "Not good, Malden. Not good."

"I will find out and report back," I replied mindlessly.

"You better," she glared at me once more before telling me I could leave.

I rushed back to the Peoria to put my finger on the pulse of the chaotic command I had inherited. Each of my department heads had worse news than the last one.

"I am missing four different critical NECs," my engineering officer told me.

"We cannot get underway in a week. We can't get underway in a year! It's just not possible," the first lieutenant shrugged his shoulders.

"Have you even been down to the engine room?" the command master chief chimed in.

"What?" I snapped alert.

"The engine room," the man of indiscernible ethnicity shuffled some papers on the wardroom table. "It's a mess down there."

"I . . ." My voice faltered as the compliment of department heads and division officers took on looks of grave concern. "You'll need to show me what you mean."

The main propulsion assistant said under her breath, "We are so screwed."

"Didn't LCDR Jones follow up on any of this?" I objected to the growing laundry list of problems with the Peoria.

The combat information center officer piped up. "Sir, I am going to be brutally honest with you. This ship is a one-legged man in a butt-kicking contest. We have half the crew we should and none of the spare parts. There's black mold in all the berthings, and your head would spin if you saw the fan room by CIC. You've inherited a basket case—the worst ship in the whole fleet," he took a moment to fiddle with his coveralls, "and we're all going to war in this tub."

My enfeebled mind was woefully inadequate for the task ahead of me. I needed the old me to snap back into existence. Instead, I was a drained, rotted husk much like the Peoria. Picked over and mismanaged, my command and my mental state were mirror images.

"The best thing that ever happened to this boat was when LCDR Jones went missing," the 1st LT muttered, readjusting the strap on his command ball cap.

The rest of the wardroom shared a stress-relieving laugh. I nervously laughed along and rubbed my still painful hands. It appeared no one knew about the beating I inflicted.

"Well, ladies and gentlemen," I tried to project confidence, "we've been dealt quite the hand. But orders are orders. Let's get this show on the road."

The sheer volume of work to be done on the filthy ship from cleaning to repairs was staggering. I was in daily fights with various supply departments, contractors, and other commands. From what I gathered about the other ships on the waterfront, all the others were in a similar state of disarray. The only ships left in port by this stage of the conflict were the basket cases and the rejects.

All the streamlined commands were either fighting for their lives or feeding the fish. The Navy was trying to breathe life into the skeleton fleet to fill unfillable vacancies in the roster. I received word the Peoria would be assigned to conduct anti-submarine patrol. I had to inform the commodore the ship was not even equipped with the anti-sub module.

I received another message the day before we got underway that our new mission would simply be "escort," whatever that was supposed to mean. On day three, the Peoria was at least cobbled together enough to have a decent chance at making it to Hawaii without capsizing. I hoped to finish up any remaining repairs in Pearl Harbor before getting sent into the war zone.

On the day before we were supposed to leave, a white bus with tinted windows showed up on the pier. A motley group of personnel in something resembling uniforms, male and female, filed out of the vehicle in much the same way an animal excretes waste. An MP hopped out of the driver's compartment and pointed at the Peoria.

"CMC," I asked cautiously, "What's this group coming aboard now?"

The useless sack wheezed, "Oh, I was meaning to tell you sir. That's the rest of the crew."

"The rest of the crew?" I stood in disbelief.

The grotesque pâté of humanity slunk aboard the ship. Not one of them were wearing the uniform correctly while more than a few sported skull caps on their head. One particularly large individual wore a soiled wifebeater instead of a uniform blouse. I understood that a small portion of the miraculous fifty thousand had shown up fresh off the prison yard.

"Sir?" A sailor came up to the bridge with a duty phone. "It's the commodore."

I took the device and put it up to my head like a loaded handgun.

"LCDR Malden, the personnel deficiencies you claimed would prevent you from getting underway are taken care of. I will see you off the pier at 0600 tomorrow," she stated curtly before hanging up.

I sat down in the captain's chair and caught my breath. I motioned for the CMC to leave me alone in the pilothouse. My onboard phone rang.

"Sir, the new . . . *arrivals* . . . are waiting for you in the galley."

I hung up and took a deep breath. I hadn't heard from my tormentors in DC since the drop-off in the desert. I was sure they had access to my underway schedule. The memory of the boy returned briefly before I snuffed it out with the crushing list of things to do on the ship. I donned my command ball cap and descended to the galley below to greet the individuals I'd be sharing a war with.

RELIEF

"Attention on deck!" the CMC called out as I stepped into the galley.

Some of the new arrivals stood up immediately while others looked around cluelessly.

"At ease," I motioned for everyone to sit down.

I finally got a good look at everyone. There were roughly twenty in all of every size, shape, color, and mental capacity. There were a few females sprinkled into the mix. One of the men was playing a beat on the table with a pencil while mumbling rap lyrics. I shot a look over to the CMC. He half rolled his eyes and told the newly minted sailor to stop.

"Good morning," I began slowly, "I'm LCDR Malden. I'm your commanding officer. I—"

"Ayo, so we going to get shot at?" one of the urchins interrupted.

I took a moment to compose myself.

"Yuh, stupid," the one next to him said, smacking his head. "We going to war."

"Just how much training have you all had?" I rubbed my face.

Deep down, I knew the answer. The fifty thousand had only been summoned a week ago.

A man named Suarez spoke in a surprisingly articulate manner. "Sir, we were pretty much taken out of orange and put straight into blue." He straightened his blouse. "We've had six days of basic training."

I stood dumbfounded. I was about to take a ship into harm's way with twenty units of deadweight.

"Hey, I need to go to medical," a skeevy-looking imp said, raising his hand.

The former prisoner next to him agreed. "Yeah, I do too, yo! I can't go to no sea. I get real dizzy."

Soon enough, the whole galley was awash with complaints and excuses. The one wearing the greasy wifebeater started pushing around Suarez who tried in vain to get everyone to calm down.

"CMC, get this mess off my ship!" I commanded and left the compartment.

I dialed the commodore's number.

"Good morning, Sir/Ma'am, LCSRON 12."

"Put me through to the commodore. This is the CO of Peoria!" I spit my words into the phone.

"One moment, sir," the sailor put me on hold.

My blood boiled as I walked out onto the flight deck.

"She's currently in a meeting. Can I take a message?"

"Tell her I'm coming over there," I hung up the phone.

I stormed over to the gangway.

"Peoria, departing," the 1MC seemed to mock me.

After a brisk walk to the LCSRON building, I arrived in a fit of rage. The sailor at the front desk tried to stop me but I burst into the commodore's office anyway. Fowler gave me a look of disdain, shock, and anger when I interrupted her phone call.

"How do you expect me to go to sea with that dreck?" I aggressively pointed in her face.

"Malden, get ahold of yourself!" she stood up. "You think you can barge into a captain's office and—"

I interrupted, "They've only had six days of training! Honestly, what possible use do you think we'd get out these miscreants?"

Fowler sat back as if I had just uttered the words of some ancient forbidden spell. "Miscreants?" she almost smiled but retained a serious character. "Is that how you refer to people of color?"

I rolled my eyes, much to my detriment, "This has nothing to do with their race. They're fresh off the prison yard! They broke out into a fight in five minutes. What do you think's going to happen when we've got Chinese missiles coming at us?"

"I think you need to examine your biases," Fowler turned to look out the window. "I knew you'd have trouble with such a diverse crew."

"The crew was already diverse enough," I sputtered.

My fried brain immediately realized the grave mistake I had just made.

"Diverse enough?" she mustered some genuine fury, "Just how diverse is *too diverse*, Mr. Malden? Do you have problems taking orders from a woman? Or am I too diverse for you?"

"That's not what I meant," I tried to backpedal.

"I can't believe you're an officer in the U.S. Navy with this attitude," Fowler clutched at her eagles again. "That's why you defied me on the bridge, isn't it?"

"Ma'am, that's ridiculous," I shook my head.

"Oh, I'm being ridiculous now?" she put her hands on her hips and struggled to form her words, "Listen here, you little—you're taking that crew to sea or I will find someone who can!"

I nearly laughed at this empty threat. Every last ship on the waterfront was missing seats in the wardroom.

"You just go ahead then!" I clenched my teeth, "Admiral Nimitz raised from the dead couldn't take that tub into war."

Fowler looked me dead in the eyes while picking up her desk phone. She dialed a number and waited impatiently for the executive assistant on the other end to read the standard script.

"SURFPAC," she said for effect, "This is Commodore Fowler down at LCSRON 12. I need to talk to the admiral."

SURFPAC was the acronym for the command over all surface ships in the Pacific. My heart sank slightly, but remained confident she was bluffing. I dared to give her a contemptuous smile.

"Admiral," Fowler took on a quiet, submissive tone, "I have a CO here, LCDR Malden of Peoria, who says he can't get underway with his crew. He says it's too *diverse* for him to work."

I opened my mouth in disbelief. She reached over and put the phone on speaker.

". . . and unconscionable!"

The delay of the transfer cut off the first part of the admiral's speech.

"I want that CO off that ship immediately. There's going to be a full investigation into that command climate. Malden was his name? Malden's conduct goes against everything we, as a Navy, stand for. . . ."

The SURFPAC admiral bumbled through a dozen more platitudes about the value of having a crew that "reflected the changing face of America." He even went so far as to say our inscrutable use of diverse human capital would be the reason we would beat a "racist" power like China.

"Yes sir," Fowler transferred the call to the receiver once more. "I will get on that immediately. Oh yes sir. A full investigation. Absolutely. I will have the preliminary report on your desk within a week."

She hung up the phone and sat with a disgusting grin across her face. I was utterly blindsided that the Navy would sacrifice a trained officer in a peer conflict over something I deemed to be so trivial. Apparently, SURFPAC and the broader Department of Defense took my comments more seriously than the thousands of American sailors lining the bottom of the Pacific.

"LCDR Jones will take your place," Fowler informed sanctimoniously. "You're transferred to LCSRON on a legal TAD status, effective immediately."

I shook my head. "Jones hasn't shown up for over a week. That was in my personnel report I gave you on my first day. NCIS is currently searching—"

My correction sent her into a rage. "I've had it with you! I'll get my dog to run the ship! Anyone will run it better than you!"

"Then you'd better call him up," I rose to leave the office.

Fowler threw a mug across the room, shattering it on the door.

"You get back here, Malden! I wasn't finished with you," she stood up.

I turned to her with sleepless, hollow eyes. We remained in a silent stand off for a few moments as Fowler tried to come up with something demeaning to say.

"Just get out!" she waved me away like a fly.

As I left the room, the realization I'd survive the war stabbed me like a knife. Green's words streamed through my mind like a ticker tape relaying the news of an immense disaster. With my relief from command, I'd be caught up in red-tape, investigations, and other consequences for the foreseeable future. The only thing they couldn't do was send me to war. They'd lost faith in my ability to command.

How did he know? I walked slowly through the halls of the squadron command.

I drifted over to the admin office to inform them of my status. I knew I'd be getting a call from them in a minute anyway. I realized the pace and intensity of the past week had managed to drown out most of the horrific memories. Now, with the burden of command lifted, they all came flooding back. My pulse skyrocketed as I leaned on a wall for stability. The mansion, Sloan, the engine room, Green, Ben, the trail of destruction from my compromised state—all of it came back to the forefront of my mind like an overfilled reservoir shattering a dam.

"But you'll be back." Green's words played over and over in my mind until I shouted "Stop!" at the top of my lungs in the hallway outside the admin office.

I realized a sailor was walking at the other end. She froze in place and looked like a deer in headlights. I rubbed my face and waved her on. I had my dream of command for all of a week. Now I'd be trapped with my thoughts while the worst sort of administrative hell played out on my career.

After checking in, I shuffled back to the Peoria to collect my belongings. Some of the former prisoners were dancing to obnoxious music with a cheap speaker on the flight deck. The sailor on duty at the gangway nearly announced my arrival, but I tersely motioned for him to stop. Without a word to anyone onboard, I grabbed my things and left. I tossed my command ball cap off the gangway on my way back to the pier.

THE VITALITY OF ITS GODS

"So, you never actually got sent to WestPac?" Edwards asked.

"Nope, that missile barrage was my closest brush with the conflict," Richard managed a defeated chuckle. "Peoria sank a week later. They caught a torpedo midway between San Diego and Pearl."

"What did they do with you at the LCSRON?"

The captive sighed. "My new job was to manage the inflow and outflow of former prisoners to the basin. They figured it would be a fitting punishment for my racism. Every time one of them got caught with drugs or assaulted base police, it fell on me."

Edwards nodded intently. "Did you get any more tasks from the woman?"

"There were plenty," Richard shifted in the chair. "More of the same. I started to hope my assistance was in some way hurting the war effort."

"But it wasn't," the guerrilla added.

Malden stared off into the darkness. "No, I came to find it was all part of the show. They bolstered the police stations with contractors to help stem the civil unrest. The so-called contractors were really just front companies for the cartels. I was running them supplies, drugs, and weapons," he said with disgust. "I was a mule."

"Why do you think Green had you do that?" Edwards stroked his stubble.

The captive put his face in his hands. "Your guess is as good as mine. Someone had to do it, I suppose. I was the patsy with enough kompromat."

"I know a better reason," the man tilted his head forward and put his hands on the table. "And, of course, ceasefire came only a short while later." Edwards began again, "Green had been establishing contacts long before that."

The captive put forward an upturned palm. "What do those things have to do with each other?"

"As strangely as the Sino-American War came onto the scene, it left. To the confusion of political scientists, strategists, pundits, and everyone else observing the situation, the war became frozen in place after a savage exchange of blows." The guerrilla leader crossed his arms, "The window for history to move had closed. They stabilized him."

"The boy?"

"Who else?" Edwards chastised, "Yes, the boy. They never lost him fully, but your intrusion caused the greatest disturbance they had dealt with to that point. They must have lost out on an untold number of cycles. The demons they serve were not happy. The ceasefire can only be explained by his stabilization."

Richard put the pieces together. "So, if the boy dies . . ."

The guerrilla nodded and interrupted, "The longer this has gone on, the more bizarre and artificial everything has become. The country itself has become a reflection of that poor wretch under the Pentagon: caught in the hellish zone between life and death. Everyone can sense something is dreadfully wrong. We have an economy propped up by fake fiat currency. Men pretending to be women, women pretending to be men. We've outsourced social connection to tapping on a phone. Our food is dyed, painted, and filled with corn products. The homes are fake. The jobs are fake. The voting is fake. Half of the population is on mind-altering medication just to bear up with the insanity of it all. Every last sacred aspect of life has been handed over to the demonic. The churches are empty, but our living hell is as full as ever. We're living in an infernal fun house mirror chamber held firmly in place by human sacrifice," he lowered his tone, "and there's only one way to put an end to it all."

The captive sat back in his chair. "But what do you mean Green was making contacts? More candidates?"

"That, among other things," Edwards continued. "Green is, first and foremost, a pragmatist. He understood the tenuousness of this house of cards they built long before you ever set foot in that basement. They all thought the boy would last forever. Not Jacob Green. While desperately looking for the next candidate, his angle has been to establish a sort of federation of the profane as a backup."

"Alliances?"

The man smiled slightly. "You're catching on. He hadn't lost sight of the vision set forth by men like Celler and Kalergi."

Richard ventured further. "You're referring to immigration?"

Edwards tilted his chin back then declared. "The demons who've long held to the newcomers deep into the dark reaches of history don't simply stay at home when their denizens arrive on our shores. Kipling put it best:

The Stranger within my gates,
He may be evil or good,
But I cannot tell what powers control—
What reasons sway his mood;
Nor when the gods of his far-off land
Shall repossess his blood."

The captive sat in silence as the words of the poem set in like dense fog.

"We've invited the broad pantheon of hell's gods to be our neighbors while forsaking the covenant of our fathers," the man clenched his jaw. "And this is all by design. Green is alliance-building while his compatriots seek to remain as haughty monopoles. In his model, though, his ilk are still on top. But he counts as friends all the most powerful santeros, voodooists, shamans, and occultists. The supplies you were running were no doubt just favors for one of Green's allies."

"Magic?" Richard scoffed. "You're telling me that someone like Green is betting on staying in power through magic? Like spells and cauldrons?"

"Presumptuous and self-willed are they," Edwards recited. "We're not talking about silly Halloween playthings or teenagers asking about their crush on a Ouija board. These are demons who walk the earth with lust to devour and destroy. They can be courted, counted upon, and ingratiated to. If the term *magic* is too much of a stumbling block to you, call it what it really is: the worship of the old gods. Green, sensing his people's golden age could be coming to a close, is courting the new arrivals to gather under him in a feudal arrangement of demonic power. With the church gone, America is in the process of becoming a spiritual vacuum. This man, like so many others of his people since time immemorial, is positioning himself to come out on top of the potentially reshuffled deck. It's an insurance policy if they can't find another candidate."

"I don't understand," Richard contested. "Why haven't they been looking for the boy's replacement before now?"

"Oh, but they have," the guerrilla furrowed his brow. "Bombing campaigns in Gaza deliberately trying to mortally wound children, human trafficking at home, abortion—they've been clawing like rats at the passage of time, desperately trying to hold everything in stasis."

"But you said the Soviets knew how to do Stimulosis. They're not around anymore." the captive reasoned.

"It's very simple," Edwards explained. "The Soviet's specimen died in the mid-sixties. The Americans' boy didn't. Our shamans selected their torture victim more accurately—or perhaps with more luck. Leonid Brezhnev, to his credit, was so disgusted by the program that he banned the search for another specimen. At that point, the demons feeding on the anguish and movement of the soul were no longer divided. They all went to feast at the Pentagon, bringing favors, riches, and all the might of the underworld. The Soviet Union teetered on for another few decades until it succumbed naturally to the forces of history. Meanwhile, the satanic empire we find ourselves under beat mercilessly on, bolstered by the destruction of its rivals and the vitality of its gods."

"Wouldn't the Soviets have every incentive to expose the Americans for doing this?" Richard struggled to wrap his mind around everything he had been told.

"For what? To then have to admit they beat the Nazis by courting the favor of demons? How well do you think that would work for national mythmaking?" the guerrilla dismissed rudely.

His captive pursed his lips. "So everyone in the American government just went along with this?"

"Almost everyone," Edwards sighed. "Those that knew about it and opposed the process were thrown out, driven insane, accused of being anti-Semites or otherwise ended up committing suicide with two bullets in the back of the head. I haven't been able to nail down a firm date of when the American program reached its full potential, but the best I can reckon is at the very end of World War II. FDR, I believe, was ignorant of the project. Truman was a full-throated supporter. I am not sure about Kennedy. They killed him for opposing the Israeli nuclear program. Maybe more. The first secretary of defense and your late cellmate, James Forrestal, was a notable opponent after the hideous engine had already been set in motion. Just look what they did to him."

Richard shuddered at the mention of room 384 at Walter Reed.

"The Jewish state in Palestine was their greatest achievement," the guerrilla took on a disgusted tone then gradually grew incensed. "They used the greatest concentration of demonic power ever gathered to one people and used it to give God the finger. A physical state called 'Israel' hadn't existed since the Assyrian exile! Haven't you ever stopped to think about how artificial it all is?"

"What does Israel have to do with any of it?" the captive raised an upturned palm.

Edwards' patience wore thin. "Don't you get it yet? The whole machine from Israel to the media to the porn industry—the unthinkable levels of control they possess that would make the tyrant kings of old blush—all of it runs on the industrialized human sacrifice under the Pentagon. They've been granted a Promethean fire to accomplish their wildest and most debased desires. Why not use it to defy the very judgments of God that they would be scattered among the nations?"

Richard didn't have the energy to contend with these claims.

Edwards concluded, "Most things in life are actually very simple. How you counter them is difficult, but the problems are all quite uncomplicated."

"But why the Pentagon? Why didn't they hide him off in the mountains somewhere?" he probed.

"Excellent question," his captor scratched at his stubble. "There's something to be said for the convenience of access. However, the answer goes much deeper than that. The very location of the capital was divined, not chosen, all the way back in 1791. Yes, *divined*. Just as with present day immigration, we brought strange gods to our shores with slavery. Benjamin Banneker, one of the original surveyors for DC, was descended from the Dogon people in West Africa. The Dogon had knowledge of celestial entities impossible to be seen with the naked eye. Banneker used the folk magic of his ancestors to guide the selection of the capital's location under the guise of astronomy. The city's planner, Pierre L'Enfant incorporated a variety of satanic symbols into the layout. Nearly all the founding fathers were Freemasons."

Richard exclaimed, "And I was the one in the mad house? You're insane. You're crazy. Are you listening to yourself?"

"Are you?" Edwards raised an eyebrow under the otherworldly light of the solitary bulb above them as he pulled a piece of paper from his bag.

The captive saw that it was a map bearing the logo of the US Geological Survey.

"This is the USGS magnetic anomaly map. Notice anything interesting?" Edwards sat back and crossed his arms.

Richard leaned forward and brought the paper closer. Pointing to DC like an arrow were two parallel zones of disparate magnetic energy.

"What's that supposed to tell me?" he pushed the map away.

Edwards shook his head. "I know you're a little uninitiated in these things. Magnetism has an enormous effect on the success or failure of rituals and scientific experiments alike. The more I've researched, the less difference I've found between the two. The planners of DC never dreamed of technology like Stimulosis, but they knew the importance of magnetism. When it came time to fully establish the engine room 150 years later, the capital happened to check every last box as a viable location."

"But why the Pentagon specifically?"

The guerilla's patience for Richard's questions started to wane, "You know, I had to risk my life for all of this information numerous times. I suppose you get to just skip to the end?"

"I've had my brushes with death for the knowledge I have," the captive countered.

"I suppose so," Edwards raised his eyebrows and nodded, "What do you know about the Manhattan Project?"

"They made the nuclear bomb."

"Correct," the militant tilted his head, "Major General Leslie Groves oversaw the program. Do you know what else he was in charge of?"

The captive shrugged.

"The construction of the Pentagon. Two projects of that scale and importance surely should have been divided between two people, right?" Edwards asked rhetorically. "So, which project was cover for the other one? What occupied more of Groves' time?"

"Obviously the Manhattan Project," Richard asserted.

Edwards smiled and leaned back. "While the development of the nuclear bomb is as equally fraught with ritual and demonic consultation—a story for another time—if everything I've told you to this point is true, which project had the greater potential payoff? An impressive weapon or unlimited favor with the serpent?"

"If," the captive began. "If everything you've told me is true . . . I'd elect for the latter."

"I came to the same conclusion," Edwards sighed. "The Pentagon was purpose-built, and hastily so. Its five sides corresponded to the five petals of the *stimulosus* stinging nettle. Congress approved the start of work on the structure shortly after Sachsenhauser's meeting with Morgenthau."

Richard rubbed his face, his head spinning with information. "But, the boy . . ." he ventured with a shiver, "Where did he come from?"

The guerrilla took the map and placed it back in his bag. "Look we're wasting time," he took a deep breath. "What happened next?"

FLIGHT, PURSUIT

I found out about the ceasefire a day after it happened. My time in legal hold caused my mental state to decline to worse depths than even my time in the mansion. I lived in base housing, walked to my assigned desk, took muster of the varying pool of convicts in my care, and then stared at a cubicle wall for the remainder of the day. They didn't even give me a computer at my desk. My "job" was glorified daycare. I'd get the occasional tasking from the woman to move things around Southern California or sometimes to the next state over. I'd wake up and do it all over again the next day. My first tour in San Diego was marked by going to the beach, going out with friends, and long days on the ship. Now, it was the repetitive deadening of my mind and soul while the Navy sought to string me up.

I'm sure the office broke out in celebration at the news of the ceasefire. I was completely oblivious and locked away in my thoughts. When I finally did find out, the information made no impression on me. I knew I wasn't going to war anyway. I supposed at the time that both sides got tired of trading blows and decided the whole thing wasn't worth it. The belligerents took the conflict to the negotiating table, both claiming victory. For the Americans, winning meant anything but losing. In a short while, everything in the country, the Navy, and the world had gone back to the way it was. The whole affair drifted into everyone's memory like some far-off historical tragedy like the Titanic.

Meanwhile, I sat rotting in my cubicle, memorizing the thread count on the cloth padding of the partitions. I wasn't even permitted a phone, because the admin space contained personal information and was deemed a SCIF. I would occasionally see Captain Fowler in the hallways. She always had a haughty look of triumph when she saw my withering form. How long I sat in that cubicle, I have no idea. One by one, the miscreants on my muster sheet were discharged, transferred, died, or went back to prison until there were none left. There was some discussion of giving me a new "job" while on legal hold, but Fowler didn't want to do me any favors. Instead, I was confined to the desk everyday with every last horrific memory.

Finally, the preliminary results of the investigation showed up on my desk. It was no surprise to me that the report found, "LCDR Malden fostered a command environment of bigotry, hostility, and intolerance. His actions are a discredit to himself, the US Navy, and the Constitution."

The investigation contained no interviews or statements from my crew. They were all dead or missing, of course. None of the diatribes or polemics against me made any effect. The final line of the report is what sent me reeling: ". . . and, in the interest of educating the officer corps and the broader Navy, LCDR Malden is hereby summoned for a Board of Inquiry at Naval Support Activity Washington. . . ."

The board was the least of my concerns. I was heading back to DC, just as Green had predicted. The report trembled in my hands as I stood up in the office. I was to report to Washington in one week. I wasn't technically under arrest. The worst thing the BOI could give me was a dishonorable discharge and order me to pay back any bonuses on unserved time. None of that mattered compared to the soul-rending fear I had of going back to DC.

I snapped. I simply got up from my desk and started walking. I shuffled out of the LCSRON building and headed toward the gate. Once I got off the base, I ignored several prostitutes on my way through the ghetto outside. I walked and walked. There was no use in running. In my declining mental state, somehow the repetitive, mindless locomotion would float me to a place far away from it all. I had left my phone in the locker at the LCSRON. As I travelled, I began taking off pieces of my uniform. First, my rank patch ended up in the garbage. Next, I gave my blouse to a homeless man. My belt, I tossed into a ditch. I went into a thrift shop, bought some shorts, and donated my pants. All in all, it was the slowest, laziest flight from responsibility ever recorded.

After shedding my clown suit, I just kept walking clear through dark. I was eyed suspiciously by a number of hostile denizens of San Diego's seedy neighborhoods but was left alone on account of me looking like a crackhead. I was thin, frail, crazy-eyed, unstable, and delirious. A cold air mass moved in as I entered the undeveloped foothills around Mount McGinty. I deviated from the roads and just kept walking through the scrub and cacti. The piercing pain of the tines caused far more mental anguish than physical pain.

The night sky had no stars. They were all points in the heavens that had been pierced by cosmic needles a million times over. A pair of brighter holes were his eyes. They looked down at me with a thousand years of agony condensed into a single moment. I tried walking faster and keeping my gaze planted on the ground, but to no avail. Between the cacti and the cold shivers running down my spine, all I could think of was the boy. I broke into a frantic run. I screamed in frustrated anguish until I ran out of breath. I stopped, dizzy and panting next to a large boulder.

"What are you running from, Mr. Malden?"

My fatigued adrenals spiked as I turned to the voice. "You're dead!" I picked up a rock and hurled it at him "You're dead! Dead, dead, dead!" I kicked my feet in the dust and pointed at him with misery.

He simply stood motionless as I uselessly writhed against the immaterial.

I fell to my knees and began sobbing, "What do you want? Why don't you just leave me alone?"

The figure observed me for some time. I couldn't tell if he was relishing my woe or taking compassion.

"You can't run away from it," he broke the silence of the frigid, dry air.

"But," I turned to him, "what is it?"

The silhouette went back to his usual habit of smoking before answering. "I was content to shuffle off into the abyss. You killed me. Now you suffer the consequences."

"Why does it matter that I killed you if you were content to die?" I pleaded while driving my fingers into the dust.

He exhaled a cloud into the darkness. "I killed that guy in Aqaba. I had to suffer the visions. I asked all the same questions. 'Why me? Why am I seeing this?'"

"Well?" I looked up from the ground to the figure.

He chuckled scornfully. "Don't look at me. I'm dead. Now I get to show you like he showed me."

"You mean you saw the man you killed after he was dead?" I leaned back to sit in the rocky soil.

The silhouette took a few steps closer and sat down in kind. "It was almost immediate. The language barrier didn't seem to be a problem. I understood everything that Jordanian said. He told me he was on his way to hang himself when I hit him. His son had gone missing. Kidnapped."

"He didn't have any hope the boy would be returned?" I furrowed my brow.

The figure leaned back on his hands and looked to the sky. "He and his son were visiting his cousin in the West Bank. All of them were Christians, curiously enough. A few IDF soldiers showed up one night during dinner. They insisted they needed to bring the boy in for questioning. The father adamantly refused. He heard stories of boys being taken for innocuous reasons and never coming back. Ultimately, his cousin convinced the father to let the boy go. He didn't want his house getting trashed or drone-striked. Well, the dad followed the IDF soldiers back to their little forward operating base—no more than ten soldiers there. He saw the Israelis take his son into a tent while a helicopter landed. Out steps a well-dressed man with a briefcase. After the new arrival went into the tent, the father started to hear screaming. He panicked and ran back to get his cousin. Soon enough, the whole extended family and neighbors had found some spark of resistance and were up in arms. Some local militants got the memo too. The hajjis started shelling the FOB. The father, worried for his son, told them to stop. They turned their weapons on him. After some arguing, he agreed to take a gun and shoot up the base if they stopped shelling. When he got close enough to shoot, his son had already been loaded up in the helicopter. The father started firing wildly into the base. When the chopper flew out of sight, he realized nothing could be done. He threw down the gun and headed back to his cousin's house. The father knew he would never see his son again. He later found out one of the IDF soldiers was killed by a stray bullet of his. After drifting back to Aqaba, his hometown, he started seeing it."

"You mean . . ." I started to shiver.

The figure shook his head. "He couldn't take it. Not only did he see it. The dead IDF soldier took a sick pleasure with it. Every last detail."

We shared a moment of silence as the distant glow of the city pulsated over the foothills.

He continued. "When I got back to the ship that night, he showed me. He showed me all of it. His tone was a little nicer than I was. But careerists like you deserve to be unsettled a little."

I chafed at his comments but didn't put up a fight. "So, he killed an IDF solider, then started seeing it. When you killed him, you started seeing it?" I leaned back and looked up at the astral pin holes. "It's like a transmitted infection."

"That's how I understand it. He was with me all the way up to the end. He tried to tell me not to do it. But I just couldn't keep seeing it. I couldn't take it anymore. He was relentless with it. He told me to do something about it, but what could I do? A junior sailor in the Navy?" The figure slipped into a frustrated tone for a moment, then lowered his voice. "Once I hit the side of the ship, he was gone. But I somehow still remained. I watched the whole debacle of you guys reeling me up by my neck. I'd think you guys would show a little more respect than that."

He flicked his cigarette into the brush.

I sat up and faced him. "Look, I'm past trying to salvage my career. But wasn't it more Fowler's fault than mine?"

"I tried contacting her," he lit another smoke. "I really did. The more I tried with her, the more I started to feel rage toward you. I came to learn you just stepped back and let her do it. Yours was the greater offense."

His accusation made little impression on me. It was one more of a growing portfolio of debts. "So, I'm just cursed with your torment until I kill myself?"

The prospect grew more attractive by the minute.

The figure shook his head. "Now that's uncharted waters. Both the Jordanian and I were killed before we could do it, remember? Maybe it's worth a try. That Chinese sub captain that sunk Peoria has no idea how close he came to a living hell." He fell silent.

I felt the enclosing clutches of fear as the figure sat in contemplation. I knew whatever conclusion he was about to draw, it would mean suffering for me.

"You know what, I've just put it together," his voice gathered steam like a locomotive pulling out of the station.

"What?" I bristled at the sadistic air of his tone.

"I've decided how I'm getting out of this!"

I could almost see a hellish grin on his face through the impenetrable shadows of the night.

"I've been too easy on you. That Jordanian only was around for a few days. I've been stuck like this since the deployment!" He stood up and rapidly approached. "You and I are going to start looking a little more often."

I scrambled to get away. As I breathlessly ran, the nightmare pursued me. My vision clouded over first in my peripherals, then everything went black. A fuzzy view of my surroundings returned after a short period of time. I was back in the engine room. There he was with his tortured wheezing. I opened my mouth but could not scream. Then came the needles.

THE MOUNTAINTOP

"Why is it when I saw him those times, nothing in the world changed?" Richard questioned.

Edwards leaned forward. "You were shown him while you were physically in the Pentagon the first time. It was a unique confluence of factors. Sloan was showing you the boy, but you also happened to be in the exact location of the engine room. I don't claim to fully understand the mechanics of it, but instead of seeing an apparition, you saw him in person. In all my years of research, you're the only one I've encountered outside of the program that's gotten that close."

"Lucky me," the captive's disposition sank low.

Edwards began a new line of questioning. "As I understand it, Sloan was trying to saturate you with visions of the boy so you'd kill yourself?"

"He certainly did his best." Richard's eyes raised to the lightbulb.

"And Sloan concluded this would release him. Why didn't you?" Edwards asked carefully.

"Oh, I tried," the wretch fiddled with his hands. "But that God of yours had other plans. A misfire, people getting in my way, losing my nerve, a vision from Sloan at the moment of decision. I tried very hard."

"When was the last vision you had?" the guerrilla leader probed.

Richard rubbed his eyes, as if to remove the residue of his last terror. "I was having one when you guys yanked me out of the room."

"And where was Sloan? Was he in the room with you?"

The captive leaned in his chair to look behind Edwards. "He's right over there," Richard gestured into the darkness. "Don't you smell the cigarette smoke?"

The guerrilla stood up rapidly, the scrape of the chair on the concrete reverberating throughout the warehouse. He peered into the shadows for a moment before yelling, "In the name of God, I rebuke you! Get out!"

He then stood motionless for a moment, like a hunter listening for sound of game. At last, he sat back down.

Richard sat back and smiled for the first time in too long. He let out a few laughs before returning to tears. "He's gone," he leaned forward to rest his head on the table, "Oh finally he's gone!"

Edwards stayed silent for a few seconds before ending Richard's joyful moment. "For now. We'll need him later," he delivered the news like a professor handing back a paper with a failing grade.

The captive lifted his head and looked him in the eye. He sighed in despair before sitting upright again. Richard felt like he could breathe again, if only for a little while. He resolved to savor the feeling, however fleeting.

"You've been very cooperative, and I appreciate that," Edwards appeared sympathetic, "But I am going to have to ask you to keep telling your story. We can't afford to get this wrong."

A group of hikers found me at the summit of Mount McGinty the next morning. Without sleep and under constant torment the night before, I was raving mad. They assumed, without too much error, that I was on drugs. A woman in the group ventured to offer me water. I gratefully took the plastic bottle with a trembling, shriveled hand. Without even thinking about it, I drank the entire container. I managed an apology, but she took compassion on me. I noticed a delicate cross necklace hanging around her neck.

"Do you have a place to stay?" the woman kneeled next to me.

I looked up at her angelic appearance and got lost in her ocean blue eyes. "Yes," I whispered.

"Can we help you get there?" she asked, taking out another bottle from her pack and giving it to me.

I looked out at the beautiful landscape surrounding us, then at her face. At the top of the mountain, the problems below were like a distant memory. The unending nightmares faded as long as I looked into her eyes.

"I'd rather you didn't," I answered her question.

"Are you safe?" the woman encouraged me to drink.

I shakily sat on a nearby rock, unable to reply. I felt I would scare her away with the truth. One of the men in the group encouraged her to move on. To my immense disappointment, she listened.

"Totally ruined the view," one of the hikers remarked loudly.

As they trundled down the mountain, the woman looked back at my wretched form. As the distance grew between us, the peace she brought me followed her down the mountain. When she turned her head for the last time, the ghastly visions returned. I got up from the rock to follow her. After a short while, one of the men noticed me trailing behind. The woman also turned to look. She was the only one of the group who didn't look at me with utter disdain. I halted while the group bickered about what to do.

One of them called out, "Where are you staying?"

I approached closer but couldn't bring myself to answer honestly. "National City, by 32nd Street," I fibbed.

They conferred once more. After a minute, one of the men spoke. "We'll give you a ride."

I had no desire to go back, but if I could spend just one more minute with the angelic woman, it would all be worth it. I gratefully caught up to the group and walked behind them down the trail. The woman fell back to the rear and walked beside me.

"How did you get up there?" she asked.

I shook my head. "I have no idea. It's been a night."

I noticed her looking for signs of needle use. She also saw I wasn't missing any teeth. "What's your name?"

"Richard Malden," I replied.

The woman smiled warmly. "My name's Alice."

She was the only person in a long time to show me any humanity or compassion. Our time together ended all too quickly. The group piled into an SUV and put me in the passenger seat. They dropped me off on a street corner near the naval base. Alice waved gently at me as they drove away. I drank in her soft, beautiful eyes as long as I could before they disappeared around a corner. I was terribly alone.

I walked reluctantly to the gate and made up a story about getting robbed to explain my appearance and lack of ID. After going through a few hoops of verification and identification, base police took a report and turned me loose on the base. I shuffled mindlessly to the LCSRON to grab my phone. I slipped in and out without anyone noticing me. I then returned to my miserable shack on base. I noticed I had several missed calls from the squadron and a voicemail from a private number. The spiritual piranhas didn't take kindly to my absence.

"Mr. Malden!" the woman on the voicemail chirped, "I can't wait for your return. You know, I don't like it when you dodge my calls."

Her voice contrasted deeply with Alice's. The juxtaposition of graceful compassion against the woman's lurid, consumptive tone crushed my soul.

"And Mr. Green has allowed me to pick you up from the airport. See you soon!" the message ended.

I took a shower, changed into a spare uniform, and trudged back to the LCSRON building. My blank captivity in the cubicle was at least preferable to sitting at home. When I arrived, the admin officer was in a flurry of activity. "Where have you been?"

"Doctor's appointment," I lied before turning my back to go to my cubicle.

She walked after me "You need to tell me with stuff like that. With your BOI going on, I thought you took off to Tijuana!" the admin officer said loudly for the whole office to hear.

A woeful disgust welled up inside me. I heaved around in the same manner an anti-aircraft gun traverses in its emplacement. I had a thousand things I wanted to say but held my tongue. Instead, I just stared into her eyes with a hollow expression of malice.

"It's just," she grew visibly uncomfortable, "you need to tell me."

I turned my back once more without a word and started walking to my cell.

"Your flight is tomorrow, by the way. The TPS order came in this morning," the admin officer informed. "The duty driver will drop you off."

I glared over my shoulder and started walking out of the office.

"Where are you going now?" the shrewish woman chased after me.

"DC," I replied without turning my head. "Or hell. Whichever comes first."

WELCOME BACK

I showed up the next morning after another night of torment. The duty driver, of some swarthy complexion, shot daggers with his eyes in the rearview mirror. I supposed the allegations of racism had made their way around the base. From the time we left base to the moment we arrived at the airport, we didn't exchange a single word.

"You'll get what's coming to you," he broke the silence as I retrieved my bag from the van.

"Oh, believe me, it's already here," I replied and shut the door.

I found my terminal and sat in a dim stupor. Flights had resumed as normal after the ceasefire. I was several hours early for my flight. After some time, an old man sat across from me. A much younger woman, who I assumed to be his caretaker, left him for a moment. He appeared to have the same sunken appearance I had. I noticed he was staring at me.

"You remind me of somebody," the old man wheezed.

I looked up at him in silence.

"Louie," he sat back in his chair and fiddled with his cane. "That's it. You look just like Louie."

"I don't know who that is," I blankly replied.

"Did they send you off to fight the Chinese like they sent us?" his voice trembled.

I looked into his grief-stricken eyes. "They tried to."

"They kept coming," the old man looked far off into the distance as the memories of a forgotten war poured out of his eye sockets like holes in a levee. "Louie and I got captured."

"Korea?" I asked in a low tone.

"You look just like he did," he leaned forward to take a closer look, "Louie? It is you!"

I grew uncomfortable as the old veteran struggled to stand up and walk over to me. He collapsed into the seat to my right and stared deeply into my soul.

"We've got to get out of here, Louie," he whispered. "We've got to get out! I thought you died a long, long time ago."

I didn't know what to say. I looked anxiously for his caretaker.

"They're starving us, but you can have my ration. You've been terribly sick," the old man extended a skeletal hand to grab my arm. "They're going to break us, Louie. We've got to get out of here!"

Mercifully, the woman returned. "Mr. Anderson, stop bothering him!" she scolded and then apologized to me.

The caretaker helped Anderson get up and took him over to another row. He gave me several more pleading looks on his way over. A short while later, another contingent of old veterans filed into the terminal. A few wore hats boasting of their service in Korea. I overheard them saying ground was to be broken in DC for a new memorial to the first war against the Chinese. After all this time, it seems the forgotten war had finally been remembered. I scanned the rows of silver haired relics. There were some White, some Black, some others—most just looked dead.

I noticed Anderson getting the attention of another veteran and pointing back to me. The other one looked in my direction and motioned for him to calm down. We all filed onto the plane around 1130. A substantial portion of the passengers were part of the veteran group. I managed to score a window seat after it became clear no one else was assigned to my row. I recalled the joyful feeling of exploration and wonder I used to feel as a child going on flights to some vacation on the coast. All those memories would glance on the nose of the aircraft before getting sucked and exhausted through the roaring jet engines as we left San Diego. My brief, abortive time in California was a strange outlier in Green's apparently unalterable plan for me. As the flight passed over the vast expanse of the continent, I was pulled back into DC's orbit.

I knew the chances of an airline disaster were low, but that didn't stop me from selfishly hoping. The ground beneath the aircraft transitioned from deserts, mountains, planes, and forests. Even the freshly sutured wound of the Mississippi River was serene. The seatbelt I had to wear during takeoff and landing felt more like the restraints of an electric chair. I was at least able to enjoy the peacefulness of the fleeting hours on the plane. Sloan mostly left me alone when I was around other people. The main problem was that I had become quite reclusive.

When the wheels touched down at Dulles International Airport, the screech of the tires sent dread into my bones. I couldn't have cared less about my Board of Inquiry. It was my impromptu chauffeur and Green that I feared. I tried to savor the last minutes of the plane taxying on the runway and docking with the terminal like a child trying to make the most of the last day of summer vacation. When the light came on letting everyone know they could unbuckle their seatbelts, I felt more imprisoned than ever. The veterans on the aircraft delayed my exit, but I knew my rendezvous with my tormentors of every stripe was inevitable.

Anderson continued to shoot me concerned looks all the way until the veteran group boarded a bus together. He was in anguish over leaving me behind. I stood on shaking knees by a bench at the arrivals lane. With every car that pulled up, my heart sank—only to be relieved it wasn't the woman.

I observed all manner of humanity arriving and departing. There were veterans of the recent conflict finally being granted leave reuniting with loved ones. There were gaggles of foreigners resuming the stream of tourism and immigration. I observed a pair of parents with their child on a leash and a dog in their arms. There was a Haredi Jewish group shuffling around until a large chartered shuttle scooped them up.

Finally, a dark luxury sedan pulled up in front of me. The tinted window rolled down just enough for me to see two different-colored eyes peering at me with a predatory gaze over designer sunglasses. Though the lower part of her face was obscured, I knew what her expression was.

Like an animal being led to slaughter, I opened the rear door and got in.

"You're not going to sit up front with me?" she prodded while eyeing me in the rearview mirror.

I tried to think of a tactful reply, but words failed me.

She scowled and started driving.

Every mile that clicked over on the odometer was like the timer of an explosive planted deep in my mental state by my first stay at the mansion.

"For your next trip, I will want you to sit up here," the woman gripped the steering wheel with a clawed hand.

Her driving style perplexed and mesmerized me. She drove at least twenty miles per hour over the speed limit on the Beltway, seamlessly weaving between the heavy traffic of the evening rush hour. What I thought I could count on being at least an hour drive slipped away rather quickly. The autumn sun had receded below the horizon when we came to that accursed mansion once more. She entered a code into the gate and turned off her headlights. When we crossed over into the grounds, it felt like a dozen hands were reaching into the car and groping at my soul. She parked the car near the cottage on the side of the mansion. Already on edge over her intensions, I mistrusted this action even more. The woman exited the car and compelled me to do the same. She waited for me to catch up and join her near the corner of the building.

"Leave your things here. I will have them sent up to your room," the woman ordered.

I placed the bags on the ground as quietly as I could, ever present of how much I trespassed on the mansion's strict code of silence. She beckoned me to follow her to the ornamental garden. As my eyes adjusted to the light, I noticed a solitary man sitting on a stone bench overlooking the sculptures and dormant hedges.

"Did you ever doubt me?" Green noticed our arrival.

I remained mute and closed the distance as slowly as I could. When I arrived at the bench, I saw that he was clutching a large leather-bound book. His eyes pierced the darkness though they had little difference in color to their surroundings.

"It appears the nice little God of the Christians hasn't willed you to die yet," Green set the book aside and invited me to sit.

I approached the bench but he recoiled.

"Not there," he gave me a look of deep offense.

Looking around, I saw nothing else to sit on. I reluctantly sat on the cold earth a few feet away from Green. The woman took her place on the bench next to him and kissed his neck passionately. The host was entirely unperturbed by this action and continued looking stoically at the gardens. She stopped and sat upright, carefully checking to see if I was jealous. I averted eye contact.

I sat as some kind of house pet by the bench for what seemed like hours. Green punctuated the silence by periodically picking up the book and rocking back and forth while he read it. There was something much different about him this time. He was both more confident and unsure. Entertaining both ideas as equals, Green held stability in one hand and upheaval in the other. He was like a great general, certain in the success of a coup but shaken by the prospect.

"After your episode in Norfolk," Green broke the silence, "you've been quite reliable."

I said nothing as I sat on the cold grass. I worried that if I sat there too long, I'd grow roots and become one of his statues in the garden. A cold wind caused me to shiver.

"I always remember those who do what they are told," he turned to face me. "For this reason, I've permitted you to stay at my estate while this trouble with the board blows over."

Green paused as if waiting to see if I would thank him.

The woman piped up instead. "You've been very gracious to Mr. Malden."

"You're saying it's going to blow over?" I spoke for the first time since the airport.

The host grabbed the book and took a deep breath. "Your time in the Navy is over. Long over."

He stood up and began to wander aimlessly in the garden while motioning for the woman and I to follow behind.

"But your time with me is just beginning, Mr. Malden. I foresee a bright path ahead if you manage to stay in line."

The air grew heavy and thick. My walking became labored like I was trudging through heavy snow. Green led us deeper and deeper into the garden until we came to the entrance of a maze.

"I've arranged for something of a test," the host caressed the face of a female statue before snapping his eyes to my own. "I know the visions that haunt you. How much would you like them to stop?"

My breathing became shallow. "At what cost?"

Green lit a torch he retrieved from beside the statue with a lighter concealed in his jacket, revealing the smile of a dangerous predatory beast.

"How perceptive you've become," he handed the light source to me.

I reluctantly took the torch in my hand; its warmth was a hollow comfort amid the spiritual cold of the mansion's grounds.

"But something tells me you'd do almost anything to never see it again," Green presumed correctly. "You see, this is what I want for you as well."

"We're really on your side," the woman's green and blue eyes flashed in the light of the fire.

"If you pass through the maze and emerge on the other side," he motioned to the exit only a few feet away, "He'll never find you again. He'll be lost in the labyrinth along with the others."

I felt a cold mass of air emanating from the maze. The temptation to enter grew by the second. Anything, even service to Green, was preferable to the constant torment of Sloan. I took slow, hesitant steps toward the entrance while the host watched me carefully.

"Go on, Mr. Malden," Green pointed to the path. "Truth is a quarrelsome and rotten thing, after all."

THE LABYRINTH

I must relay with great shame how briefly I contemplated my options. Sloan had pushed me too far. I had to get away. I had to make it all go away. Even if it meant a lifetime of servitude to Green, I needed some kind of respite from the horrific visions that tortured me.

When I entered the maze, I briefly looked back at my prospective master and the woman. She had a look of rapturous joy over me choosing to enter the labyrinth. As I rounded a corner in the dark hedges, I saw a long pathway open up before me. The moon was just barely providing enough illumination before a dense fog rolled in. My torch sputtered before pathetically going out. I discarded the item shortly after.

The mist was ice cold and left a coating of condensation on whatever it touched. Curiously, I was be able to see more than before, at least at closer distances. The maze was lined with gravel which made loud crunches as I inched through the fog.

"Malden!" A voice echoed in the labyrinth. "Malden, you coward! Where are you?"

I froze and looked around in fear. The only things visible were the hedgerows on either side of me and the ground below.

"Malden . . ." he called out once more. "I'll find you and make you pay!"

Sloan's voice was getting closer. I did my best to walk faster through the long corridor with my arms outstretched. I glanced over my shoulder just before stumbling into the thorny hedge. I disentangled my clothes and saw that the path split at a T.

"There you are!"

I saw his silhouette approaching out of the mist. As he got closer, visions like I had never had before danced before me. I broke into an all-out sprint deeper and deeper into the maze. I made random turns and loops in an effort to lose my pursuer. Finally, his haunting cries were far away. The visions were gone again. I stopped to catch my breath briefly before resuming my journey. The fog lifted slightly, and I could see much farther than I could before. The cold never left, however.

As I rounded the next corner, I froze dead in my tracks. A man was sitting on a concrete bench doing his best to look through the mist at the sky above. He noticed me before I could retreat back around the corner.

"Habibi," he shouted to me. "How long have you been here? I have not seen you before."

I decided to run the other direction anyway. I came to a series of switchbacks before entering a large courtyard. The man was there too.

"I see. You're trying to shake the visions," he approached. "Ya sadeeqi, you cannot do it."

I stood frozen and clenched my teeth.

"They never let me look away," the man drew nearer with each crunching step on the gravel, "Here let me show you."

"No, no!" I tried to get away. "I don't want to see!"

At once I was trapped in his memories. Just as Sloan recounted to me, I saw his son, the IDF soldiers, and the helicopter. As the vision progressed, I saw the unspeakable torture of both his son and the boy. He depicted much more vivid detail than Sloan. I was shown every last needle and every last puncture amidst the cries of anguish.

"Look!" He grabbed hold of me. "You cannot look away!"

I broke free of his grasp and ran deeper into the maze. I gave up all hope of getting out. I just wanted to get away. Whether he pursued me, I couldn't tell. I weaved a tapestry of panic with my path through the labyrinth. As I was running, a hand reached out and grasped my shoulder. The figure spun me around and was only an inch or two from my face. From my peripherals, I could tell he was wearing a military uniform and body armor.

"So, you're the next one, hmm?" His thick Israeli accent formed a grotesque staccato.

I pushed him away and stumbled back. "Get away from me!"

"You're staying," the man walked after me, "You're going to love it!" he said with a sadistic bent.

I shoved him away once more.

"Yes, fight! Fight some more," he mocked. "You'll break soon enough."

We heard the encroaching sound of a helicopter. A rope dropped down through the mist and dangled between us. We both lunged for the apparent lifeline and wrestled with each other. Finally, the man managed to get the rope around my neck and fasten it tightly. He shouted something in Hebrew and the helicopter gained altitude quickly. I started choking violently as I was lifted higher and higher. I reached up and managed to grab the rope and pull myself up a little to relieve the pressure. When I got above the fog, I saw the boy. He was screaming in misery as the recording of the German female played. His form was enormous as if his presence hung like a storm system over the whole continent. The sound of his shrieks vibrated deep in my chest. I started to cry out in turn as my hands became fatigued.

Suddenly, the rope went limp. I fell back into the fog as the vision of the boy was obscured once again. While it felt like I had been dropped from a great height, the impact was no worse than jumping off the roof of a car. I still called out in pain when I hit the ground out of anticipation. The rest of the rope followed after me and coiled like a snake by my leg. Finally, the bitter end tumbled to earth. After some harried pulling, I got the loop off my neck. It had left quite the burn on my skin, but otherwise I was physically unharmed.

I was hopelessly lost before the hellish airlift, but now I was even more so. I sat on the gravel for a moment. I deeply regretted my decision to enter the abyssal labyrinth.

"How many others are there?" I whispered to myself while looking up at the impenetrable fog.

I realized there was no way out except to keep going deeper into the heart of darkness. I was reminded of being trapped in the supply closet at the Pentagon, both by this realization and the fact the pathway led into a tunnel of hedges. I looked in the other direction and saw a silhouette approaching rapidly. I ducked into the tunnel and was shrouded in total shadow.

Not even the fog permeated through the thorny arches above me. As I shuffled anxiously into the throat of some unknown beast, the ceiling became lower the deeper I went. I was reduced to a crawl before finally having to slither along the ground. The surface transitioned from gravel to concrete as I came up against a corner. I contorted my body through the Z-shaped intersection and observed an amber light at the far end of the tunnel. My heart sank when I realized where I was. I knew the space was too narrow to turn around.

I gasped in terror when I was grabbed roughly by the ankles. Instead of pulling back to the maze, the unknown entity pushed me forward. I cried out in pain as my skin and clothes ripped in equal measure. I was propelled deeper into the tunnels until I reached where the vent opened above me. That same sickly green light filtered through the grates onto my horror-stricken eyes. I turned to see what had pushed me through the tunnels. The slats of light from the vent darted across Sloan's face. A burning hatred filled his countenance.

"You think you can take the easy way out?" he chastised.

I shook my head as the tears began flowing once more. "I need it to stop!"

"You think you get to just pull the ejection handle instead of going out like a man?" Sloan shoved me violently.

"I've been offered a way. Wouldn't you take it?" I pleaded.

He stepped back into the darkness and faded away.

"Sloan?" I called out.

I received no response except some kind of shuffling above me. I tried to exit back through the tunnels, but the opening was nowhere to be found. I gingerly put my face up to the grate and tried to look into the decontamination room. Suddenly, the vent was removed and an individual wearing a hazmat suit pulled me up from the space. There were three others in similar garb. Their faces were unknowable due to their tinted visors. One of them hit a switch on the wall. A mechanical whirring began just before I was doused with a high-pressure stream of water. The flow stung the cuts and abrasions on my skin, and I howled in pain. The others set about removing my clothes and putting me in a hospital gown. I was dizzy and limp from the aggravation of my wounds. Once they picked me up, they carried me over to the door to the engine room.

"No!" I called out in a muffled tone. "Don't take me in there!"

The rushing of the positive pressure inside the room sandblasted the very core of my being. As the door opened, I noticed the bed where the boy ought to be was empty. I began screaming and writhing like I never had before. I slipped out of my gown and scrambled naked down the hallway past the decontamination chamber. The suited pursuers ran after me with outstretched arms. I was filled with such terror and adrenaline that it felt like my hips were going to shake out of their sockets. The sound of my bare feet made a pitter patter on the linoleum floor of the hallway that resembled the dropping of rotten, unharvested produce from the vine. I rounded a corner and discovered a series of doorways. Using up what precious lead time I had, I checked the handles to see if any were open. Just as I managed to open one of the doors, the squeaking arrival of my pursuers' rubber boots compelled me to enter and lock the handle behind me. They shook and battered on the door as I cowered in complete darkness apart from the sickly light leaking through the frame.

"God, get me out of here!" I called to heaven in a last-ditch appeal.

I continued backing away from the door as the group's efforts to follow me intensified. A brief hiatus was followed by enormous impacts on the barrier by what sounded like a battering ram. Each blow let more light into the room as the gaps between the door and its frame widened. I put my hands up to my mouth in a rapidly strangling sense of dread while I continued stepping backward. Just as the door flew off the hinges, the floor gave out beneath me. I tumbled through branches and thorns until I was deposited panting and soaked in sweat onto the gravel floor of the maze.

I let out a series of panicked yelps before I realized the suited pursuers could not follow. I sat for a moment in the tortured, frigid silence of the labyrinth. I looked down and saw I was wearing the same clothes as when I had entered. I shakily got on my feet and started walking again. With a leap of joy, I saw an opening in both the hedges and the fog. I could see Green and the woman waiting patiently.

"I made it!" I cried and broke out into a run. "I made it!"

When I crossed the threshold of the opening, I collapsed on the ground. My airways hurt from the blind sprint, but intense relief washed over me.

"What do you think you're doing?" Green shook his head.

I looked up at him with a crazed grin. "It's over! I made it through."

He sighed deeply and told me to get up. "Look where you just came out of," Green compelled.

Pangs of fear started to return and swelled into unbreakable dismay when I stood up and viewed the maze. I had stumbled back out of the entrance.

"Back in you go."

BACKSTABBER

I pleaded and begged until at last Green slapped me across the face.

"Be quiet!" he pointed in my face, "You failed! You're done!"

Even though I knew the consequences of my choice, the verdict shook me anyway.

The woman wrinkled her nose in disgust at me. "I can't believe you, Malden," she hissed.

I sank to my knees and looked back at the path through the maze. The exit stood only a few feet to the right mocking my inability to find it from the other side.

Green started to walk away but turned toward me once more. "You had such promise!" he let a rare slip of emotion.

I could sense he was under a fair amount of stress.

Green continued, "Because you couldn't handle a little bit of discomfort, I will see to it you rot in a cell one way or another! You'll never see the light of day again—only four walls and the company of innumerable needles."

At last, his tirade was finished. He returned to the stone bench where I first found him and read once more from his book. Green periodically looked up to the stars as if checking their progress. The woman's repulsion turned to grief as she walked me toward the garage.

"Richard," she started coolly. "Can I call you Richard?"

My mind was too awash with adrenaline to answer.

She continued as we trudged in the cold autumn night. "I do wish you'd go back. I so very dearly wish you'd stay with us."

I looked into her disparately colored eyes with curiosity. "I won't be staying here?"

The woman flipped to disgust again. "You coward! I hope you rot!"

She continued to berate me all the way until I reached the loft. She unlocked the door and shoved me inside. The woman hovered for a moment on the threshold thinking about coming in. Finally, she shook her head and slammed the door. I heard her curse me as she locked it from the outside. The lights in the loft lingered for another few seconds before cloaking me once more in darkness. I laid back on the floor right where I stood and whimpered. The visions I had been subjected to in the labyrinth were even more terrible than anything I had seen. As I laid limp on the floor, I paused to remember that my BOI was the next day. That was the least of my worries. I didn't bother prepping my uniform or rehearsing what I would say. My mind had been packed to the brim with abominations beyond my wildest nightmares.

"How dare you, Malden!" another voice bellowed, joining the accusing chorus.

I scrambled to get up and saw Sloan sitting on the couch, smoking as always.

"You backstabber!" he stood up and approached me menacingly, "I went so easy on you, and this is how you repay me? You were going to trap me in there! I was just going to wander that maze for all eternity because of you."

"But I didn't make it out," I bargained with a tremor in my voice.

"But you tried, Richard," Sloan materialized directly in front of my face.

I did try. I was fully willing to sell him and anyone else I needed to down the river to get a moment's rest from the torment.

"You've been trying to get me to kill myself for your relief!" I counter-accused.

Sloan became incensed. "So then you're dead! You were going to send me to hell!"

"You're already going to hell," I muttered.

He became filled with an otherworldly rage. Sloan grabbed me by the neck and forced me to the ground. "I'll show you hell," he hissed.

&⁊&

"And that's just what he did," Richard lamented, "All night, over and over again. Vision after vision, nightmare after nightmare. There was no respite until morning when the woman came to collect me and drive to my board."

Edwards listened intently. He let a small shimmer of empathy cross his face.

"Doesn't he get it, though?" he shook his head in dismay, "He'd end up in that maze with the others anyway."

Richard looked up with a confused look.

Edwards continued, "The Jordanian, the IDF soldier, who know how many others—they all ended up there even after they were supposedly released."

The captive sat back in apprehension. "So, that means I will end up there too."

The man across from him lowered his tone. "If you help me, I will make sure that never happens."

"How could you possibly do that?" Richard pursed his lips and gestured flippantly.

"We're going to put a stop to this," the militant made a fist and shook it confidently. "By God's grace and power, we'll put an end to all of this."

The captive, formerly interested in what he had to say, slumped back in his chair at the mention of God.

Disappointed in Richard's reaction, Edwards pressed on. "We're almost at the end of your story. Just keep going."

THE HEARING

On our drive to NSA Washington, the woman got a call, presumably from Green. After she hung up, we made an abrupt course change.

"Where are we going?" I asked impotently from the back seat.

I had attempted to sit in the front per her previous request, but the woman forbade it with contempt. She made no reply to my question besides a look in the rearview mirror that communicated an incongruous mix of desire and hatred. After an additional twenty minutes on the Beltway, I realized with trepidation where our new destination was.

"Last minute change of venue," the woman spat her words. "Green said you'd be more comfortable here."

The sight of the Pentagon crushed what was left of my battered soul. From the road, it appears to most as an enormous office building. To my eyes, however, it was a rotating blade obliterating and lacerating the fragile cords tethering me to sanity. I began breathing rapidly as she pulled up just outside the gate.

"Get out," she snarled.

I was frozen in place. The woman resorted to getting out of the sedan and dragging me out. The gate guards looked on in amused bewilderment. I stumbled a few steps before gathering the wherewithal to put on my cover. I was wearing what was left of my dress blues for the rotten occasion. The woman softened her demeanor and approached me. Her hands drifted to my lapels as she straightened my uniform jacket. The woman's green and blue eyes met mine as they shined two natures in the early morning sun.

"Get away from me!" the woman pushed me harshly and returned to the sedan.

When the door closed behind her, the tinted window obscured my view of her face. She made a rapid turn before speeding once again toward the Beltway. In my beleaguered state, I had developed something resembling a sick attachment to her as she had to me.

"Trouble with the missus?" the gate guard prodded when I approached on foot.

"Among other things," I stared at the Pentagon with a hollow gaze.

It was 0800 and my BOI wasn't until 0900. I had time to find the room and get acclimated to the space. I knew they had selected NSA Washington to make my board a public spectacle. The move to the Pentagon was perplexing for the Navy's motives but entirely predictable for Green's. I knew he intended to unsettle me ahead of my hearing. My awareness of this fact had no effect on my reaction. Every step closer I took to the doors heralded new anxieties.

The second I got inside, everyone in the building was strangely aware of me. Hushed whispers and sneers followed me throughout the colossal structure. I asked around where the BOI was and eventually found a large conference room capable of seating fifty or so people somewhere on the third floor of B-Ring. I sat meekly in a row of chairs outside the door. There were still another thirty minutes before the charade was to start.

As I watched the nameless streams of people pass by, I became unsettled by a low wheezing I heard from a nearby vent. I had mostly been able to avoid the fact I was in the physical location of that horrific vision. The sound brought it home in the worst possible way. I looked around to see if anyone else noticed the noise. Everyone went about their day as normal. Suddenly, a doddering flock of captains and admirals showed up. They each gave me look of varying levels of disdain before filing like ducklings into the room. After this group, a spattering of officers of various ranks and services filed in. Lastly, a petty officer sporting a video camera and a notepad slunk past me into the room.

At last, the hour of my board arrived. The wheezing in the vents stopped for a moment before I was called to enter the room. All eyes were planted firmly on my sunken face as I made my way to the small table between the two sections of seating. In front of me was a wide table with the panel of senior officers I saw earlier. They were all shuffling through papers seemingly without direction in the hopes of giving the show trial some air of legitimacy. The petty officer with the camera pressed a button, and a red light indicated the whole affair was ready to begin. I stood stiffly at attention until the admiral at the center of the table motioned for me to sit down. A nameplate in front of him read VADM Mike Kellum.

"LCDR Malden," he began with an officious tone, "you have been summoned to this Board of Inquiry to determine if the results of the preliminary report regarding alleged behavior of racism, bigotry, and conduct unbecoming of an officer are founded. Do you understand?"

I settled into my chair just as the wheezing resumed at a deafening volume.

"Do you understand?" Kellum repeated.

"Yes sir," I managed before shooting a nervous glance at the air vent on the wall to my right.

"Captain Blake," the admiral looked over his reading glasses at the officer at the far end of the table, "the floor is yours for questioning."

Captain Blake was an obese woman wearing a maternity uniform, though I suspected she wore that cut regardless of if anyone was unlucky enough to impregnate her.

"Mr. Malden," she wiped away sweat from her brow, "what is your view of women in the US Navy?"

I closed my eyes for a moment and tried to drown out the racket coming from the grate.

"Ma'am," I began shakily while my eyes darted to the vent, "I believe—"

A loud cough erupted from one of the audience members, causing me to startle and lose my train of thought.

"Are you quite alright?" CAPT Blake put a chubby hand on the table.

"Yes ma'am," I regained a small modicum of composure. "I believe that women can contribute just as much to the mission of the Navy as men."

I elected to kowtow. My smallest, fleeting chance of escaping Green was to possibly be retained by the Navy. I knew he could still harm me and my career, but I held to some hope that the institution might protect me at the end of the day.

Blake appeared satisfied with my answer and continued. "When you were on the bridge with CAPT Fowler, did you ever distrust her judgment?"

I clenched my teeth and tried to come up with an acceptable response. All the while, the labored respiration filled my eardrums.

"Per the safe shipboard principles, I always placed a high degree of importance on forceful backup." I spewed a semi-believable answer.

The obese woman, however, was unconvinced. "You didn't answer the question."

The wheezing grew to an unbearable volume. I began to sweat in the stifling layers of my dress blues. The sound seemed to be amplified directly into the nerves connecting my ears to my brain.

"There was a time when I logged an official—"

Another cough caused me to jump.

I suddenly became acutely aware of everyone's eyes on me. My gaze wandered around the room while the sound grated my soul.

"Mr. Malden," the admiral in charge of the hearing frowned, "do you have somewhere else to be?"

"Sir," I wiped my brow, "is it possible for us to close those vents?" I pointed all around the room while the attendees shook their heads in disbelief.

"The vents, Mr. Malden?" the admiral stared at me with incredulity.

I attempted to loosen my collar and make a reasonable reply. Instead, words failed me altogether.

The admiral scoffed and directed one of the sailors at the back to comply. The room sat in pregnant silence while the vents were closed. I, on the other hand, continued my unwilling soak in the hellish noise. With each grate closing, the volume lessened slightly. I wiped my brow once more as the sailor took care of the final vent. At last, the ghastly noise was reduced to a low hum just above the register of what I could perceive.

"More comfortable now?" the admiral sputtered.

"Yes sir," I replied.

Blake resumed her questioning. "You were in the middle of telling me about an official disagreement you had with CAPT Fowler. Recount it for the board."

I nodded meekly and took a deep breath before telling the story of Sloan's death to the best of my recollection.

"Is that really how you're going to spin it?" a voice said with disdain in my right ear.

I turned slightly and noticed Sloan standing just over my shoulder.

"Tell them what really happened," he prodded.

Reluctantly, I acquiesced to his demands. After all, painting Fowler in a positive light and myself as a newly reformed respecter of women could bode well for me. "Ladies and Gentleman," my voice fluttered, "that was my original story. After much reflection, I've come to the conclusion that I was in the wrong."

"So, you think Captain Fowler made the right decision regarding MM3 Sloan?" another captain interjected.

"Careful how you answer this one, backstabber," he took a step forward and lowered his face to be even with mine. He stared with murderous intent at me while I tried to pretend nothing was wrong.

"Sir, I believe proper procedure was followed."

Sloan shook his head and straightened up.

The admiral in charge flipped through some papers on the table. The tortured respiration returned at an even louder volume. "I've called your former CO, Vice Admiral Kevin Simmons, to answer a few questions," he waved his hand at the sailor by the door.

The underling complied and escorted Simmons to the table next to mine. He shot me a contemptuous glance before taking his seat.

"Thanks for coming down." Kellum gave Simmons a moment to settle in before asking, "What was your relationship to LCDR Malden?"

The rotund senior officer glanced at me briefly before answering, "LCDR Malden was an executive assistant for my office briefly before the conflict with China."

"Was there anything about his demeanor that indicated he was intolerant of others not like himself?" Kellum clicked a pen and sat poised to take notes.

Simmons adjusted his jacket then continued. "As a matter of fact, there was."

He recounted my outburst at Katz, and my apparent lack of professional demeanor toward him. I would have been enraged at his account if I could pay attention. I shut my eyelids tightly several times. Despite the closed vents, the rising and falling of the dreadful breathing found a resonant frequency in my skull. The noise reverberated in the space my brain should've been as I put two closed fists up to my head in anguish. My eyes darted to and fro in the conference room looking for any kind of relief or escape.

"Mr. Malden, are you covering your ears?" The admiral let a hand go limp on the table making a tremendous boom in his microphone.

I blinked rapidly and tried to answer. "No sir, just . . ."

"Just what? Are we boring you?" another senior officer on the panel interjected.

"My apologies," was all I could manage.

Admiral Kellum exchanged an offended look with the rest of the panel before proceeding. "Thank you VADM Simmons, that will be all," he dismissed.

Simmons to chuckled at me as he waddled away from the table. I was breathing rapidly and looked visibly disturbed.

"Let's take a five-minute break," Kellum half rolled his eyes and shuffled some papers around for effect.

Everyone got up to stretch their legs or use the bathroom. Hushed chatter filled the room as the gawkers speculated about my bizarre behavior. The sailor with the video camera was loving it. The frazzled racist cowering before the noble arms of neoliberal power made for great propaganda.

I rushed out of the room to find a water fountain. The sound of the breathing was muffled in the hallways by the streams of personnel going about their business. After taking a long drink, I noticed a group of service members sneaking pictures of me with their phones and sneering. All too soon, the five minutes was up. I reluctantly returned to my chair as the room quieted down. The tortured respiration remained.

"Let's get this show back on the road," Kellum put on a folksy act. "Rear Admiral Jones, the floor is yours for questions."

Jones' black eyes muddled over a piece of paper for a moment before venturing to look into mine. "Do I offend you, Mr. Malden?" he opened his salvo of questions.

"No sir," I replied in between the hellish breaths.

"Would you describe me as a . . . ?"

He paused to put on reading glasses and looked at what I assumed to be the preliminary report to make a point.

". . . a miscreant?"

"No sir," I repeated mechanically.

Shortly after replying, I heard a soul-rending scream emanate from every gap in the vents. Every synapse in my brain saturated with an unquenchable dread. I started to shake while trying to keep a veneer of sanity, desperately holding out for the end of the shriek. No matter how long I waited, the volume only increased. My ears started to ring from the ever growing strength of the noise. At last, I broke.

"Make it stop! Somebody please make it stop!"

When I opened my eyes, I found myself standing with my hands over my ears. The conference room was in a shocked silence. The scream subsided as well, but the labored breathing remained. I found my own panicked respirations rising and falling in phase with the horrific noise.

"Malden, what on earth is wrong with you?" Kellum took off his glasses and raised his volume.

With trembling legs, I slumped back into my seat unable to reply. CAPT Blake leaned over in her chair and whispered something in the admiral's ear. He shot a few confused glances at me while she talked. After a short period of time, he nodded.

"Five-minute recess while the board confers," Kellum shooed everyone out of the room.

I ran to the bathroom to vomit. A few individuals pounded on the door of my stall with malice.

"So, you can talk a big game until the hammer drops?" One of them mocked.

"I guess you're about to find out," another joined in.

I heaved once more into the toilet. All the while, the sound of the breathing grew louder. I managed to stand up, flush the toilet, wipe my face, and return to the room in the time allotted.

"LCDR Malden," Kellum took a grave tone, "It's obvious you're under some kind of distress. We've decided to suspend this Board of Inquiry until a full psychological evaluation can be completed. Given how obvious your psychological state is, I am shocked they didn't order one for the preliminary report."

"I am not crazy!" I burst out.

The room erupted in laughter.

"None of you get it!" I put my face in my hands. "You have no idea!"

"I'm going to have you transferred for observation to Walter Reed at least overnight," Kellum commanded. "Once they've given you a full round-up, we can resume the BOI."

After a short while, the audience filed out of the room, content they had seen their fill of entertainment for the day. The sailor with the camera, however, was displeased with the turn of events. His propaganda career-making film was ruined by the offender just being a simple lunatic. I was sure he could salvage something though. The breathing quieted down to a low hush. Sloan shook his head with a derisive smile as he sat in one of the chairs along the wall.

The news managed to extract another ounce of terror from my fatigued mind. I was grateful for my time in the Pentagon to be suspended for now, but the prospect of getting prodded by "mental-health professionals" sent my head spinning. I knew I wouldn't be able to squeeze through the system unscathed. After a short while, an MP entered the room to escort me out of the building. I was met with disdain and haughty remarks throughout the whole of the facility until we exited into a light autumn rain. When the door closed behind us, at last the breathing went silent.

THE PROPHECY

The MP brought me to a group of white vans where a duty driver stood milling about. She was a marine private first class with tightly slicked black hair and a sour expression. The MP instructed her to bring me to Walter Reed and escort me to the mental health wing.

"Keep an eye on him," he whispered conspicuously. "He's nuts."

The marine shot a nervous glance in my direction and nodded. She directed me to get into the back seat of the van. I wordlessly complied. The whole drive to the hospital, the woman eyed me warily, as if I was going to pounce at any moment. I had no intentions of escape or resistance. The only thing I could do was try to salvage what was left of my sanity before seeing a white coat.

When we got to Walter Reed, the marine briskly exited the vehicle and ordered me to do the same. The imposing concrete tower at the center of the complex stood as a prism, refracting what sunlight that made it through the clouds into uncanny frequencies. The woman handed me off to a nurse and egressed from the building as quickly as possible. The nurse brought me through a series of hallways until we arrived at room with a window facing the parking lot. She told me I could keep my uniform on, but everything with a sharp edge would need to be taken off. I watched in understated disappointment as I handed her my ribbon rack, the expression of so many of my former accomplishments. She unceremoniously put it in a plastic bag along with my name tag, wallet, and phone.

"Oh, and your shoelaces too," she stopped just before leaving.

I bore up with the indignity without a word. I wondered why they didn't just put me in a straightjacket and be done with it. The window was conspicuously riveted closed, just like the ones in Bancroft Hall at the Naval Academy. I remembered coming to Walter Reed as a plebe. I had passed out from a raging fever as the result of a strange viral infection that swept its way through the brigade of midshipmen. Until now, the profuse sweating and shooting body aches of that sickness was one of the worst agonies I had experienced. In my newest, foremost malady, I returned once more to Walter Reed all these years later.

After a short time, the door opened. The woman from the mansion slipped in and closed the door behind her. Her bobbed hair sat neatly over a pilfered lab coat. She took a seat across from me and crossed her legs.

"Oh Richard," the woman started with a sympathetic tone, "I hate to see you like this."

I crossed my arms and made no reply.

"But you understand, right?" the woman got up to look out the window. "You did this to yourself."

"How do you reckon that?" I contested.

The woman's green eye caught a sojourning glimmer of sunshine before it retreated in the shadow of a cloud again.

"You should've gone back into the maze," she tapped on the window sill with perfectly manicured fingernails. "Instead you're here." The woman returned to looking outside. "I begged him not to change the venue. I knew it would lead you here."

I was in the car when she received the call. I knew she didn't protest even a word.

"Why don't you guys just kill me and get it over with?" I looked up at the drop ceiling tiles.

Suddenly, I found my neck being constricted by her arachnoid fingers. Her sharp nails dug into my skin.

"Because it is not permitted!" she hissed into my ear.

I tried to pry away her hands but the woman's strength was belied by her spindly form. Finally she relented and took a step back, as if in shock at what she had done.

"So, I suppose this is goodbye," the woman conjured a tear. "I will miss you."

I rubbed my neck as the shock subsided. She left the room with a soft touch on my shoulder. Only a few minutes later, a real doctor entered the space. He immediately noticed the marks on my neck. In a panic, he looked at his clipboard.

"When did that happen?" the doctor pointed at the red ring and fingernail marks. "It's not on your intake paperwork."

Without giving me time to answer, he poked his head into the hallway to call for backup. "Self-harm!" he called out.

In a few seconds, an absurd number of nurses and orderlies rushed into the room. Each one placed their hands on me to restrain any movement as they moved me to the bed. The sudden rush of stimulation and restriction caused me to panic. I thrashed violently as yet more nurses came in to assist. The doctor prepared a syringe and put a stop to the imbroglio.

I awoke in another room restrained to my bed. I was wearing a hospital gown now. The space was without windows or color. Just a harsh, buzzing fluorescent light presided. As I awoke out of the drug-induced haze, the gravity of the situation set in. I was trapped in more ways than one. Anything I said or did would be passed through the lens of a self-fulfilling prophecy of their impression of my insanity. I tugged at the restraints but they were cinched down tight. I assumed I was being monitored, so I didn't do this for very long. After fifteen minutes of me being awake, the door opened. It was just beyond my field of view as my head was strapped in place.

When the figure approached, I saw that it was Sloan. I did my best to ignore him, but he stood close to the bed.

"You think you're the only one who can make deals?" he leaned down and spoke directly in my ear. "I can play that game too."

I remained silent, though my heart pounded.

"I know. Damned if you talk to me," Sloan chuckled. "Damned if you don't. Since you seem so unable to speak, just listen."

I clawed at the palms of my hand with my fingernails to try to distract myself.

"Mr. Green and I had a lovely conversation. You know, he's the first one besides your sorry self I've been able to talk to since my death? He's a very special, powerful individual. We've struck a deal of sorts. I no longer want you to kill yourself," Sloan informed as he paced to the foot of the bed.

I strained my eyes to look down but could just see the top of his head.

"Don't get too excited," he shifted his weight in my peripheral vision. "My program for you hasn't changed. Green didn't need to do much convincing. You almost trapping me in that maze was enough. Now I get to make you pay for that. I'm going to take immense pleasure in making sure you live as long and as miserable of a life here."

I struggled at my bonds once more. My heart beat rapidly in concert with my breathing.

"I've stumbled into the fountain of youth, Malden," he approached the bedside and looked me directly in the eyes. "And you're the wellspring."

"Get away!" I at last broke my silence.

Sloan laughed, "Oh would you rather see something else?"

I thrashed and screamed while the orderlies rushed in. Though they tried to sedate me, the visions commenced nonetheless. Through it all, Sloan snickered and whooped.

"Get 'em boys!" he called out. "He's gonna be here a while!"

My eyelids felt leaden as my limbs went limp.

I awoke in a different room with my arms bound to my side. I sat in a reclining chair in a wood-paneled office. I looked to my right and saw an older man sitting at an ornate cherry wood desk. He had slender glasses and a notepad, pen poised to write the next chapter of my life.

"State your name, please," the man instructed.

I closed my eyes tightly for a second before turning in the chair to face him. "Richard Malden."

He looked at me incredulously, then scribbled something on his notepad. "I am Doctor Montgomery," he stated as if for the record.

I nodded carefully and prepared for what might come next.

Montgomery leaned over and pressed a button on his desk phone. "Janice, come in here and undo Mr. Malden's restraints," he tilted his head courteously in my direction with a small grin.

A moment later, a nurse came in and set my arms free. I stretched them out and rubbed my shoulders. A terrible stiffness in my neck had set in. Once the nurse left, the doctor got up from his desk and sat on the couch a few feet away from my chair.

"Are you reasonably comfortable?" Montgomery asked.

"I- I suppose so," I stumbled.

He adjusted his weight on the couch before crossing his legs. Montgomery rested the notepad on his lap while twirling the pen. "Richard, I believe this is all a big misunderstanding," he began. "I looked through your service record. You were under enemy fire shortly before your relief from command, correct?"

"Yes," I stated.

Montgomery nodded and wrote once more. "And do you suffer from nightmares?"

"I do."

"How often?" he peered over his glasses.

A sound startled me. I noticed Sloan rushing into the room and plopping on the couch next to Montgomery. "Sorry I'm late," he put his arms behind his head and grinned lasciviously, "You would not believe the things I've been getting to do."

The doctor noticed the jolt and my gaze follow apparently nothing to the couch. "Richard?" he asked, "What just came into the room?"

"Nothing, sorry. I just got distracted." I tried to ignore the observer.

Montgomery lowered his brow. "Distracted by what?"

I sputtered to think of an answer.

"Go on, Richy, tell him," the man next to the doctor jeered.

"I just . . . I've been under a lot of stress from this whole affair," I clenched my teeth and attempted to slow my breathing.

Montgomery appeared to be genuinely well-meaning. Unfortunately, I knew he would unwittingly become my jailer. "That's very understandable," he ran his fingers through his greying hair. "But I'm having trouble understanding something."

My eyes lifted from the floor to meet his.

"Why did you need the vents closed at your board?" He started to chew on the end of his pen as he moved his glasses to the top of his head.

I managed to create a somewhat believable alibi. "I was cold. I just came from California where it was a lot warmer."

Sloan waved at me and pointed to the vent above. In short order, I began to hear the low rasping again.

Montgomery nodded along. "But why did you cover your ears and then have that outburst about making it stop?"

I did my best to keep my eyes firmly planted on the doctor. I knew this was my last chance to not appear unhinged before I would be locked away forever.

"It's like you said," I played along. "The stress of the attack really got to me."

Montgomery lowered his glasses and wrote vigorously in his pad. "I think I am starting to get a clear picture here." he shook his head, "You'd think, after decades of awareness about PTSD, that we'd be treating our veterans a little better than this."

A glimmer of hope scintillated behind my eyes until I noticed Sloan getting up from the couch. He walked behind the doctor like a well-known magician waltzing on stage. I knew exactly what trick he was about to perform.

"Are there any other experiences contributing to the potential PTSD?" Montgomery looked up for a moment.

His gaze met mine just as Sloan wheeled a hospital bed from behind the couch. The boy's slackened jaw hung agape while his piercing, wretched blue eyes started to burn holes in my soul like a magnifying glass capturing the sun's rays. Montgomery waited respectfully for me to reply. In reality, I had forgotten all about his question. Sloan reached down and pressed a button on the side of the hospital bed. In unthinkable waves of anguish and agony, the boy was tormented by the piercing and stabbing. All the while, the tragic victim maintained penetrating eye-contact with me.

"Richard?" Montgomery prompted.

"Yes?"

The sounds of the screams and wails filled the office.

"Are there any other experiences?" he repeated.

"No," I resorted to monosyllabic responses.

Montgomery was unconvinced. "Are you sure?"

"Go ahead, Malden," Sloan walked over to me while the boy writhed. "Tell him everything."

"There's nothing," I said tersely.

"What do you keep looking at over there?"

I snapped, "I said it's nothing!"

Montgomery's good will soured. "It certainly seems like something."

The boy, the noise, the stress, the doctor, the torment, the hospital, the vents, the restraints dangling by my side—I utterly and totally snapped.

"Shut up! Shut up! Shut up!" I yelled at the top of my lungs. "You *really* want to know? Well take a look! Can't you see it? Oh, but you won't believe me, will you?" I stood up and waved my arms wildly to get him to look where the boy was laying. "They're torturing him beneath the Pentagon. I saw it! Sloan led me to it, okay? Is that what you wanted me to say? Well, I suppose there's no point in concealing what everyone knows is there. I already know I've gone mad! I guess it's time reality caught up to me!"

Montgomery sat frozen on the couch with a shocked and grieved expression on his face. He looked at me as if I had just commit suicide right in front of him. A sudden click of the pen sounded the death knell of my freedom. I sank to my seat in dark despair at what I had let slip. Sloan rolled the boy behind the couch and left the room. The doctor averted eye-contact while writing the last strokes of the unalterable prophecy of my fate.

JUDGMENT

"How long were you at Walter Reed in total? Edwards rubbed his eyes. Dark circles, already pronounced, grew deeper on his face.

"Heaven knows," Richard slumped in the chair and looked up at the dark, invisible ceiling. "Do the souls rotting in hell know how long they've been there?"

The guerrilla leader raised his eyebrows. "I suppose not."

"Why did you pull me out?" the captive kept staring blankly above him.

"God told me you were there," Edwards said matter-of-factly. "He told me what you had seen. That's all we knew."

"So, you risked your life and the lives of whoever helped you to pull some random whack job because a voice told you to?" Richard said with a mocking tone. "I don't think Walter Reed was at capacity. Maybe you should've stayed awhile."

"Blasphemer," the militant shook his head. "But the natural man receiveth not the things of the Spirit of God."

Richard rolled his eyes, pounded on the table, and shouted, "Stop it! Stop your quoting! It doesn't mean anything to me!"

"I know," Edwards crossed his arms, "but the truth is always worth speaking."

"There's that word again," the captive got up from his chair and paced angrily at the frontier of the lightbulb's reach. "May this God of yours smite the truth! I want the truth gone. All of it! If I was living a lie before," he swore, "give it back to me. I will swallow it hook, line, and sinker. I don't care if it rots me from the inside out. I will take anything but the truth!"

"Sit down," the guerrilla let him finish his tirade. "We're not finished yet."

Richard walked over and placed his hands on the back of the metal chair. "What else is there to know? That's the end of my story. You know what happened next. You yanked me out of that hell and put me in another one."

Edwards looked around the room. "I don't see anyone tormenting you here."

"That's because you'd have to look in a mirror," the wretch shot back.

His captor pursed his lips and raised his eyebrows. "I suppose I can hand you right back."

"Do it then," Richard said defiantly.

Edwards at once got up from the chair and walked rapidly into the shadows.

The captive panicked as the prospect set in. "Wait! Wait, stop!"

He was met with dim silence as the darkness of the warehouse yawned in his face.

"Edwards?" Richard called out.

A silhouette emerged.

"Edwards!" the captive shrank in terror. "He's back!"

A voice called out, "I need something first."

"What is it?" Richard put up his hands as the figure continued to approach.

"The truth." Edwards rebuked Sloan once more. He motioned for the captive to sit down and took his own seat.

"But I've given you the truth," Richard contested with a trembling voice. "Every last regrettable detail."

"You've told me the truth, yes," the militant put his hands on the table and leaned forward, "but you've not committed to the truth."

His captive slumped his shoulders. "I don't have any energy for cryptic sayings or riddles. Neither do I have anything left to commit."

"There's still your soul, Richard."

"And what's left of that?" he retorted. "Take that boy for instance. Do you really think there's anything left of his soul?"

Edwards lowered his gaze and took a contemplative breath. "I no doubt will incur the wrath of this nation's gods for even uttering this, but my God is greater," he clenched his fist. "That boy, contrary to the designs of his tormentors, has a name. He had an identity, a face, a family. He laughed, cried, and played just like any other boy. He went to his mommy when he got hurt. He got excited when there was a holiday. Through summer, fall, winter, and spring, Helmut Grenzer loved and was loved by others."

The name hung in the air like some unspeakable secret that had been brought out of concealment by a sudden burst of light. Richard's eyes began to well as he thought of the boy in his wretched state.

"And you would join with the architects of his torture in depriving him of that humanity? Of course he has a soul left. They would've disposed of him long ago if he didn't," the militant let a rare gust of emotion take his speech. "You know that recording you heard? The German woman? That was his mother. Hilde Grenzer. She used to write and illustrate children's books before the war."

Edwards pulled another item from his rucksack.

It was a dusty old thing with the title *Durch Anstrengung habe ich meine Sünde überwunden* in colorful block letters adorning its cover over an illustration of a line of children prancing in a row. The man tenderly opened to the first page where a small note was written: "An meinen Sohn Helmut."

"They granted her passage to West Germany if she made the tape. She had no idea what it would be used for. All she knew was that her little Helmut was killed in the firebombing of Dresden. Just nine years old. In reality, he was recovered from the wreckage by a special commando team sent to look for specimens among the flames. These satanic individuals we call our leaders use the recording of his mother to enhance the boy's anguish. Hilde died in 1971 only to find her son was not there to meet her in the afterlife. Whether the recording made Stimulosis more effective—or if it was just for their perverse pleasure—I never knew," Edwards wiped away a tear. "But I won't stomach you telling me he has no soul left. That very soul you profane is what we're going to release to the Father when this is finished."

Richard sat back in amazement. "So, that would make him nearly 100 years old," the captive put a hand over his mouth.

The pair sat in silence as they reflected on the horror still going on at that very moment.

"But you said they were worried about him expiring," Richard inquired. "Why don't we just wait them out? It can't be much longer."

Edwards lifted his gaze to meet Richard's. His eyes were ablaze with the summed agony of ten decades of torture. "I have reason to believe they have located a viable replacement candidate," he said in a hushed tone.

The captive felt a twinge of anxiety course through his veins.

"I don't suppose you know what day it is tomorrow, do you?" Edwards folded his hands.

"No."

The guerrilla leader stood up and paced in the flickering reach of the lightbulb. "It's election day tomorrow," he began. "We are also only a few days after the most sacrosanct day of their demonic calendar. We are in a time of heightened spiritual activity, the highest of the year besides Passover. I believe they are going to be performing a gear change in the engine room very soon. We may already be too late. The only thing that gives me hope that we have more time is that you're still seeing visions of Helmut."

Richard clenched his teeth. "Why not try to end the life of the new candidate?"

Edwards shook his head. "Because I don't have an open door to him." He halted at the table and leaned in, "God has willed me to come into the possession of both the lock and the key for the current specimen. This chance won't come again."

"What do you mean, the lock and the key?" the captive questioned.

"You're going to have to be the one to do it, Richard," Edwards took his seat once more and delivered the news like the strike of a dead blow hammer.

"Do what?"

"You're going to kill the country. This whole artificially sustained machine is going to be deprived of its lifeblood," the guerrilla leader said quietly yet assertively. "I don't have any way to find or access the new candidate. You know as well as I that the access point is not purely physical." His countenance took on a look of grave importance: "It has to be Helmut, and it has to be now."

Malden suppressed a shiver as the weight of the task passed over him like a crashing ocean wave. "What would happen? I mean, if he did die before they could make the swap?"

Edwards clenched his fists and looked to heaven. "There would be such a reckoning on this land as has never been seen in the history of the world."

"But wouldn't they just be able to get the new candidate up and running after some time?" Richard asked impatiently.

The man across from him shook his head. "The sum total of our sins would come due in a moment's notice. It would be as if the parachute worn by a man descending to hell were suddenly cut. There's nothing that could be done to slow the free-fall. Not all the demons on earth or under the earth could even manage that. Take the electrical grid for example. If it was destroyed early, the rebuilding would be easy. If suddenly it were to be taken away today, it would be pandemonium. It is the same with the rewards extracted from Stimulosis. The synthetic arrangement of favors and protection they've concocted built upon itself like a house of cards. If it collapsed, there would be nothing left to salvage. Every last one of us would be touched by the fire, praise be to God." He lowered his hands and looked into Richard's eyes, "Mighty and swift will be the retribution. The nation's suffering will fall on deaf ears in heaven, and I thank the Lord for it. We will deserve every last lash on the whipping pole."

"You're a psychopath," Richard pushed away from the table. "How could you want that for everyone?"

The militant grew frustrated, "There's your disdain for the truth again! Every last one of us has benefitted from Helmut Grenzer's suffering. While we all slept peacefully at night, they tortured him. While we stuffed our faces with food and plenty, he was deprived of all love and affection. While we complained about the mundane travails of modern life, he put roofs over our heads and food on our tables. While we conquered the world and gathered its riches to us, Helmut Grenzer toiled in the basement of the Pentagon. From the youngest to the oldest, knowingly or not, we all have drunk the poisoned chalice of this ghastly arrangement!"

"I thought God was all about forgiveness," the captive sparred.

Edwards lowered his tone. "Many are called but few are chosen. The way is narrow, Richard," he shook his head slowly. "And the debts are coming due very soon."

A different kind of fear ruminated in the captive. It was not the product of mere intimidation or danger but the inexorable gravity of the divine.

"But all that suffering I'd cause," Richard's voice broke with the weight of his words.

"It would be incalculable," Edwards finished his sentence.

The captive looked up at him with anguish. "Isn't that worse than letting them continue?"

"It's all about the truth, Richard." The man replied, "The truth is a concept that knocks the foundation out from under such utilitarian considerations. The so-called greater good often runs contrary to the truth. If we were to minimize suffering in this world, we would also have to maximize lies," he paused for a moment as the statement festered in the captive's brain. "And that's exactly what we've done. I will always choose an uncomfortable truth over a comfortable lie. That's the most important lesson I've learned through this journey."

Richard raised his hands in disbelief. "Thousands would die!"

"Millions," Edwards corrected.

"And all of this will fall on my head," the captive let his arms go limp. "How do you think your God would forgive that?"

"God never punished His prophets for bringing about the destruction of the wicked," the guerrilla leader countered.

"So does that make you or me the prophet?" Richard said with contempt.

Edwards closed his eyes for a moment before continuing. "You've been placed in my path as a sword of God's judgment just as he raised up Nebuchadnezzar or Titus. But you can still join the ranks of heaven if you cease your resisting of the Lord's will."

Malden began to break down. "How is it that a loving God could do this?"

"How is it that a loving God would tolerate this demonic empire any longer? I've wrestled in my prayers over this," Edwards turned his eyes to heaven once more. "How much longer, Lord? Like the martyrs crying out under the altar, I cried, 'How much longer?'" He lowered his eyes to the table. "But, in His divine timing, here we are. I no longer need to ask that question. He has answered me: 'Their foot shall slide in due time; for the day of their calamity is at hand, and the things that shall come upon them make haste.' The time is now."

Richard looked down at the hands that would kill the nation. "Why me?" he yelped.

"He appoints the times and places of our habitation," the militant recited. "Who are we to say to the potter, 'Why me?'"

"You mean to say I don't have a choice," Richard rocked in his chair.

"God's will is inevitable. But He may harden the hearts of men. I pray you are not in the latter state." Edwards gave a look of pleading, "I shudder to think of what would happen to you on the day of judgment if you turn away from this ordained crusade. It is a fearful thing to fall into the hands of the living God."

The captive gripped his chair. "I've read the Bible. I went to Sunday school. I've never heard any pastor or Christian talk like you."

The guerrilla leader nodded slowly. "Your personal disdain for the truth is not unique to you."

Richard's soul became caught in an irresistible pull. He put all his effort into pushing against it. The sum total of the agony he had witnessed, experienced, and caused crumbled in the face of that unstoppable force. The closing noose of judgment constricted his breathing while the weight of his impending task poised at the trapdoor. Every pierce of the needle in Helmut's body lanced Richard's conscience in turn. At last he broke, his face awash with dread and fear of God.

Edwards interrupted his contemplation only for a moment. "You and Jacob Green will share the same cup of wrath stored up by your rejection of the Lord. It has only been through the God's mercy that you do not this moment descend into hell."

The man's soul was brought low. Reflecting on the many times he could have been killed or sent to the abyss, Richard rest his head on the table with his hands up in surrender. "Then what must I do to be saved?"

BAPTISM BY WATER AND FIRE

Edwards directed Richard to wade into the icy waters of a river outside the warehouse. He had spent the last hour praying over the afflicted soul and answering his questions. At last, the former captive, now a brother, trembled amid the churning current. Edwards had taken him out of the warehouse where he discovered they were far out in the country somewhere. The cold autumn night air felt more pure than in the city. Outside of the building was a contingent of four other militants at the ready. They all looked at Richard with a piercing gaze on his way down to the river.

Edwards took hold of him and prepared to administer the rite. Richard looked to heaven and begged for strength and forgiveness. "I baptize you in the name of the Father, the Son, and the Holy Spirit," Edwards said in a cool, rhythmic tone before submerging him in the river.

The frigid water rushed in around Richard. He felt as if a layer of rotten flesh sloughed off his body as new skin emerged. When his head broke the surface of the water again, the man that rose up observed the old self float dead and bloated down the stream.

Edwards embraced him tightly. "Welcome home, brother."

Richard started to shiver violently as the pair waded to the riverbank. The four other militants were waiting for them, their faces aglow.

"The angels in heaven are rejoicing over you," one of them declared.

Another was on his knees with arms stretched to the sky in thanksgiving. Never before in his life had Richard ever seen such an earnest expression of faith. These men could only be described as foreigners to the decadent time they found themselves in. It was as if God had plucked five men from the army outside Jerusalem in 1099 and brought them to that autumn night for a final assault on the ramparts.

Edwards guided Richard back inside and gave him a towel and black combat fatigues to wear. Richard shed the sopping, filthy hospital gown in much the same way he had shed his former life. The visions never left, but they gained a new purpose in his mind. Once he had finished changing, he came out from behind a partition. Edwards had also donned the same garb. The five men were loading up weapons and praying.

"What are you doing?" Richard asked carefully.

"A better question is what are you going to do?" the guerrilla leader slung a rifle over his shoulder. "I have no doubt many of us will become martyrs tonight, but your mission rises above it all."

"I understand what you want me to do," the new initiate sat back down in the chair by the table, his legs shaking from the cold and the adrenaline. "But I don't understand *how?*"

Edwards exchanged a look with one of his men. "Sloan," he said matter-of-factly. "We let him go free. I had bound him in the name of God to stop tormenting you and commanded his spirit to stay in place. For as it is written, 'Whatsoever ye shall bind on earth shall be bound in heaven.' Now, he's off to warn Green that you've escaped."

Richard's eyes widened. "Why would you do that? He'll have all of DC looking for me in a minute!"

"And they'll find you, surely," Edwards motioned for his men to start leaving the building.

"Where are you going? You're just going to leave me here to get captured?" he followed the group outside where a running van was waiting.

"We're going to force Green's hand. If he knows you talked to us, he'll panic and make his move to swap the victims," Edwards said quickly, "Helmut will be vulnerable. Green will be distracted. If you can't put a stop to it all, we'll at least destroy this agent of Satan. Your account has been invaluable. In God's name, we'll come back for you." He shut the sliding door of the van and hopped into the driver's seat. "Your faith is about to be tested. You must remain strong! Be not afraid of them that kill the body, and after that have no more that they can do!"

With this remark, the van sped off on a gravel road that meandered along the river. Richard was left shocked, bemused, and betrayed. The man who had just brought him to the faith was now becoming its greatest test. He yelled after the vehicle as it disappeared into the night. Richard felt used and abandoned as he trudged aimlessly on the gravel road. He was still wearing the flimsy moccasins from the hospital. The thought of returning to that hell made him wish he had never left and had a small taste of relief.

"What did you tell them?"

Richard saw Sloan approaching from far off. He remained silent.

"What did you tell them?" the figure was filled with an unspeakable fear.

"What do you care?" the man kept walking. "My fate will be the same won't it?"

Sloan grew vicious with cursing. "You're going to mess it all up for me! I've been the happiest I've ever been and all you had to do was lay there like a vegetable."

"And you contributed nothing to my suffering?" Richard contested, "Just what is Green offering you that you've become such a devil?"

"Don't you judge me," he snarled. "You were going to become Green's servant and backstab me before you failed your test."

"That is true," the man noticed police sirens in the far distance. "But I won't fail the test of my new Master."

"What are you saying?" Sloan began to panic. "You don't know who you're dealing with now. I can call upon a legion to deal with you if you don't stop what you're doing!"

Richard stopped walking and took in a deep breath of the night air. "I'd wager that's them now," he pointed to a police vehicle that had just crested the ridge in front of them.

Sloan began showing the horrible visions to Richard, but they had little effect anymore.

The police rushed in and scooped up the escaped patient into the backseat of a squad car. The nameless police officers brought him to a rural police station where they instructed Richard to wait for a van from Walter Reed as he sat handcuffed to a chair.

He closed his eyes and prayed as he never had before. The man's closed eyes and muttering words only confirmed the police officers' impression of him. After all, no one prayed anymore. When the van arrived, Richard clenched his teeth and prepared to go back to his torture chamber.

"Oh Lord," he repeated under his breath as he was loaded into the back seat by law enforcement.

"There's something quite different about you," the woman in the driver's seat turned around. "Your circumstances have certainly changed."

Richard bristled at the sight of her as she started the vehicle and drove away.

"I think it's terrible, this news," she appeared to wipe away a tear. "How did he manage to change the mind of God? I always knew Jacob was stronger. He demanded a blessing and received one!"

The man in the backseat gradually realized they were not headed back to Walter Reed. "What news?" His voice shook.

The woman glanced at him in the rearview mirror as a street lamp passed over head. The brief period of illumination made it seem as though her eyes flashed like a signal light of some distant ship. "You're to be killed. The God of the Christians is allowing it," her voice modulated between ecstasy and grief.

Richard sat back on the cloth bench seat as more streetlights caused peculiar shadows to dance in the cabin. The idea of death over going back to Walter Reed was far preferable. The mode of death, however, he knew would be unthinkable. He resolved to pray once more.

"Stop it!" the woman shrieked. "Stop doing that!"

Richard hadn't made a sound. He only closed his eyes and communed silently.

"If you do that again, I will kill you myself," her darker nature had fully taken over.

This threat made little difference either. Richard had made his peace to shuffle off this mortal coil and end his earthly suffering. The pain and agony of his lengthy tribulation wore heavily on his body and soul. Richard longed only for eternal rest. As they neared the mansion, something disquieted him.

There was a sudden rush of trepidation over dying that had been conspicuously absent for some time. He knew if he died, the boy would suffer on. Worse still, there was likely another to take his place. The fear of death, smothered first by self-hatred then by a desire for relief, came back roaring in to his mind like an escaped predator cooped up in a zoo. It tore through his psyche and consumed every thought it could catch.

Edwards, where are you! Richard screamed in his inner self as they pulled into the driveway of the mansion.

To his surprise, the grounds were lit up in all their splendor. The front lawn was littered with the hastily parked limousines and cars of the summoned elite. It seemed Green had called an emergency meeting.

As they pulled up the driveway, something else caught Richard's eye. A lone figure was set atop a tall pole. He was whimpering and screaming—a noise so terrible it easily penetrated the interior of the van. The woman pulled into a parking spot next to the horrific display, opened the door, and grabbed Richard by the hair to drag her captive out. He fell to the ground in a muddy puddle.

"Get up!" she kicked him. "I can't believe what you've become!"

The man looked up at the pole and saw a face he recognized.

"Malden!" he cried in between agonized breaths, "Malden! Get me down!"

The woman paid him no heed and brought Richard to his feet. He could see the wretch was being impaled slowly by the pole. As she marched her captive toward the bronze doors, Sloan continued to call after him with grave entreaties.

"You coward! You've got to get me down," his shrieks filled the whole mansion grounds. "You did this! I hope they string you up right next to me!"

Richard looked back at him with a detached sense of pity. Before he knew it, he found himself in the mandible, consuming jaws of the mansion's doors. When they closed behind him, Sloan's screams were extinguished.

THE LABORS OF JACOB

Richard turned from the bronze gate to face the foyer. Every inch of the hallway was lined with individuals in robes. Their faces were all obscured by masks and shadows. A rush of cold air sapped any warmth from Richard's body. The woman stood next to him in silence for a moment. One of the figures silently gestured for the pair to advance with a swoop of a robed arm.

As they walked, each obscured face followed them through the hallway. Richard's breathing advanced rapidly but could make no sound at all. Any wayward vibrations seemed to be caught and strangled with extreme prejudice. Even the impact of the pair's shoes on the mirror-finish floor dissipated into the abyss of supernatural silence.

Oh Lord preserve me, Richard prayed silently.

At an instant, one of the figures struck him on the head. When Richard turned to see who it was, he was greeted with the black eyes of a red decorative mask. The figure stood motionless before putting up a finger to its downturned mouth. Richard shuddered and stood frozen until the finger dropped and pointed down the hallway. At last, the chthonic procession arrived at the all too familiar blue and white striped doors. One of the robed individuals extended a gloved hand to the door handle before looking at the woman for approval. She nodded before giving Richard the oddest smile he had ever seen.

In contrast to his previous encounters with the great hall, a blinding light emerged from the growing gap between the two doors.

Richard's eyes fluctuated in pain as they attempted to adjust. He was caught up in the swell of acolytes rushing in with ravenous abandon.

They tripped and stumbled over each other to get to the prospective meal first. When they reached the table, however, it was barren. A new structure had been erected on the long wall opposite the door. It was a high podium with two sets of stairs leading up to it. At the very top sat a figure of immense importance. He slammed a fist on his platform causing the rabble to cease their squabbling. Though he only just removed his mask, Richard knew who it was. It was the first time he had seen him in the full light.

"Partakers in the sacred rite," Green raised his arms, "the table is empty!"

This announcement was met with ear splitting wails of anxiety. One figure fell to his knees and beat his chest.

"But what of this visitor?" one called out. "No one is permitted to enter the chamber during a time of light and not partake!"

Oh Lord Jesus! Richard prayed intently.

The accuser pointed his finger at the new arrival. "Do you not hear what he is doing? You've invited one of theirs to our space!"

"Remove him," the leader commanded.

Richard winced thinking the order was for him. Instead, the group set on the defiant one with an animalistic hatred. He observed the robed crowd surround the man and form a wall of people around him. In a minute, it was all over. After considerable thrashing and screaming, the acolytes returned to their places. All Richard saw where the challenger had been was a picked over corpse missing most of its flesh. Though he was unbound, the visitor remained cemented in place by fear and spiritual oppression. Green lifted high the leather-bound book Richard had seen him flipping through before his ordeal with the labyrinth.

"You all know of the labors of Jacob," he kept the tome above his head with one hand and motioned expressively with the other. "Behold! Once more I have wrestled with God and won!" His free hand came to rest as an outstretched signpost pointing directly at Richard. "This one has trespassed in our sacred places and interfered in the reverence of our gods. For this debt, I bested Hashem in contest over his soul."

Through the speech, Richard noticed the one wearing the red mask taking quick looks at him from across the room.

"For his myriad of offenses, what is the penalty?" Green gestured to the crowd from his podium.

The visitor expected the great hall to erupt in shrieks of condemnation. Instead, the only sound was a rapid moving of fabric as every individual in the room pointed a finger at Richard. They began to walk slowly toward him with their accusatory appendages extended like harpoons at a long sought after prize. The visitor stepped back until he came up against a wall. When the tide of acolytes drew closer, their pace slowed and their arms lowered. Richard breathed rapidly as he scanned the grotesque forms under the hoods. The woman had left the crowd and stood at the feet of the podium while Green watched keenly from his perch. The group formed a neat half circle around Richard. He shifted along the wall and the acolytes adjusted their half-orbit in kind.

"Oh, but what host am I? Asking you all to do this work on an empty stomach?" the dark pontiff clapped his hands before descending to the floor below.

Richard got a closer look at his robe. Where the others' were dark hues of blue, brown, and black, Green's was a shimmering, golden white. Decorative piping of the same azure that adorned the columns of the space formed the Tree of Life on his chest.

"There is another, better reason I have assembled you all here today," the host walked among them.

As he passed each believer, they bowed their heads in reverence.

"The light in this hall has been sparked by the breaking of a new dawn just beyond the horizon," the pontiff walked contemplatively to the head of the table. "The gods of old have demonstrated their power. Awoken from their slumber by the striking of a hammer on the hot iron of fortune, we have assumed our place as the avatars of their resurgence."

Richard suddenly felt a new surge of dread.

"Tonight," Green motioned for the faithful to gather at the table, "we, the blessed few, the knowers, the adored and beautified body; We are about to witness the coming of an even greater age than what is already here."

A few more acolytes shot glances at Richard. Green noticed the growing sense of disquiet that the visitor was witnessing the intimate details of their mysteries.

"Do not be troubled by him," the pontiff knocked on the table three times with his fist. "He too must bear witness."

With this noise, the two doors on either side of the roaring fireplace opened. The dark man Richard had last seen taking compromising pictures of him entered escorting a small girl. From the other door first emerged a gurney with a young boy in restraints. The decrepit cargo was wheeled in by a man following close behind.

"You see, faithful?" Green drew attention to the outsider. "As Malden's God would say: Thou preparest a table before me in the presence of mine enemies."

The scripture fell from his mouth like a precious jewel fished out of a sewer.

"Oh, flock," the host returned to addressing the crowd. "Tonight, we will secure better guards for our future security. The old is yet passing away, but do not despair! Look, a child has come to us!"

The crowd erupted into ecstatic cheers. The child who had walked in looked utterly terrified. She tried to cower away, but the dark man kept her in place. The boy on the gurney looked like he was just on the threshold of death. He had gauze wrapped around what appeared to be a sucking chest wound. Richard wasn't sure which child Green was referring to. He knew the girl could not be viable candidate. The visitor knew her fate would not be much better, however.

"Do you understand, Malden?" the pontiff mocked. "You've failed. Your God failed. The thousand years are over now. I demanded a blessing and He couldn't help but give it! The older shall serve the younger, indeed."

The acolytes took a moment to laugh at Richard who had taken a few steps away from the wall. An intense anger against the blasphemers welled up within him.

"We will separate the spinning plates and suspend the engine in motion," Green stretched out his arms. "The old and worn out will be supplanted by the vital!"

The crowd made muffled claps with their gloved hands.

"But first, let us whet our appetites," Green pointed to the guest. "Let us take God up on His vanishingly reliable word!"

The acolytes rushed toward Richard in a frenzy of hatred.

Overtaken with panic, the prospective victim called out, "Get back in the name of God!"

The robed individual at the spearhead of the formation recoiled as if burned by scalding water. The rest behind him wavered in their charge.

"Faithful!" Green left his place at the head of the table and walked aggressively to where Richard was standing wide-eyed and trembling. "God may have forgiven his sins, but we haven't."

The sounds of his hard soled shoes echoed throughout the great hall until he was face to face with the visitor. Green looked back at the crowd before a blade formerly concealed in the sleeve of his robe extended to his hand. In a swift upward motion, he slashed at Richard's face. Blood spattered the floor as the victim recoiled in pain.

Green turned to face the crowd with the pommel extended in invitation. "Who will do it?" the dark priest challenged. "How much do you really believe in the old gods?"

The acolytes still hung back in hesitation.

"Look how he bleeds!" Green's tone became frustrated. "Whoever blots out this worm out will have his soul as a personal plaything. I swear it!"

Richard clutched at his face in pain. The cut ran from his right temple down to his left cheek. By only a half inch had Green's ghastly blade not blinded him. The blood poured profusely as he stumbled back.

"I will do it!" one of the acolytes budged his way to the front of the pack. "If it pleases you, sir. I will do it."

It was the same robed figure wearing the red mask with the downturned mouth that had cautioned Richard to be quiet before entering the great hall. The voice had a strange and forced character to it as if the individual wore a mask over his voice as well.

"Come and see!" Green took hold of the man's hand and led him in front of the congregation. "One of our newest faithful shall yet put the rest of you to shame."

At this statement a number in the crowd shifted with indignation.

"I have one request, if I may be so bold," the figure kneeled before Green while he held his hand, "May I perform it in private? It is not right that a humble initiate put my elders to shame."

The pontiff raised him to his feet and smiled as he handed over the knife. "Go and do as you have wished."

The figure rushed over to Richard and whisked him out of the hall. As the captive turned to look once more into the space, the woman had cut the throat of the girl and set her body on the table. The crowd at once set upon her like rabid dogs until the closing of the doors blotted out the horrific scene.

AND JACOB WAS LEFT ALONE

"Thomas, John," Edwards said in a hushed tone as he observed from a concealed position on the slope of an adjacent hill to the mansion grounds through a spotter's scope. "Take up your positions near the gate. When you hear my shot, that's your signal."

The two militants gathered their gear and set off into the darkness. Matthew and Simon laid prone on the ridge with their leader. The news had inflated their figures to hundreds, perhaps thousands, in the imagination of some. Through many operations, battles, attrition, and betrayal, the Temple of God's numbers were just five in all with Edwards included.

Their leader shifted from the spotter's scope to a rifle on a bipod. They were 600 yards away from the smallest gap in the curtains of the great hall.

"I thought you said they would have the curtains open," Simon took up his position as the spotter.

"Patience," Edwards whispered. "They'll open the curtains and the windows soon enough. They need to for the ritual. Something they believe about ushering out the old energy and bringing in the new." He paused before continuing: "We can't bet on Malden getting to the boy. We at least have to make sure we cut off the head of the snake!"

Simon nodded and looked closely into the small gap in the curtain.

"Edwards!" he gasped. "I just saw Malden. He had a huge gash on his face!"

"Lord have mercy," the leader said coolly. "A martyr's death so soon. I envy him."

Matthew, a boy of no more than sixteen, clutched his assault rifle tighter. "Sir?" the youngest asked.

"What is it?" Edwards adjusted the power on his scope and practiced his breathing.

Matthew tried to keep from shaking. "Why don't they do this in secret? Don't they know we're coming?"

The leader kept his eye glued to the view in the optic "All they know is that Richard told us everything. They assume we'll be headed for the Pentagon. Besides, this is where it has to be done anyway. This is where they feast."

"Oh Lord!" Simon put a hand to his mouth and looked down from the spotter's scope.

Edwards chastised him. "Keep looking! I need eyes on the target when it happens!"

The man shook his head. "They're eating her!"

"Did you think I was lying? This is who these people are," the leader gripped the stock of the rifle while maintaining a harrowing gaze on what little they could see of the horror.

Matthew strained his eyes in the night at the mansion. All he could see was the narrow sliver of light like the pupil of serpent anxiously searching for its next meal.

"I can't!" Simon looked away. "Jesus save me, I can't look!"

Edwards snapped, "Matthew, get on the spotter's scope!"

The young boy set his rifle aside and felt his stomach turn just before looking into the optic. The other militant, the veteran of a dozen close brushes with death, vomited in anguish. Matthew took his place just as one of the acolytes paraded a section of small intestine across the opening.

"Look, Matthew," Edwards said roughly. "Take it all in. Store what you're seeing in your trigger finger, but not your soul. There will soon be justice for more than just this girl."

After fifteen more minutes of the repulsive consumption, the curtains widened suddenly and the windows flew open.

"Where is he? Where is he?" the leader swept the view of his scope through the crowd quickly.

Matthew's hands trembled terribly on the optic. "I don't see him!" Edwards showed a rare sign of panic.

"Wait," the young militant felt a shot of adrenaline as if a prized buck approached his tree stand after hours of waiting. "Second window from the right, at the base of the stairs of that podium, ascending!"

The leader adjusted his view and found his target. As his scope swept the crowd, he caught a view of the boy that would become the next victim of Stimulosis. He knew if he did not put an end to Green, they may find another candidate, and he would never get another chance to end the horror. Perhaps another would take the pontiff's place, but there were none even half so erudite or in tune with the profane. Green was one of those rare forces of history who built his empire in and by the shadows, scorning the public eye and human recognition.

At last, his crosshairs rested on the six-pointed star motif on Green's back while he ascended the stairs at a steady, ceremonial pace. The dark man carried the new candidate up the opposite stairs, IV bags and all. The pontiff was reading from the leather book and clutching at a glass container holding the delicate five-petal flowers and stems of stinging nettles. Edwards inhaled and lowered his finger to the trigger. His quickly accelerating heartbeat caused the reticle to pulse in his vision.

Lord, guide this shot by your will, he prayed as he exhaled.

Edwards increased the pressure on the trigger slowly until a mighty thunderbolt of noise rang out in the darkness.

The figure escorted Richard quickly through the hallways of the mansion, leaving a trail of blood as they went. Finally, he brought him to a drawing room with exquisite couches. The whole space was covered in mirrors. Surprisingly gently, the robed man guided his captive to a seat. Richard closed his eyes and clenched his teeth. He prayed as he had never prayed before—not for physical safety, but for the safe voyage of his soul. The sound of the knife falling to the floor caused him to jolt.

"Oh Rich," the man sobbed and removed his mask.

The captive opened his eyes to see his own father. The man staggered over to a nearby couch and collapsed.

"How did you get caught up in all this, Rich?" he whimpered.

Richard wiped away the blood from his eyes to verify what he had just seen. To all his revulsion, disgust, and disappointment, there sat Vince Malden—prospective senator and father.

"Dad?" he widened his eyes. "I was right! I did see you!"

"Oh Rich." The elder Malden put his face in his hands, "I never wanted any of this! It was just an innocent invite. How could I have known where it would lead?"

"You monster!" Richard stood up and pointed.

"Keep your voice down!" his father gestured with his hands. "And stop praying! They can sense it."

"You mean you can sense it," blood and tears began to mingle freely on the son's face, "You're one of them, dad!"

"You don't understand," the elder Malden wailed. "They were going to kill me if I didn't join in!"

"You looked into the pits of hell and decided to take a swim. All for your own benefit!" Richard accused.

His father became combative. "But I saved your life! That's got to count for something."

"How you groveled before Green—I don't doubt you really did volunteer to kill me. You just lost your nerve!"

The elder Malden remained deathly quiet.

"He knew who you were," Richard's shaking legs guided him back to the chair. "He knew you were one of the new initiates! And he knew who I was. Green's not stupid! What better way to gain favor with the profane than to murder one of your own offspring!"

His father stood up quickly as darkness overtook his face. "You have no idea what you're talking about! I won't be lectured by you! Do you have any idea what I've gone through? The people I'm involved with?"

"Do you?" Richard stood up in kind.

Silence permeated the mirrored space while their reflections bounced around the room like wayward photonic particles. The father shot a glance over to the knife.

"What now, senator?" the son shook his head slowly, "Will you sacrifice your son too for power?"

The elder Malden picked up the hellish blade slowly while maintaining eye contact. "You have no idea what you've done," the father's voice became like it was in the great hall as his eyes glazed over in shadow. "It's in everyone's best interest for this to continue. Would you sacrifice the blood of millions for petty truth?"

Richard stepped back while an otherworldly aura descended on the room. In his peripherals he could see the robed man inching toward him in the multitude of mirrors lining the space. The knife moved through the air like a glowing hot piece of metal removed from the furnace.

"The God of the Christians has said you may die," the robed figure widened his darkened eyes. "Who am I to disagree?"

He lunged at Richard like a coiled snake. The son flinched and put up his hands. The elder Malden raised the knife with murderous intent. At the tip of that blade was power, prestige, and all the things he ever desired. All they needed to sprout was the fertile soil of a worthy sacrifice.

Richard backed away just as his father tripped on a rise in the carpet. The elder Malden tumbled ignominiously to the floor before yelping in pain. The son crouched to turn him over and found the knife buried deep in his father's chest.

"Oh, Rich," he wheezed and grabbed at the younger man's face. "Oh, Rich, forgive me!"

His voice, though saturated with pain and regret, had lost the chthonic character once more. Richard knelt and cradled his head. A sanguine rush soaked the robe his father had earned through a debasing series of poor choices leading to his abortive attempt at murdering his own son.

"Please forgive me!" he clutched Richard's shirt as he went pale.

The younger Malden could only look on in silent horror as his father's soul slipped into the abyss. In a moment, his life was gone. Richard sat back and cried aloud in anguish.

"Why, dad!" He put his hands to his face as he laid next to the fallen man. "Why!"

The soul-crushing feelings of betrayal and grief caused Richard to writhe in agony. The sum total of their life together—the good and the bad—was blotted from the page by one last ill-fated grasp at recognition.

Suddenly, Richard was overcome with anger. His rage was not directed at his defiled father, but at those who had violated him. Richard grabbed the knife and heaved. With considerable effort, he extricated the blood-soaked dagger from the elder Malden's chest. His father's eyes stared lifelessly in the latticework of reflecting mirrors. Richard took one more glance at the despicable corpse before taking off at a gallop toward the great hall. He was resolved to make Green pay.

When Richard burst into the space, the commotion caused the pontiff to scramble up the steps in alarm. A bullet found his hip at the end of a six-hundred-yard journey.

THAT HE MAY SEE

"He moved! Why did he move?" Edwards tried to find his target in the scope again.

"You hit him!" Matthew cried out. "You got him!"

The leader surveyed the chaos in the great hall. The robed acolytes were scrambling to form human shields around both Green and the new candidate.

"He's still moving!" Edwards said with dismay, "I think I only winged him!"

The other two guerrillas, Thomas and John, appeared under the threshold of the window and started lobbing explosives inside. Edwards caught a glimpse of Richard shielding his eyes and retreating from the room. A series of flashes, followed by delayed percussive blasts, whittled the crowd down considerably. John attempted to climb into the great hall but was riddled with gunfire as soon as his head appeared in the window. Green's security detail had joined the fight. Thomas retreated to the gatehouse and returned fire.

"C'mon, let's go!" Edwards grabbed an assault rifle and compelled Simon and Matthew to follow him.

The trio ran headlong down the slope of the hill and across the field. The six hundred yards which the bullet had traversed in the blink of an eye felt like an eternity while their comrade was pinned down and encircled. They reached the fence and observed a growing firefight erupting across the grounds.

Edwards directed Simon and Matthew to spread out and lay down suppressing fire. The leader flanked left toward the gatehouse to gather his embattled comrade. He could hear the security forces chattering excitedly in Spanish. When Edwards reached the edge of the fence near the gate, he called out to Thomas to retreat.

"I've got you covered!" the leader directed several bursts at the maneuvering silhouettes on the front lawn. He saw one get knocked down by the crossfire from the other two guerillas. "Get out of there!"

"Edwards!" Thomas shouted. "Look!"

The man gestured to the center of the front lawn where a pole stood. Atop the torturous spire was the form of a man writhing in agony.

"We couldn't see it before," the guerrilla raised a hand to heaven with his back to the gate's pillar. "And Elisha prayed, and said, *Lord, I pray thee, open his eyes, that he may see!*"

When he finished this sentence, a launched grenade landed next to his cover and martyred him. Edwards turned to look at the previously unseen spectacle. He could hear the miserable soul even over the increasingly rapid and accurate fire.

"Get me down! Somebody please!" the wretch howled.

"Sloan!" the leader put a hand next to his mouth to direct the sound of his voice. "Sloan, is that you?"

"Ask your God to let me down! Please, I am begging you!" he replied.

The security forces directed a light machine gun at Edwards' position, causing him to duck down. It appeared Green's men could not see Sloan.

"If the Lord wills it," the leader yelled amidst the firefight. "But you must do something for me! Go find Richard and get him to the engine room!"

Sloan let out a tortured laugh. "Green's too powerful! It wouldn't matter!"

Enfilading fire from Simon and Matthew took their toll on a few of the security detail.

"Sloan!" Edwards' voice took on an eschatological character. "Your time causing problems is at a close! You've seen the torture the devil can do to you. Wait until you fall into the hands of a righteous God! You owe a debt! Not to me, not to Green, but to God!"

"Ask your God to get me down!" Sloan nodded slowly and hung his head in surrender.

Edwards prayed that it would be so. At once, the pole vanished beneath him. Sloan's form shapelessly fell to the ground. He lay there for a moment before stumbling to get up. Edwards observed the silhouette stand motionless for a moment before turning to head into the mansion. The leader proceeded to heave several smoke grenades into the front lawn. As the obscuring mist filled the grounds, Edwards retreated to find the other two.

"Simon, Matthew!" He stumbled next to them while the smoke continued to dissipate. "We've got to get inside! No doubt, Green is still attempting the ritual in an alternate space deep in the mansion!"

Simon nodded and got up from the prone position.

"Matthew, get a move on!" Edwards lightly kicked the young boy's side.

He rolled over with a glassy expression in his eyes and a bloody hole between them. The remaining two guerrillas said a brief prayer over Matthew before climbing the fence. The security forces were firing wildly with small arms and grenade launchers in their blinded state. Edwards directed Simon to throw his last smoke grenades toward the opposing forces as they flanked right. One of the fragmenting projectiles landed perilously close to them as the mansion's flood lights' rays illuminated the growing cloud of white smoke. The scattered light gave the scene an ethereal, supernatural character. The pair dispatched one of the guards at the rear of the house before entering through a broken window.

❧

Richard stumbled back from the great hall, blinded and deafened by the explosions. Blood flowed from his sinuses as well as the gash across his face. He still clutched at the knife, but could only wander aimlessly as the dust stung his eyes. Richard felt several bodies rush past him but could only flail the blade uselessly in their direction. The rushing people paid him no heed.

"Malden, you worm!" a familiar voice approached from amidst the impenetrable dust and ringing of eardrums.

Richard felt fingers tighten around his neck. In response, he slashed with the knife. The man yelped in pain before trying to wrestle the weapon away. The pair ended up on the ground with Richard on the bottom.

"How dare you! How dare you trifle with this!" the heavyset man pinned down the hand holding the knife.

The dust began to clear from Richard's eyes just as he recognized the voice: Admiral Simmons.

He struck the senior officer's face with a savage upward palm-heel strike. Simmons recoiled but kept his grip on Richard's hand holding the knife, desperately trying to pry it loose. In the corner of his vision, he noticed Green and the new candidate being wheeled down the hallway, escorted by a strong contingent of security personnel. Richard bucked his hips and struck the admiral again, causing him to fall over. He rolled with the rotund man and wrested control of the knife. Richard raised up the blade and plunged it toward Simmons' neck. The admiral managed to put up an arm in defense. The knife sank into his wrist as he cried out in pain. Richard was sprayed with blood from the ruptured artery but attempted another strike. Simmons put out his hands and caught the killing blow before it could reach his neck. Richard adjusted his body on top of the knife to lend his weight to the descent of the blade. Slowly but surely, the admiral's strength failed. The knife entered his neck at a reduced, but inevitable pace. Simmons writhed and wheezed as his airways were pierced. Richard gritted his teeth and heaved his body weight into the fight once more. Once the entirety of the blade had been buried in the man's neck, he retracted.

"Kate" the admiral wheezed as blood gurgled in his airways. "Kate. . . .'

Richard stood up with trembling legs with the knife dripping in his hand.

"Kevin!" a female shrieked and approached rapidly.

The woman's hood was down and was clearly Jennifer Katz. Richard retreated and raised the knife, but the woman ignored him. She caressed Simmons' face tenderly as the sound of gunfire around the house intensified. The admiral was choking violently and could say nothing in reply. Richard left the dysfunctional pair to their mourning and set out after Green.

The dust cleared the further he followed the pontiff's trail of blood deeper into the hellish mansion. Richard turned down a corridor with a noticeable downward slope. The appointments of the hallway changed the deeper he went. It less resembled an exquisite mansion and took on the appearance of a hospital floor. The buzzing fluorescent lights brought back Richard's memories of the corridor just outside the engine room.

"Malden!" Sloan yelled after him.

"In the name of God, I rebuke you!" Richard replied fiercely as he continued to run down the hallway. "You will not inhibit me!"

"Stop for a moment," the figure called out. "I know I am hell bound, but let me at least help you. You'll never get to the engine room without me!"

The man turned to the apparition and caught his breath. "You're in service to Green! How could I trust you? Now go to the abyss and leave me alone!"

"He betrayed me!" Sloan continued to approach, "Once he was told he could kill you, he had no further use for me. I was shown mercy on that pole and let down. Let's show mercy to that poor boy and put an end to it."

The figure pointed to an air vent. The sound of tortured breathing filled the spacc.

THE DAWN OF A DIFFERENT DAY

"He's losing a lot of blood!" Simon said breathlessly as they pursued the sanguine trail through the mansion's labyrinthine structure.

"There's no saying it's all Green's," Edwards huffed as they sprinted. "He's still going to attempt the swap!"

A shotgun blast knocked Simon across the space as they turned a corner. The calavera tattooed man trained the weapon on the guerrilla leader. Edwards managed a quick burst from his assault rifle and neutralized the threat.

"Go Edwards!" the martyr waved with a bloody hand. "Finish it!"

The leader nodded and shed his backpack to reduce the weight. He ran at a fevered pitch as his breathing grew shallow and rapid. Edwards knew this was his last chance. The hallway seemed to go on for miles as the sound of chaos at the mansion faded behind him. Now, there was only the noise of his boots against the floor and the buzzing of the lights. The blood trail ran cold, but there was no way to turn. Edwards pursued with reckless abandon deeper into the bowels of the machine. The time was running short. The electricity in the hallway shut off apart from an intermittent series of emergency lights. They passed over Edwards like the buffeting of waves on a ship's hull. Millions of souls crying out in anguish swelled under his feet and carried him forward.

After an unknowable period of harried progress, he saw Green carried by his men and the gurney slink into a door. The woman with two different colored eyes closed up the space behind them. He could hear the groans of both the pontiff and the boy as they suffered from their wounds. Edwards slowed his progress and approached the door. He tested the handle and found, unsurprisingly, it was locked. The hallway continued to stretch in a downward slope to his right. In front of him was the Tree of Life sigil in all its demonic fury. Edwards could hear the panicked sound of voices behind the door.

"I can still do it!" Green shrieked. "Prepare him and open the ventilation shaft. The energy must be permitted to escape and reenter."

Edwards tried to formulate a plan, but knew the time was close at hand. He shot the handle of the door several times with his rifle. The bullets had little effect as the barrier remained stubbornly bolted in place. However, Green's men rushed to sortie and dispatch the threat. Edwards stumbled back from the entrance and hid behind the door as it swung open toward him. He waited a split second for more of them to exit before opening up.

Edwards managed to down all but one before his magazine ran dry. He leapt up to wrestle the last guard and managed to take his gun and kill him. Edwards turned to face the room before a withering blast from a small submachine gun pierced his body. The woman stood holding the weapon with a look of shocked pleasure next to Green and the boy. The space was filled with medical equipment for the procedure and, strangely, a roaring fireplace. The dark pontiff, leaning on the gurney and gushing blood from his hip, gripped the stinging nettle in a gloved hand and prepared to administer the rite.

❧

Richard wormed his way through the ventilation shaft. Green's knife remained firmly planted in his waistband. The blood continued to pour from his face. The flow aided his slithering over the smooth metal surface. The sound of the breathing reverberated through the corridor. Sloan crawled in front and admonished him to keep moving. At last they reached the concrete tunnel with the amber lights Richard had witnessed what seemed like an eternity ago.

"Not far to go, Malden," Sloan crawled faster. "We have to hurry!"

Richard's elbows were a tattered mess of missing skin and blood. His flesh screamed at him to stop—yet his soul propelled him onward.

"Helmut!" he cried out. "I am coming for you! It's all going to be over soon!"

They reached the grate underneath the decontamination room as the leaden weight of the spiritual atrocity seeped from the engine room like noxious gas. The breathing, labored as ever, beat on a tortured tempo as it had done for decades. Through wars, crises, and plagues, the latter day priests harvested their fill of anguish from their victim to satiate the gods of old.

They had discovered an eternal wellspring of good fortune with which to conquer the world. As the power accumulated, the blasphemers ventured thoughts of vanquishing God Himself. All the mustered forces of Antichrist drank from the profane waters of Helmut's travail as they advanced over the earth. The earth was at its darkest, but the dawn was soon at hand.

Richard squirmed through the grate into the chamber as Sloan followed shortly behind. The figure stumbled to the door. The Hebrew inscription sat mockingly to the right. The entrance to the engine room unlocked and the portal to unknowable misery opened. Richard put a hand over his mouth as he carefully approached. The harried noise of their flight became swallowed by the oppressive quiet of the engine room. The only remaining sound was Helmut's breathing.

"Forgive me, Malden," Sloan grabbed his sleeve just before he entered. "I am about to go to eternity."

Richard turned to the decrepit figure and embraced him. "Sloan, I need you to forgive me instead," he sobbed. "I could have saved you."

"It's too late for me," the apparition rasped. "But, for what it's worth, I do."

Richard turned to look at the boy. His pallid blue eyes longed for the final, sweet release.

"Go now!" Sloan compelled. "Time is running out!"

The recording of the Helmut's mother started again as the needles rose up from the bed. Richard rushed into the space, awash with tears. He removed the knife from his waistband to put the ailing boy down. Helmut eyed the blade with disgust. Richard dropped the weapon and chose another path.

"Helmut!" he started to unplug and tear at the spider's nest of wires and tubes lashing the boy to his torment.

When the boy heard his name, it was as if the last tortured spark of life still in him animated his body. Richard undid his restraints and shoved his hands underneath his body to lift him from the bed. The needles lanced and punctured Richard's arms as he lifted Helmut. He cried out in pain, not only at the lancing, but also at the small taste of the boy's almost unending agony. Richard fell to the floor with the bony figure limp in his arms.

"It's over, Helmut," the rescuer gently stroked the boy's face as the tears streaked his own. "You're finally free."

The boy's horrific breathing continued, but relief did not cross his face. Through a titanic effort, Helmut pointed at the door. Richard understood what he meant.

Green's hand descended rapidly with the stinging nettle. The new candidate writhed in pain as the Stimulosis began. Needles rose up from the gurney as the medical equipment caused a hellish din. The fluorescent lights all flickered, and some exploded from the surge in energy. The dark pontiff limped over to the fire and scooped embers into a ceremonial vessel before sprinkling them over the boy.

"Ummy!" the wretch cried in Arabic, "Ya ummy, sa-adini!"

Edwards looked on in desperation as he bled out.

Green chanted in Hebrew before smiling at his would-be assassin. "You're too late," he spit. "It's done!" Green laughed as he raised his hands. "Oh gods! A new and better sacrifice!"

The woman dropped the sub machine gun in her hands. Her face took on an entirely different character as if one of her natures had just overpowered the other.

Edwards grinned as blood seeped from his mouth. The militant raised his head with all of his remaining strength.

The woman began convulsing and shrieked, "It's not enough, Jacob! You failed us!"

Green's countenance turned to horror as he clutched at his hip. "No! Here it is! Everything is ready! The sacrifice is here!"

"We're starving!" the woman lunged toward the boy. "We're starving! We're starving!"

Edwards wheezed as his vision began clouding over. "In the holy name of Jesus, come out of her!"

She was thrown against the wall as the lights flickered. The boy's heat rate monitor indicated he was flat-lining. The woman foamed at the mouth while Green tried to restrain her.

"Would you send us to torment before our time?" she cried out to the militant.

With his dying breath, Edwards commanded, "Into the pigs you go!"

The woman collapsed where she stood as Green contorted in agony. Gesticulating and straining, he rushed into the fireplace. First his body burned, then his soul.

⁚

Richard carried the boy in his arms out of the engine room for the first time in nearly a hundred years. When they left the decontamination chamber, the ground heaved beneath them like pangs of labor just beginning. The lights flickered and dust came down from the ceiling. He stumbled for a moment but kept his footing.

"What are you doing?" Sloan questioned. "Why didn't you do it?"

Richard shuffled down the hallway while Helmut starved for air. He turned toward the figure and shook his head. "They can't feed on him anymore," the man wept. "But I want him to see the sun one last time!"

Sloan nodded but seemed to fade with every second. "That door right there is an elevator. I will open it for you, but be quick! He doesn't have much time left."

Doors separated in the hallway with the mournful tone of the elevator's chime. Richard sat down in the compartment and clutched at Helmut's face. His mind returned to the graffiti in another elevator early on in his journey: The essence of human interaction is the short contract. As they prepared to ascend from the depths, Richard made a covenant.

"Just a little while longer," he sobbed. "I promise. I promise you'll get to see it!"

Sloan waved goodbye as the elevator doors obscured him from view for the last time. Richard bid his former tormentor farewell and prayed for his soul. The feeling of rising to the earth's surface caused the boy's weight to become leaden in the rescuer's pierced arms. The faintest glimmer of a smile spread on Helmut's slack jawed face, but the long suffocated light of life was nearly out. When the doors opened, Richard stood with the boy and exited the elevator, his body racked with grief for the shadow he held in his arms.

They were in a supply closet like the one Sloan had led him into ages ago. A thick curtain concealed the hidden elevator. The door was propped open as personnel were beginning to buzz through the Pentagon's hallways in the early morning. The otherworldly pair stepped out into the corridor and walked toward the stairs. A female service member shrieked at the sight of them and dropped her stack of papers.

Richard was still dripping blood from his face as Helmut choked and writhed. Everyone stood back in horror and failed to impede their progress. Some fainted. Others wept. Most just stayed silent. It was as if the collective knowledge and shame of their unknowing benefit flooded into their minds and paralyzed them. Helmut's eyes began to close when they were just within sight of an exit door. His body seemed to disintegrate in his rescuer's hands.

"No, Helmut!" Richard cried. "Not yet!"

The armed guard at the door dropped his weapon and fled. The boy held on a little longer as the icy bite of the outside air caused his eyes to flicker. A small glimmer of Helmut's boyhood returned as he felt the breeze on his face like a long-lost mother's caress. Richard fell to his knees as the morning autumn wind greeted them. He was breathing rapidly from exertion, but the panorama before them caused him to go silent.

They were on the east side of the Pentagon overlooking the Potomac. The sun had had just begun to rise as a few birds flew across the black silhouettes of the nation's monuments to its strange gods. Delicate clouds caught the breaking of the new day and weaved a tapestry of gentle longing and farewell. Richard shivered as their breathing formed small wisps of mist.

"Oh it's beautiful, Helmut," Richard sobbed.

Richard propped up the boy to see the sunrise and hugged him tightly from behind. He tried to give every last bit of love and tenderness he had left in his body to the tormented boy as they rocked back and forth. Tears flowed freely from the rescuer's face as he rested his chin gently on Helmut's head. Slowly but surely, the boy placed a skeletal hand on Richard's and held it tightly. A heavenly quiet like a time of dutiful prayer and petition blanketed the scene. Even the perpetual whirring of the infernal Beltway faded into nothingness. The only noise that could pierce the silence were the last words of Helmut Grenzer.

"Mutter," he said in his native tongue, his voice gathering the last disfigured and mutilated remains of his soul to itself: "Es ist endlich vorbei."

As Richard held Helmut in his arms, the boy's form strained against the cosmic cables that had long overdue held him in place. He was caught up by a supernatural gust. The force of his impending exit built until a final release like moored ship snapping its lines in a hurricane.

Slowly at first, then all at once, his soul broke free of its bonds and sailed from the place of his torment to the arms of Providence. Helmut let one last labored breath escape his lungs. The condensation of that exhale dissipated into the air as he shed the memory of every last moment of misery. The sound silenced the world over as creation froze in awe of the boy. His body rapidly decomposed until Richard held only his bones. The ground moved once more beneath them as the earth groaned.

He sat in stunned silence, weeping, and awaited the drop of the executioner's blade on the neck of the beast system. The warm glow of the rising sun bathed his body and soul in equal measure. The shivers of cold turned to a shaking anticipation. The nation clung uselessly to the transient, evaporating securities which were now rapidly disappearing. The wind picked up at an imperceptible rate until it became a mighty gale.

Richard carefully set Helmut's remains aside and stood up to take it all in. He could no longer hate the truth. The truth, in all its woeful and repulsive forms, was about to be told in the impending cut of heaven's terrible, swift sword.

This was the dawn of a very different kind of day. This was only the beginning.

ENJOYED THIS BOOK?

TO READ MORE, VISIT US AT

ANTELOPEHILLPUBLISHING.COM

www.ingramcontent.com/pod-product-compliance
Lightning Source LLC
Chambersburg PA
CBHW030123010826
48973CB00002B/397